Merlinda Bobis has had four novels, six poetry books, and a collection of short stories published, and ten dramatic works performed. Her novel *Locust Girl, A Lovesong* received the Christina Stead Prize for Fiction in the NSW Premier's Literary Awards and the Philippine National Book Award. Her poetry collection *Accidents of Composition* was Highly Commended for the ACT Book of the Year Award. For her, writing is homecoming: a return to roots, a retrieval through memory, and a reckoning with loss hopefully with care and grace. She lives and writes on Ngunnawal Country (Canberra).

Other books by Merlinda Bobis

THE
KINDNESS
of
BIRDS

MERLINDA BOBIS

First published by Spinifex Press, 2021

Spinifex Press Pty Ltd
PO Box 5270, North Geelong, VIC 3215, Australia
PO Box 105, Mission Beach, QLD 4852, Australia

women@spinifexpress.com.au
www.spinifexpress.com.au

Edited by Pauline Hopkins and Susan Hawthorne
Cover design by Deb Snibson, MAPG
Cover notation by Lynne Kowalik
Owl drawing by Merlinda Bobis
Typesetting by Helen Christie, Blue Wren Books
Typeset in Albertina
Printed by McPherson's Printing Group

 A catalogue record for this
book is available from the
National Library of Australia

ISBN: 9781925950304 (paperback)
ISBN: 9781925950311 (ebook)

Supported by

For all the grieving
and all the kindness.
May they keep holding hands.

CONTENTS

O BEAUTIFUL CO-SPIRIT

Strand by strand, we coloured her hair.

Lydia Nichols

There's a quiver in her voice, then a lilt as she says her name. 'I'm here, Lucia.' It's echoey here with no windows, so 'Lucia' reverberates. Farah says it again, walking forward. 'Lucia, I'm here — and Pilar's with me —' then swallows and breathes out.

But Pilar is holding her breath. She stares, feet rooted at the door.

Cuerpo presente: Body lying in state.

'Remember Pilar?' Farah continues, 'Our neighbour upstairs.'

She wants to run back to her car.

'Come, Pilar, come in,' Farah beckons to her.

She wants to drive home.

Farah sets her large bag under the steel trolley bed. Last night, she asked Pilar to please come. For support. Because there's no one else. But Pilar didn't expect *this*. At a Belconnen funeral parlour, Lucia with only a white sheet on her, lying in state.

1

It all began last night, quickly, at the stairwell of their apartment building. Pilar was rushing down with her garbage and Farah was going up slowly, head down as if examining her every step.

'Hi,' Pilar greeted her. They're just polite "hi-hello" neighbours now, barely speaking to each other after that thing with the birds.

Farah looked up without looking at her, mumbled something and continued up, then called out, 'Excuse me,' in the dark. The stairwell light had done its duration.

Pilar stopped.

'You're Filipina, aren't you?' Farah called out from a few steps up.

'Yes.'

'So you're Catholic?'

'Well, yes, but …'

'My friend Lucia died this morning.'

In the dark, the announcement sounded as if already made from the grave.

'I'm sorry.'

'Lucia is Catholic.'

'Oh.'

'Like you.'

Their voices had dropped to an echoey whisper.

'May I talk to you for a second — please?'

The light came back on. Pilar looked up from several steps down. Farah had pressed the stairwell light button and was now standing in front of her door. Under the yellow light, her face looked shiny.

'Sorry, I — I forgot your name.'

'It's Pilar,' and she started walking up to her, still with the garbage. 'I can't remember your name either.'

'Farah — oh, you go and organise those first —'

'It's okay, these can wait.'

It's the shine of tears, Pilar realised as she came closer.

'So sudden, her heart.'

Her hands were full so she couldn't really put her arms around her, could she?

Sob after sob sounded louder in the dark. The stairwell light had done its duration again.

What's it with duration and distance? The duration of light and of seeing, the distance of steps from each other. Even if they're all Australians under one roof. Lucia, Italian Catholic. Pilar, Filipina Catholic, well, baptised so. And Farah?

'I'm Malaysian Muslim, so I don't know how —'

'But you don't wear a—a —'

'A hijab? Not all Muslims are the same.'

'And not all Catholics are the same. I really don't know the prayers. And maybe Italian Catholics do things differently.'

'Doesn't matter. Compared to you, I know nothing. But I know it would mean something to Lucia … to have someone from the same — she was a believer.'

'I'm not — I mean —'

'Please?'

Pilar nudged the garbage with her feet, rustling the bags, reminding the other that she has a job to do and she really must go. It was past eleven.

'I know it's too much to ask, after that fight about the birds — I'm so sorry, we're so sorry.'

Pilar shrugged.

The weeping was over but not the pleading. 'You can just — I mean, just be there … please.'

Of course, it was a lot to ask. And why her? Inside Farah's and Lucia's bedsit, Pilar felt her arm being twisted by 'the same religion' and this imposed grief. It's not that she's heartless. It's not that her neighbours a floor down had been nasty with her when she'd just moved in from Wollongong last year, because of the birds. It's not that she's against birds. It's not that they had heated words then. It's not because of this sneaking irritation-awkwardness-helplessness-sadness, or whatever it is.

'Lucia's so sorry about *that* time,' and she sighed.

Sigh filled the bedsit: lounge set that doubled as dining, half-kitchen tucked in a corner and a double bed against the wall with Catholic rosary and Muslim prayer beads hanging together from a nail. Only one bed? Pilar shook off the thought.

'Cup of tea?'

'No, thanks — my garbage's smelling, must get rid of these now.'

'We've no one else.'

It was the way she said it. Or maybe the way it fell in her ear. It made her think of an empty street. So she said yes, she'll come, but she'll drive her own car.

But she didn't expect *this*.

The name echoes again in the room with no windows. 'Lucia, we're here.'

Last night Pilar thought she's going to be 'just here', lay flowers by the coffin and that's that. She bought a bunch from Woolies.

'I've two of your best dresses to choose from.'

What? Pilar swallows as she finally steps forward from the door, only a step, gripping the bunch of white chrysanthemums.

'So which will it be? The white lacy thing that we bought from that DJ sale or the gold gown which you wore at that Italian ball … was it fifteen years ago now?' And she whispers, 'Both long, so your feet don't stick out.'

Pilar doesn't know whether she's going to laugh or protest.

In a fainter whisper, Farah adds, 'Got knickers too — you can't go without.'

Pilar giggles.

Farah turns around to face her, face pained but purposeful, and silently mouths: 'No one should go without.' Then she takes out the white dress from the bag, puts it up for her to survey, and next, the gold. 'What do you think, Pilar?'

She doesn't know what to say. She's been asked to do something beyond what anyone should be asked to do. Here. This way. For a stranger, really.

Dresses laid on one arm, Farah turns back to Lucia, strokes her hair. 'You've gone grey … I remember you in this gold … when we first met … you had all that long, dark hair … so beautiful.' Then she falls silent, grows still, how still.

Pilar freezes too. She thinks, it's like watching a strange yet familiar tableaux. Woman bending over her dead.

Labaran. Bestihan. Ayusan. Para hermosa.

In the silence, it's her mother's words that she hears from all those years ago, bending over her own mother laid on the bed in their old house in the Philippines.

Wash. Dress. Groom. So she's beautiful.

Mother did all these as she said the prayers, which Pilar can't remember at all. But the curved back, she remembers. Mother was wearing something blue. Grandmother was covered with a white sheet. She was her mother's handmaiden then, ready with the basin of warm water with lime leaves and jasmine. She was thirteen.

The back returns to life, straightens, and Farah turns towards her again. 'Please, will you help?'

Para hermosa: So she's beautiful.

Farah drapes the dresses across the body then takes out a pair of white silk knickers from the bag and stands at the foot of the bed. 'Please.'

Pilar hesitates.

'She's clean, she's been washed.'

So now, *bestihan*, dress.

Pilar lays down the chrysanthemums on the floor and looks for the first time.

Sixty-year old skin alabaster and wrinkles in calm repose, like the shut eyes and lips. The body is still covered from the shoulders down.

'Like she's only sleeping,' Farah says, then starts slipping on the knickers under the sheet. It's a struggle, so Pilar finally comes to her aid, lifts the sheet slightly, her face turned away. Farah has just gestured, please don't look. Now she has enough room to lift each leg and finish the job. 'Decency for dignity, you understand?'

Pilar nods. She is, after all, not family or friend. But she hopes the dressing up won't also be a struggle under the sheet.

'Thank you. Very kind of you to come — and we're really sorry about that bird stuff, and sorry we never said so.'

Pilar shrugs.

Nowhere to lay the dresses, so Farah returns them in the bag and goes to the side of the bed, then starts folding the sheet upwards from the feet.

Pilar goes to the other side, follows the folding. Thank god, this will be simpler. 'Years ago, I did this with my mother. For grandmother in the Philippines.'

'I did this too. With my sister. For our mother in Malaysia.'

The rustle of fabric fills the pause.

'You also dressed her in her best?'

'No, we wrapped her in white cloth called *kafan*. It's how we do it: shrouding.'

'*Kafan*? Sounds like *kaban*, meaning "coffin" where I come from.'

'Oh.'

Sheet fully folded now. Nowhere to put it, except under the head, like a pillow.

'You have very fine skin, dear Lucia, like a baby's.'

'Fine and fair. Alabaster.'

Farah smiles. 'I like that word.'

'So why the dresses then?'

'Lucia is not Muslim, I mean, our shrouding practice is not her practice.'

'Of course.'

'And she always wants to look her best.'

'Oh.'

'Even when she's dead, she said.'

Like Pilar's grandmother who chose her own death dress years before she died. '*Ay, alembong si Lola*' — Grandmother's vain and bit of a flirt, her grandchildren said, but affectionately. Her hips swayed as she walked, still in high heels at eighty. 'I think, the gold gown.'

Farah takes it out from the bag, lays it on top of Lucia. 'Uhmm … I think so too.' Then she lifts the gold satin from the body, cradles it, unsure. 'They don't usually allow this here, but it's only right that I do it myself with your — but I've already asked too much of you, so if you'd rather not —'

'I'm here now, Farah,' but she swallows. She handled grandmother when she was thirteen, but *this* — 'might as well get on with it.'

'I'll hold her, you put it on. That okay?'

They both hold her, slipping on the dress from feet up to buttocks then hips, pushing-pulling left then right — 'She's only small but so heavy now,' Farah says.

'Maybe all that living collected to take to the other side …' Pilar murmurs.

Farah pauses, holds the other's gaze. 'Aren't we supposed to be lighter when we leave —?' her voice cracks.

'But we're strong, Farah, so if I lift her from the waist and you support and pull, she'll be right,' and on it goes, propping back,

7

then shoulders, struggling with satin and flesh, until finally, whew — but the back won't zip!

They stop, both sweating now.

'How's it to be womanhandled, Lucia?'

Pilar giggles, Farah giggles.

'Shhh …' both hush each other.

'It doesn't have to zip.'

'No, it doesn't.'

'Won't be seen.'

'Won't, when she's inside —' Farah swallows, then quickly, 'Okay, let's rest her down — gently now — there!'

They look.

'I think we did okay.'

'Uhmm … you're kind, Pilar. Despite.'

'You're kind, Farah. To organise this — and me.'

Both laugh.

'*Diit na kabootan, diit na kagayonan bago maghalè*' — a little kindness, a little beauty before leaving — Grandmother used to say when they forgot to kiss her goodbye at the end of a visit, pointing to her cheek awaiting the peck. And as they did their filial *besos,* she'd add in her affectionate singsong, '*Nunca maglingaw — las amabilidaditas, las hermositas.*' Never forget — little kindnesses, little beauties. Her mother was from Malaga so she often mixed Spanish with the local language. Sometimes her "inventions" were quite a mouthful.

Pilar straightens the beaded hem of the gown. '*Las hermositas.*'

'What did you say?'

'How do you say "kindness" in Malay?'

Farah smooths the hem further, making sure no feet sticking out. 'In Bahasa Melayu, it's *kebaikan*. In yours?'

'*Kabootan*, I think literally "co-spirit". That's in Bikol, my birth tongue. In Filipino, it's *kagandahang loob*, "beautiful inside" or "soul" or "spirit".'

'Beautiful co-spirit … you,' Farah whispers.

Embarrassed, Pilar waves away the remark but it travels across the body, hovers around her, wanting to be let in, to be owned.

'Yes, we did well, Pilar — she's beautiful, look.'

Lucia all frocked up for the ball.

'Wait —' Pilar gets a chrysanthemum from the bunch at the foot of the bed, lays it on Lucia's breast. 'Maybe?'

Farah arranges the hands so they seem to be holding the white flower.

Both consider.

'I don't think so,' Pilar says.

'Agree.' Farah takes the flower away, folds hands over breast. 'It was she who swore at you … I remember.'

'Because of the birds.'

'She has — had a temper. But she loved those cockatoos.'

'I didn't drive them away.'

'Well, you wrecked our bird seed holder.'

'I didn't mean to, I'm sorry.' She remembers the racket of sulphur crests and white wings, the screeching and shrieking that drove her nuts. 'I was so exhausted after weeks of not sleeping because of their visits every early morning, and I begged and begged you to please stop feeding them because they went on and on right below my bedroom window and I worked night shifts.'

'So you said.'

'But you didn't believe me.'

'She didn't.'

'She called me "a fucking bird killer".'

'I'm sorry.'

'I killed no bird.'

9

'I know, we know.'

Both breathe out.

Farah pats the folded hands, as if to reassure, then caresses the face. 'When we shroud back home, we leave part of the face open so family can say goodbye …' She bends down, kisses the mouth. '*Selamat jalan sahabat* … farewell, my dearest.'

Pilar looks away.

'It's okay, we're okay now — aren't we, Lucia?'

'I'm sorry … that your birds never came back.'

'They were not really our birds.'

'Nothing is ever ours for good.'

They go quiet.

Breaths synchronise, make air. White wings unfurl, take off.

They look again.

'Dress really suits her.'

'I thought so too. The first time I met her.'

'At the ball?'

Farah nods. 'Her hair was all dark and long … now so grey.'

Ayusan. Para hermosa. Groom. So she's beautiful.

Pilar remembers how her mother made up grandmother with great care, 'So she looks beautiful.' At eighty-five, in the coffin. 'But we're not done yet, Farah.' She opens her handbag, takes out her mascara. 'You use one too, don't you?'

Farah smiles, and keeps smiling as she takes out her own.

Strand by strand, they colour her hair.

'And maybe, a little lipstick?'

'Cinderella off to the ball.'

'No. Just Lucia. My golden Lucia.'

WHEN THE CROW
TURNS WHITE

I want to bring grace, I want to bring kindness.
I think — I'm sure those things exist.

The Hon. Linda Burney, MP

Before it happens, if it really happens, she's vacuuming the chamber of the House of Representatives —

They'll stop the fighting?

(When the crow turns white.)

They'll stop the spin?

(When the crow turns white.)

They'll do something about climate change?

(When the crow turns white.)

Ay, they keep running in her head, those questions from Orla who's vacuuming the other end. Corazon sighs. She knows the answer. But she doesn't say. She pauses beside the podium of the Speaker of the House to take it all in, as she's always done since

11

she started this cleaning job at Parliament House. From floor to seats to those balconies up there, what sprawl of green the shade of gum leaves, and hanging lights like mid-air angels watching over the house, then up, up into that very high ceiling, a recess that looks like a diamond with so much light, as if God might come down any time. This great house fills her with awe, makes her feel small but proud. When she vacuums, it's like she's helping run this country that's now her new home. But Orla's questions, *ay*, if only there were no doubts!

Her phone rings. She checks it. Dave. Her tummy flips, she hesitates, then ends the call before it begins. But is it going to stop?

Pagputi kang uwak: 'When the crow turns white.'

It's what they say back home when something will never happen. And her gut tells her that it will never stop. See, her phone's buzzing. A text. She doesn't want to look but finally relents. It's not him. It's Orla: 'hail! cm lk.'

So when it happens, if it really happens on that fated day of January 20, 2020 in Canberra, she wonders if she's conjured it herself. And she remembers her mother.

'*Lahing uwak kita* — we're kin of crow,' her mother Asun told her when she was little. 'It's not just people that's family, Coring. I tell you, we're crow through and through, we pass on knowledge to each other. From great-grandmother to grandmother to mother to me, and now I pass it on to you. A precious gift: *pag-aram*, knowing. *Aram ta ang diklom, kaya aram ta ang liwanag* — we know the dark, so we know the light. We have the gift of healing. Comes from crow. But it's secret. You don't tell outside family, you just do the work when it's needed.' She said they're from a long line of *albularyos*, of healers. 'You have it, Coring, but you have to practise so it doesn't leave our family.'

But young Corazon was more interested in knowing "the real world". She wanted so much to go to school. 'It's the only way to get ahead in life, *Nay*.'

It made her *Nay*, her mother, sad. 'Careful, Coring, life could get ahead of you …' Then she died, so the gift of crow must have left the family and Corazon thought no more about it. But the local saying about crow stayed with her. Her *other family* made sure she never forgot it.

'I'm going to be a policewoman.'

'When the crow turns white.'

'I'm going to be a lawyer.'

'When the crow turns white,' the cousins teased. 'How can you be any of those, *bobo ka* — you're dumb, Coring, as dumb as your daydreaming!'

She hears them now, their derision in that big house, as she rushes out with Orla to have a look at this hail because she's never seen snow — her phone rings again, the tenth time since this morning. Might as well answer —

'No, Corazon, no more of that husband of yours.'

'He texted he's sorry. He'll come to take me home.'

'What — again? All this to-ing and fro-ing — he's bloody playing you! Told you, time to get that restraining order — now, quick!'

So she lets it ring as they run out of the chamber.

'You must see this, white balls falling like snow!'

'Lordy, look at the size of them!'

'Like golf balls!'

'They're stripping off the leaves!'

'That wind, ugh!'

'And the sound!'

'Glad I parked in here.'

Two men in suits gape through the glass at the elemental havoc in the courtyard. Corazon and Orla join them, dumbfounded by the growing whiteness of the grass. Winter wonderland in summer!

'Hope it doesn't hit the glass,' the bigger man says, stepping back.

'Don't think so, mate — but I've never seen hail like this — bloody awesome!'

'Not beautiful,' Corazon whispers, she's thinking snow. 'It's scary.'

'Climate change is scary,' Orla says, distressed. 'Drought, fishes dying in the rivers, bushfires and floods, smoke-clogged air, and now this — what next?'

'Next is: the climate change deniers in this house should cut their crap!' A pissed-off voice from behind.

One of the men turns and frowns at the speaker, an elderly woman wearing a white scarf. 'Hail is not climate change, madam, it's weather.'

'That's bull—' her retort cuts short as she steps close to the glass, 'Omigod, look at that —' pointing to a black thing falling amidst the white — 'See that?'

Orla and Corazon step close too and the bigger man opens the door and wind and hail rush in as he runs out then scoops it up.

White balls dissolving on him, inside he holds out his palms to the others who utter a half-cry, almost in unison.

It's a crow, dazed, head bloodied and shivering.

Quickly the woman takes off her scarf, wraps the bird in it.

'Wildlife Rescue,' the other man says and starts searching for its number on his phone.

Corazon grips Orla's arm. No, it does not turn white. It dies.

'C'mon,' Orla urges her to follow as the small group rush to the lobby to get help, and she hears her mother again.

'Every living creature is your *kapwa*, your kin, Coring — the birds, the flowers, even this little *kalibubog*.' She had just spanked her bottom with her slipper. Twice. And she cried and cried. 'I didn't kill it!' But the little chafer beetle looked very dead as it dangled from the string that she tied it with, at the cousins' orders. So they could whirl it around. '*Layog, layog pa* — fly, fly more!' It flew and buzzed for nearly half an hour, then stopped. And just dangled. The cousins ran back to the house while she held the still beetle on her palm and felt very, very sorry. It was the only time her mother ever spanked her. 'Remember, Coring — *kapwa*, kin.'

She hears her now as she looks at crow, no, as crow looks at her. It knows.

You won't amount to anything, the family told her. So it was best to marry the Australian. He was 42, she was eighteen.

'*Magayon ka* — you're beautiful — that's your asset. Use it!' *Tiya* Carmen made sure she looked right and ready to meet Dave, her husband's business partner. 'Breasts out, Coring, and don't forget to smile.' And that sealed it.

Corazon's 35 now. She's in bed at Orla's in Gungahlin, reading the text from Dave: 'sori 100x lv♥. wl cm tk u hm. ♥xxxx.'

Her tummy flips. She holds it, holds herself together. *Ay*, why did you have to die, *Nay*? Her mother would have known what to do. She always knew what to do. She had *pag-aram*, crow knowing. But even that couldn't save her in the big house where she served as maid. Asun was made pregnant by Ricky, *Tiya* Carmen's married brother, and when Corazon was born, it sealed their fate. Family said they'd take care of them, but all the while, they probably thought they'd grow another maid. They sent her to the public school around the corner, though, paid for by Ricky, and once a month, he visited from Manila to claim his rights. He'd lock their bedroom under the stairs as little Corazon waited outside, listening to her mother plead, 'Tama na, tama na — enough, enough!' Tummy flipping again and again, she told herself, when I grow up, I'm going to be a policewoman. So I can make it enough for Nay. And when Ricky died in a plane crash, she dreamt she'd be a lawyer to claim her own rights: support for her schooling from his estate. She cried so much when family said he left nothing for her and her mother so, no, the bastarda cannot go to high school, what with too much work around the house now that your mother's grown sickly. So Corazon became the new maid at thirteen, but she never gave up her dream to study. She'd "borrow" her cousins' books and read after midnight when all her chores were done, but soon they found out and locked in their books. The big house was an unkind house, a cruel house, and Dave, she thought, was her way out.

She looks at his text again. He was sweet with her in those early days and he promised to make her dream come true: study here in Australia. He sent her to English classes and was surprised she picked up the language so quickly and so well. He didn't know that back in the big house, she read every printed thing she could lay her hands on, including anything in English. Then he said maybe he'd send her to uni too. If you're nice to me. He's dangled this carrot since they married and settled in the South Coast. And now he's driving over to take her back there. Why did I tell him where I am? Ay, why were we born poor, Nay?

On the white shawl, crow's wings are scrunched up, still. Its beak is half open, like it's about to speak, and its eyes too large and sharp, like it's querying them. Corazon lowers her own eyes but Orla stares back.

'There, there, poor thing,' the woman says, wiping the blood off its wet head, where the feathers seem to have stood on end, with the corner of her shawl.

'Don't touch it, could be concussed,' the bigger man, who rescued the bird, whispers and tries to be as still. We can't distress the animal any further. He's set it on his belly, 'because it'll warm up here,' as they waited for help.

'That's why we've got to do something about climate change — all those animals lost in the fires and the thousands of fishes that died in the Murray, then *this*!'

'That was bad water management or nature's cycle, like fires or freak weather like this,' argues the other man, who finally spoke to Wildlife Rescue. 'Said they'll come, so many casualties around, but can't drive in his hail yet,' he informs the group, then continues, 'Look, madam, it's just nature, not climate change.'

'Spin! That's what those climate change deniers put out there. Spin!'

'Spin? You don't know what the word means —'

'Well, this government knows and knows how to make it! Oh, you poor bird.'

Poor bird begins to shiver again.

'This House knows best. Our MPs and Senators work bloody hard!'

'Ah yes — to advance their own interests, their ideologies, their spin!'

'That word again — *spin*! Easy to whinge when you're not in their shoes.'

The man with the bird on his belly has had enough. 'This House serves the people of Australia, it knows what the country needs —'

'A lump of coal waved around at Question Time?' Orla snaps.

All three stop, note her cleaner's uniform. Shouldn't you be working?

Spin. Corazon thinks of the first time she heard it from Orla as they sat in the balcony watching Question Time in the chamber that they'd vacuumed so many times. They'd finished their shift half an hour ago, grabbed a sandwich and quickly changed clothes, then rushed to the House of Representatives 'as concerned citizens like everyone else,' Orla said.

'But we're only cleaners,' Corazon worried.

'The House of Representatives is The People's House — *Our House.* So we have every right to sit here and watch, while they do their thing down there.'

And what a thing it was — or things, Corazon thought. They fought and shouted, mostly the men really, maybe because there were only a few women, so does this mean that "people" are mostly men? But she worried more about those school kids in the upper balcony watching all these and maybe thinking, if I shout the loudest and fight the most, I can be Prime Minister. Hard to follow what they said but not the aggression in their voices, the sneer and smugness on their faces, because she knew all these when she worked in the big house. Then beside her, Orla snapped, 'Look, always politics and spin!' Later, she said, 'I don't take those things sitting down, I'm convict stock and Irish!' then explained what *spin* means. Corazon said the word reminded her of *trumpo,* a top spinning. Orla laughed and laughed. 'Trump-oh — yes, spin!'

'Corazon, Corazon.' She's shaking her arm now. 'Are you listening to all this?'

The argument around crow's gotten ugly, but she's switched off, like crow closing its eyes and burying its head on its chest. It knows, Corazon thinks. It has always known and would rather not hear any more.

Some years ago, Corazon and Orla met in Wollongong when she took her daughter Sinéad to the university to check it out. She was in Year 12 then and maybe she could study here? They stayed at the motel where Corazon was cleaning. She didn't really need to clean. Successful in real estate, Dave had a big house and drove a new Mazda, but he was so *kuripot*, tight-fisted. She never had a penny in her pocket, except when she did the shopping, which he meticulously checked. How much did she spend from the shopping money he gave her, did she follow his list, did she spend it all? He had to get his money's worth and any leftover cash must be returned to him. It was *his* money. So she decided to take on some casual cleaning, thank god for Pilar, a Filipina who managed one of the Wollongong beach motels. Then there was Pilar's friend Nenita, another Filipina who taught at university and sometimes hired her to clean her flat. The Filipinas in the South Coast were a solace when it got too lonely. But Corazon couldn't come to their community events all the time. Because sometimes she had marks. Dave was a rough lover, and when she said no, he grew rougher.

Ay, Nay, why did I have to repeat history — or why did history have to repeat itself on me? Surely with *pag-aram*, our crow knowing, we could have stopped it? But Dave was always contrite, 100 times sorry after, and he'd tell his sob story all over again: that his mother had abandoned him when he was little, so please don't leave me. Then he'd gift her a dozen roses and promise that someday he'll send her to university. So she stayed and stayed. Until she met Orla.

Corazon was nearly done cleaning the bathroom when mother and daughter got into their motel room. Mother was racked with coughing and couldn't breathe — then she fell over, clutching her chest and looked like she was breathing her last. 'I think it's her asthma,' daughter was crying, 'but she hasn't had an attack for years and we don't have a puffer or meds, oh god, please help us!'

Quickly Corazon sat her upright, turned on the air-conditioner and gave her a whiff of the little bottle of White Flower oil, a bracing menthol-eucalypt-wintergreen mix that she always carries, then whispered something in her ear and breathed with her. When she calmed down, she made her a strong tea with lemon to further clear the airways. Her mother used to do this with *Tiya* Carmen in the big house. Pity, they don't grow the five-leaf *lagundi* here.

Later resting in bed, Orla asked, 'Are you okay?' Strange that the patient should ask the healer. 'I mean — that —' nodding at Corazon's black eye and bruised lip.

'I fell.'

'Fell?'

Corazon nodded as she tucked her in.

'And — and what did you whisper to me then? I didn't really understand.'

Corazon shrugged, smiled. She couldn't say. 'It's secret. You don't tell outside family, you just do the work when it's needed.' She heard her mother's counsel, and as she left the motel, her whispered incantation for anyone losing breath:

'*Ilayog, ilayog ang ilo sa bagà*
Ilayog, ilayog ang sakit ni padabà!'
Fly, fly away the poison in the lungs
Fly, fly away the pain of the beloved!

'Coring, think of the patient as beloved,' her mother once said. 'Only then can you heal her.' But cruel *Tiya* Carmen as beloved?

'Please stop,' Corazon says, voice shaky as she echoes her mother's usual caution: 'Unkindness makes you unhappy. Unhappiness makes you sick.'

Everyone is silenced. The man with the bird finds his return insult stuck in his throat and the woman, who just called him stupid, bites her tongue, and like the other man, Orla is struck dumb by this sudden remark from her who's not spoken throughout the furious bickering at the lobby of Parliament House.

'You made it sicker, look,' Corazon points at crow now trembling convulsively, eyes tightly shut and beak opening-closing as if speaking but can't get its voice out.

'Omigod, it's dying!' the owner of the scarf half-screams.

Then it froze and toppled over.

'It's gone … gone to the other side,' Corazon whispers.

This time, it's the man's belly that shivers.

The day before she ran away from the South Coast to Canberra, for the final time, Orla hoped, Dave shivered. The bushfires were raging and the sky was clogged with smoke, so they were locked in the house for nearly two weeks. Dave was bored, restless, horny, nothing else to do, and even more cruel. Each day she'd look at the brown sky wondering if it would ever clear up. If you want to clean the air, first you have to clean up the hearts. A sudden thought from her mother's words when the river near the big house got covered with thick algae and started to smell: 'If you want to clean the river, first you have to clean up the hearts.' As she worried about the sky, Dave came up from behind, lifted her skirt and pinned her against the picture window. He likes taking her by surprise, from behind. 'No, please,' she begged, she couldn't move, splayed on the glass — then suddenly, amidst the brown vista, a black thing zipped from tree to tree, then the drawn-out cry that she recognised but without the mournfulness. It was strangely pitched this time. Then like a black rocket, it fired itself towards the glass and hit it. Behind her she felt the heaving man's belly shiver, and crow flew off to a tree then back, hitting the glass again and again until he stopped. But it took a while for his shivering to stop.

Again the man's belly shivers and grows still. 'Dead,' he murmurs. Gone the pugilistic tone. He can't move, eyes locked onto the unmoving bird.

Corazon picks up crow. 'I'll take care of it — here, your shawl, ma'am —'

The woman steps back, 'No, it's okay — what will you do?'

'I'll take care of it,' she says again and the woman starts to cry, and Orla puts her arms around her as the men mutter, 'Sorry,' then Corazon's phone rings.

Orla shakes her head, don't answer. It rings and rings.

Corazon returns to the chamber with crow. Because it urged her to, she felt it as she picked up the dead bird. Or maybe because of the mid-air angels up there and the lit diamond from where God might descend anytime. Or maybe it's *pag-aram*, crow knowing: this is the right thing to do. This death must be witnessed in The People's House. So she told Orla she'll finish the vacuuming herself. Now she sets crow on the Speaker's podium and looks around the seats the shade of gum trees. Here they fought and shouted and sneered during that Question Time. 'It's all performance, grandstanding, and troublemaking for the other side!' said Orla as they watched from the balcony, and Corazon sighed. Her sigh sounds louder now, echoing around the chamber as she arranges crow on the white shawl. She whispers a prayer for the dead. 'Human or animal, you lay their dead, you pay respect,' her mother used to say.

Her phone rings, again! As she grabs it from her pocket, cool air brushes her arm — where from? Ah, she's just imagined it. But her skin's moist, she smells it. Eucalypt? She lets it ring. Shrill, wrapping around the chamber. 'Ay, this is not a happy house,' she remembers telling Orla as they watched the fighting down here.

'Maybe they're unhappy, unkindness makes you unhappy,' and someone from behind hissed, 'Shut up!'

Later that night, Orla said, 'Your unkindness thing, uhmm, I wonder ...'

She tried to explain. 'It's mostly the men who shout at each other, Orla, so maybe if there are more women, it will be a kinder house.' But wasn't the big house ruled by *Tiya* Carmen and her three girl cousins? But she couldn't say as Orla clapped her hands.

'Yes, a kinder house. Heard of Linda Burney, the first Aboriginal woman to be elected to the House of Reps? When asked what she'll bring to the Parliament, she said, "grace and kindness" — now that should make you happy.'

The ringing has stopped.

Grace and kindness, grace especially. It's that inner graciousness that helps us to be kind. But for her mother, it was the grace of the Lord. When she complained of their lot in the big house, she'd say, 'Coring, it will come.' It never did. She looks up now at the diamond filled with light and sighs. No, God will not come down to make it right. And those mid-air angels are just hanging lights. She returns to crow. *Ay*, this stillness, this ending. Her next sigh tarries. It fills her lungs, circles there, making her tremble. When she finally breathes out, she knows. *It is she who must make it right.*

She begins to wrap crow with the shawl. She'll bury it in Orla's garden. And yes, that restraining order — her phone rings again! She grabs it from her pocket to switch it off, but then changes her mind.

'I'm sorry a hundred times, love, I heard about the hail, are you okay, oh my darling, I'll drive over and pick you up, I'll make it up to you,' and on and on into her ear as she breathes in, recalling her just-released sigh, filling her lungs with it and all the air in the chamber to scream, '*Tama naaaaaaaaaaaa!*' — Enouuuuuuugh!

'Enough!' catapults from where she stands beside the Speaker's podium onto the green seats, wraps around them, rises to the balconies, making the hanging lights tremble, then, up, up to the lit diamond where it whips up air that smells of gum leaves and trees and all of the bush, then descends, circling like an *ipo-ipo*, a tornado changing the climate of the chamber and a house in the South Coast.

She breathes in this new climate, deeply, and picks up the bundled white shawl, then breathes out an incantation, her mother's —

'Ilayog, ilayog ang pusò kang gadan
Ilayog, ilayog, dae nanggad pagbutsan!'
Fly, fly the heart of the dead
Fly, fly, never ever drop it!

The bundle shivers. She chants again. The bundle opens, like a white efflorescence, then wings open — white wings? Crow has become the colour of the shawl. *Crow has turned white!* It looks at her, she looks back. They both know. When you hold anyone's heart, you never ever drop it. And when you hold the people's heart, how could you drop it?

So crow flies on, up into that diamond, through the roof and out. The wind and the scent of the bush follow, returning to their own homes, and The House returns to order. But the house in the South Coast will never be able to restore Dave's order. Balance lost, he can't drive to Canberra to reclaim his wife and no specialist will ever figure out what happened to his shattered eardrum and atrophied middle ear.

It's late when Corazon finishes vacuuming. She's been more thorough than usual. She's made sure there's no trace of crow. As her mother said, it's secret.

So when it happens, if ever it happens on that day of the hailstorm, no one knows it does. Except a woman and a bird. But Corazon doesn't know that infinitesimal white feathers have stuck to the carpet and the seats. Only crow knows its own body.

So on that sitting day of the House of Representatives when COVID-19 has turned the country and the world upside down, none of the parliamentarians know that bits of crow have stuck to their sleeves and the soles of their shoes. The people are amazed as they watch Question Time on TV. How polite, how bipartisan, how caring our MPs have become. Only crow knows, of course. Grace and kindness. They could stick to you. If given the chance.

THE KINDNESS OF BIRDS

"Hope" is the thing with feathers —

Emily Dickinson

The *kiyaw* of your Papa — they visited and sang for him.'

In Legazpi, her mother is telling the story about two orioles that came to sing for her father. He's oblivious to her awe. He is dying.

'They roosted there,' she points to the neighbour's tree across the house.

Nenita looks out from the window of her parents' bedroom that's now a mini hospital. Yes, the golden shower tree. It bursts into deep yellow flowers every summer, like the colour of orioles.

'When he was still well, your Papa would sit on the porch and wait for the couple to visit and sing.' Her mother knows orioles travel with their mate. 'Sometimes we'd sit together and wait for them in the back garden. Their favourite spot, on the coconut tree. *Ay*, the brightest yellow among the green fronds.' Then she whispers to him through the tubes and monitors, 'They visited you yesterday … they know you love their song,' and grasps his hand. As if it could be sung again by touch. *Ki-kiyaw, ki-kiyaw.* How they worded their song. *Kiyaw.* How her father nicknamed the pair.

It's this memory that makes Nenita think of the kindness of birds five months after he died. As the thought sneaks in, two rosellas fly up the cedar outside their Canberra apartment. It's early July, very cold and still a fair way until spring. She has just put the phone down after a long overseas call with her mother who's a little off-colour. A few months later, she'll undergo surgery.

The weight of the phone is still in her hand, a ghost, as she tries to imagine them listening to the orioles in the garden. Then the rosellas flash crimson and blue outside. Between the Philippines and Australia, flight of birds with flight of thought. Memory is migratory. One bird recall recalls another, then another. Serendipity, resonance, magic. We're here too, do not forget us.

Yes, they're here. Crimson and blue darting in and out of the very bent crab apple. It's spring in her old suburb, some years before the move to the Canberra apartment. The tree is in full pink bloom. And they're here: the early lovers. Two rosellas feeding on nectar. More will come as the flowers turn to fruit.

'They never fail to return.' Her husband Arvis is wistful as he sips his coffee.

'They never really leave,' Nenita says.

In a month, they will scatter the ashes of his mother's sister in the Blue Mountains. His mother, father, brother passed away years ago. But Lucy, his godmother-aunt, his "other mother", was always there after. Lucy: Light. What's left in the cup when you've finished your coffee.

The rosellas call to each other among the blossoms.

'She'll be apples — soon,' she whispers over her coffee.

'Ah, that old Australianism,' he chuckles.

'I love it.' She always has, since she heard it from her ex-husband. During their courting days, whenever she worried about anything, he'd assure her 'she'll be apples.' That all will be okay. He too passed from her life, as she, from his. But why *she* and who is *she*? Who knows? What matters is the gift of apples, the flash of russet whenever the darkness came. Maybe we should also say, 'she'll be birds,' and resolve to fly into the light.

'Lucy lived in her own home until her last days,' Arvis says. 'She was growing blind, but she still made me tea when I visited, served with her *pīrāgs*.' Sometimes these little Latvian meat pies came all the way from her oven in Gosford to their table.

Yes, this is how to remember: remember the kindness, remember kindly.

Next door, their neighbour Terence is feeding a magpie. This swooping bird is like a baby trusting his hand. But from what she's heard, he's not a kind man. His wife Karlen told her about their son who killed himself. Shot himself in the open field in front of their house. She filled in the silences and thought, maybe unkindness and kindness are umbilical. Karlen met Terence in London after he was wounded in World War II. She was a refugee from war-torn Germany volunteering as a nurse for the other side. Oh yes, she'll be birds. His hand on the trigger at the trenches, her hand nursing his gunshot wound, his hand feeding a bird.

They're both gone now, flown away from each other's lives.

There's a shadow of a magpie about to swoop at her and Nenita's returned to her own parents. To her mother and her hands as quick to hit as her tongue. Always the blame, sometimes a bruise. 'You're the eldest, you're to blame!' For her mother, it's always the fault of the eldest if anything goes wrong in the house or among her children. Even if they're all grown-up adults responsible for their own hurts and hurtings. Even if the eldest is now living an ocean away. That dark wing of blame still flaps around her and she's almost always undone. On the phone in Canberra or at every homecoming, still receiving her militant dressing down.

She has a photo of her hand. Veins like greenish, swollen rivers running turbulent from wrist to fingers with nails clipped short, precise. How quiet the hand now, how still against the whiteness of the sheet. She has an earlier photo of their hands when he's dying: hers cupping his. Father's three fingers rest on Mother's palm, her thumb presses them. A press of assurance: I am here.

Two hands, two wings intertwined.

We're here, do not forget us.

Her father forgets how many children he has, their names, but he remembers what her mother was wearing when they first met 60 years ago: a dress with green leaves. Like a shadow, his dementia lengthens towards the day's end, towards the ending. It's afternoon back home and they're telling her stories. No, they're telling each other stories. Lest they forget those early lovers and the green leaves.

Suddenly a rustle outside. 'Shhh ...' mother hushes father, takes his hand and leads him to the jalousies that open to the back garden. The leaves rustle again and she whispers, '*Hilinga* — look.'

Nenita looks but does not see.

'*Dangoga* — listen,' her mother continues, pointing to the *madre de cacao* tree.

Her face lights up, his face lights up — this Nenita sees so well.

Then she hears the singing.

'The husband-and-wife,' her mother whispers, 'they're telling stories.'

'*Tagbaya*,' her father names the storytelling birds, tiny but big-voiced: the pied fantails. He points and they all look, breaths held as they watch the crazy acrobatics. In and out of the green they dart, black aerialists with white throats and breasts. Then the husband roosts, spreads his tail — a black fan edged with white — and the pair are off as a new chirping starts.

'*Ay*, Mama, they're gone! The *mayas* drove them away,' she protests, a child again. The *mayas*, the Eurasian tree sparrows, have usurped the roost, the air, her ear.

'They'll return,' her mother smiles and pats her hand.

When a bird flies off, what remains? It's the song, if she listened enough. It's the colour, if she looked enough. But what did she really hear, what did she see?

Those hands. She wishes to be restored, a child again. Six years old. Mother's combing her hair until it shines, preparing her for the first day of school. She smiles at her on the mirror. She's proud. This is her eldest.

'Think good things,' Arvis says his favourite line. 'Yes, *mīļotā*,' he croons in Latvian — 'yes, sweetheart, always remember joy.'

It's nearly spring again and they're walking around Lake Burley Griffin. The sky is the kind of blue that makes her go 'oh', and all she can do is look and look and soar. But other stories keep swooping into her head. All in present tense. They fly into each other, wings intertwining, songs syncopating.

'Look at all these — and I mean, *really look*,' her husband says, sweeping an arm across the gleaming eucalypts, the white cherry flowers just starting to open, the Pacific black ducks and Australian wood ducks foraging in the pond where green shoots are pushing up. A pair of pink and grey overtake them: galahs heading straight up a blue gum, their call reproachful. Has she not really looked?

'Life is good, and it's healthier to remember good things,' he continues, picking up his step. This is their morning exercise. 'Good for the heart,' he adds.

What really is good for the heart before that final flight?

She remembers a moment that still disturbs her. Grandmother Catalina is dying in a hospital in Manila. Her eldest son, *Tiyo* Rex, sits by her bed, holding her hand. 'Mama,' he whispers, 'Remember when you used to beat me as a child?' She holds back a gasp. Why say this now?

Acknowledge that broken kid, mother. Please. Perhaps this is the heart's need: recognition of its hurt and, if unsaid all those years, recognition that it's still hurting. For redress. Remembering the unkindness as much as the kindness, or the other way around. For balance. Oh the little flutters of the heart, its unlikely turns.

At the funeral mass for grandmother, the priest gives the final blessings. Suddenly *Tiyo* Rex begins to sing Connie Francis' *Mama* — 'I miss the days ...' His baritone grows louder, fills the church. His siblings stare, one shakes her head, another stifles a giggle. How strange, and funny, coming from him.

Even *Tiyo* Rex has flown away. But the orioles linger.

She remembers this, on the phone. Mother's awe is so big, it swallows her up. 'I visited your Papa's grave today, and they were there, the husband-and-wife up on the old hardwood, singing!'

They sang for him in life, in dying, in death.

The kindness of birds.

And the rosellas flew up in Canberra.

The constancy of the kindness of birds.

They fly and sing wherever and whenever, and to whoever.

'You're anthropomorphising again,' a friend once observed. 'Don't you know, birds can be very unkind, they can peck your eyes out.' Nenita knows: they were both anthropomorphising. 'But you see,' she reasons to Arvis now, 'even if the orioles sang not out of kindness, my father received it as such. As did my mother and me. It's a precious cross-line for which this humbled human is forever grateful.' She's fallen in step with his stride along the lake where a cormorant is sunning itself, wings open and so, so still. They stop, hold their breaths and watch, then quietly walk on.

'Trust the sun to do its thing,' Arvis murmurs.

'Y'know, last night I dreamt I'm back home. Mother takes me shopping for the best fabric, then off to the dressmaker, again a new dress for her eldest daughter. Our usual date each time I came home, it was bonding, fun … and she never ever forgot to send me a birthday or Christmas card, always with "Your loving Mama".'

'Yes, mīḻotā, think good things.' He does not miss his stride.

Up ahead, a new song. Before they even see them. She strides faster but they're too quick. All she can make out is a dash of blue, then brown. Again a pair keeping up their scales in the air, long after they've disappeared from her sight. How can such tiny bodies hold so much song? Later, she'll read something extraordinary. Superb fairy-wrens sing a special note to their unhatched chicks. Like a secret code. The chicks learn it by heart and it's threaded into their begging call. So mum knows these are her babies, perhaps wherever they are, and she feeds them.

Fairy-wrens. Fairies. Magic. That trust can be built on a single note.

Are You My Mother? The title of a classic children's book that her mother bought them when they were little. It's about a baby bird that fell from the nest and went in search for its mum. It kept asking everyone and everything, from a kitten to a cow, a boat to a plane to a crane called Snort: 'Are you my mother?' The book was part of a small library that her mother saved up for, for so long. Paid in slow instalments while keeping a very tight home budget. What an accomplishment. How she and her siblings loved those books, read and re-read them as children, then read them to the neighbourhood's children, and later to her siblings' children. Are you my mother? Yes, and I'm proud of you, Mama.

That little bird found its mum. Was it because of a single trusted note? That survival bond. So does one stop singing when it breaks?

'The husband-and-wife oriole always travel together,' Nenita tells her husband. 'Maybe that's why Mama flew away too … so soon after Papa.'

Arvis stops walking, takes both her hands, then all of her. He holds her.

A mother grey teal leads her chicks to the water. Further on the bank, a crowd of dusky moorhens peck away at the ground.

'Look, *Gallinula Tenebrosa*.'

The name rises in her head like a Spanish song, she hears guitars, she hears flamenco. She's flown to another moment, even further away. She's waking up in the Albaicín in Granada and she's recording early morning sounds, whispering to her phone as the birds sing the light in. 'The birds like a prayer in the morning, the birds waking us, telling us that life goes on. And the voices in the periphery in a language I can't understand. But always the language of birds, that ticking of time in the throat of birds … maybe birds understand better than we do.'

They do: that morning goes on its way to evening then to morning again. But she's no ornithologist, not at all bird informed. So what does she know? She knows she wants to know hope.

They keep walking to where the Exhibition Centre stands, white against the grass against the endless blue.

Then on the slope, she sees her. The lone black swan pecking away.

'Where — why?'

'What d'you mean?'

'It's the fourth time we've seen her, alone. Swans travel with their mate — but her — she's on her own, again!' Her distress spills. 'What happened to him?'

'Probably feeding around the corner — and why do you think *this* is a she?'

Because *she'll* be birds.

They keep walking, up and around the slope. No *he*.

She hangs onto his hand. 'I keep seeing them … at their deathbed. I keep seeing their suffering faces.'

'Look up,' he says. 'The sun, the best antiseptic.'

She follows, to focus. Against the startling blue, a gleaming gum tree with two galahs curiously checking out this intertwined pair.

And suddenly the orioles fly all the way from a memory.

The rosellas follow, resolving red and blue against the cedar.

Then more of them, gracing the very bent crab apple.

Then the magpie feeding from a tender hand.

Then the pied fantail spreading its tail.

Then the sparrows.

Then fairy-wrens.

All of them singing, 'She'll be apples, she'll be birds.'

THE AIR OF THE TIMES

Düfte sind die Gefühle der Blumen —
Fragrances are the feelings of flowers.

Heinrich Heine

Belen traces the intertwined doves on the bottle cap.
Remy opens the perfume. 'Smell it.'

'Uhmm … flowery — if you like that sort of thing.'

'Nina Ricci's *L'Air du Temps*.'

'High-class, huh?'

'I think literally "The Air or The Spirit of the Times" to mean current trend.'

'Ah, little Aussie sis is giving me a language lecture.'

'Please, Áte Belen —'

'And she can afford high-class now.'

'It's a gift.'

'From an admirer?'

'Not in *that* sense. Try it.'

'*Burgis na burgis* — ultra-bourgeois,' Belen says, but she sprays some on her wrist and smells it. 'Too sweet.'

'No, it's subtle and fresh,' Remy counters.

Girl talk in a hotel room in Manila, or so it seems. Remy is unpacking her suitcase. She's just flown in from Sydney. Belen lounges on the bed, examining each unpacked item, cigarette in hand. She's just come down from the hills.

'So who's the admirer?' Belen smirks, blowing smoke at her sister.

'Still can't help yourself, can you? It's a grandfather in his 80s. Werner, an admirer, yes, of my work. He said this gift is not the perfume but the doves of peace.'

'Flying in the air of the times, very trendy — la-la-la. So he's a poet too?'

'At heart, yes, he *was*. Went to his funeral before I flew here.'

'But you didn't go to father's funeral.'

'You didn't go either.'

'You know I couldn't come home.'

'You think I could?'

Their father died a year before and it was his sons who buried him.

'How are they?' Remy asks.

'Our brothers are doing well, I heard.'

'You haven't — *encountered* them?'

'And have you, little Aussie sis?'

'I'm visiting in two days' time. Going home.'

'Home … where is it?' Belen whispers the awkward question.

Both go quiet. It's difficult to find an answer for the daughters who left home, while the sons stayed and cared for their ailing father.

Remy folds and unfolds a pair of pyjamas, then folds it again.

Belen blows smoke rings as she holds up the bottle of perfume to the light. A lambent glow: the opaque glass doves come alive. 'Expensive doves of peace,' she says and sets it down on the side table. Beside it, Remy lays the rest of her toiletries in a neat row.

Belen nods at the perfume. 'So, little Aussie sis must have made an impression on this Werner.'

'He loved poetry and hated war.' She made sure to enunciate the last words.

'Like my little Aussie sis —'

'Stop calling me that, Áte! And can you please not smoke in here?'

But Áte — big sister — just takes a long puff at her cigarette.

'Werner smoked twenty packs a day then went cold turkey at 77.'

'Ah, it's Werner who's made an impression on my little sister.' She appraises her sibling kneeling before the bed, unpacking and repacking her things. 'Still obsessive compulsive.' But her face softens and she reaches out, touches the doves. Finger lingers on the curve of a wing. 'Your hair … it's grown so long.'

'We haven't seen each other for some years.'

Big sister withdraws, shrugs. 'I sent messages.'

'No, grandmother sent messages.'

'It's the same.'

'No, it's not — and can you stop smoking?'

Belen crushes her cigarette on a saucer set precariously on a pillow.

'You'll burn the place down.'

'That's what I do,' Belen says as she gets up.

Remy faces the other squarely. 'You're really back? Is *it* over?'

'Is it ever over?' Belen mumbles as she rummages through her backpack. She finds it: a small .38.

Remy sucks in her breath. 'With you, it's never over.'

Belen checks the revolver, tucks it into the front of her jeans and puts on a jacket then heads for the door.

'Don't go.'

'Don't wish to pollute your air.'

'I'm sorry for being so … please stay.' Remy grips her arm. 'We've never been good at this, have we?'

'Never.'

'Always passing each other by.'

Belen stares at the hand on her arm.

'Except now. So please stay. Just this once.'

'My sister grew up with grandmother, like you.'

Werner nods. '*Gott segne sie* — God bless all grandmothers of this world.'

Above them at the open-air restaurant, the harbour sky is grey. But the view of the ocean wrapped around the Sydney Opera House is still majestic. Werner said so several times when she arrived for their lunch date. As usual, positive and dapper in his designer suit and tie. Remy felt shabby in denims and t-shirt.

'My grandmother was a kind woman — to me, to the neighbours, and to her flowers. *Ja*, she talked to them, so they bloomed beautiful. "Don't hurt the flowers, Werner, they have feelings," she said when I played in her garden in Kassel … so many birds … *ja*, where there are flowers, there are birds.'

'Where there are birds, there are flowers,' Remy rounds up the fact.

'Beside the beautiful Fulda river — you must see it if you visit Germany.' He turns to the water around them, wistful. '"*Düfte sind die Gefühle der Blumen* — Fragrances are the feelings of flowers." Heinrich Heine. Have you read him?'

'No, but I've heard of him.'

'Grandmother Edith loved flowers, they make the air sweet, "*Ach*, sweet, sweet gifts," she said,' he whispers in earnest, as if sharing a prized secret, then raises his glass to the sky, hand a bit shaky. '*Das Leben ist gut* — life is good!'

'You're so positive, Mr Werner.'

'The only way to live.' He savours his French red. 'So, you like it?' he nods at her barely touched glass.

'Nice, but I don't know anything about wine, sir — back home, we drink beer and Coke.'

He frowns at Coke. 'So, tell me about your grandmother.'

'Grandmother Natividad. She's no longer with us. My sister was her favourite.'

He nods, knowingly.

'She lived with grandmother in the village, on and off then for good.'

'And why was this?'

'She and father couldn't get along since we were kids.'

Werner nods again.

'Difficult time. There were six of us, with no mother.'

'You said your mother died when you were little.'

'Yes. I'm the youngest, after her.'

'Your sister.'

'Uh-huh. My only sister. She's clever. But headstrong.'

'And you, you're clever too, *ja* — but not headstrong?'

'I'm for peace, sir, I don't like fights.'

'I believe in a good fight if necessary — like your warrior woman, *ja*? I told you I worked in the British army, quartermaster in Normandy —'

'Quartermaster?'

'Logistical support. For the fighting, the living ... and the dying ... a decent dying ... when we can.' His glass of red shakes, he steadies it on the table. 'A good fight, *ja*, when we can — but I prefer peace. *Frieden!*' and he downs his red.

'Sounds like "freedom".'

'Ja, ja. To be free is to be at peace, to be at peace is to be free.'

This time, it's she who nods.

They met at the New South Wales Library in Sydney. She was in an Asian panel of arts students speaking on how art can shift hearts and minds. She spoke about a book of poems that she was writing on the *amazonas*, what they call the Filipina revolutionaries who went to the hills to join the NPA, the New People's Army, in their fight against the Marcos regime. The war lasted for twenty years and grew into a Total War, the government's "purge of communists" in the countryside and many disappeared, fighters and civilians alike. She spoke about the fighters' dilemma, to fight or not to fight, and those they left behind, their own war never ending as they waited for loved ones who never came home. 'There is always another war after every war ...' As she read from her poem, she noticed the impeccably dressed, grey-haired gentleman on the front row. Eyes closed and hands clasped over his wooden cane, whole body leaning towards the stage, towards her, she thought. It felt like she was reading only to him, for him. Afterwards he hovered around the artists. Gait slow, frail, she noticed. Finally he approached and his first words were, 'I understand.' Then he told her he had lost his whole family in the Holocaust.

'War is ugly, Remedios. We must fight for peace.'

'Fighting and peace — how can they mix?'

'Na ja, they mix when it is necessary to mix. Now drink. This is very good red — and what would you like to eat?'

'What was that French red like — what's it called?'

'I don't remember. I didn't really drink —

Belen slaps her thigh. "What a waste! I would have discussed *Frieden* with him over a whole bottle!' She's having another beer and Remy is cleaning up after dinner, picking up crumbs, rearranging the stack of empty plates and wiping the side table for the nth time. They ordered room service an hour ago: *pancit* and *siopao* — noodles and pork buns demolished in no time.

On a full stomach now, there's almost *Frieden* in the air.

'*Frieden* is freedom — *kapayapaan* is *kalayaan* — peace is freedom. Wow, Áte, the words sound almost the same too in Filipino!'

'It's never the same, Remy. There's peace and there's peace. After a war, the question is, who gains after peace is declared? Who loses out? Who's really free? And *whose peace is it* — who enjoys it? And who's made to live with a fake peace? Ah, you don't know anything.' She lights another cigarette.

'C'mon, Áte, no smoking.'

'Now, you're breaking the peace, little sister.'

'Breaking *whose* peace, yours or mine?'

Belen pushes her cigarette pack towards Remy. 'Have one, let's break the peace together — I remember you smoked when I visited you at your high school,' but Remy turns away, returns to picking up crumbs while nursing her own beer.

'*Dios mío* — will you stop that obsessive cleaning, drives me nuts!'

Remy is silent.

Belen gets up, lights a second cigarette and offers it to the other crouched on the floor. 'Or, let's smoke the peace pipe together. For once.'

"For once" reverberates in the room, echoing history.

Remy turns around and stares at her sister as if about to cry. She takes the lit stick. 'For once.'

Belen returns to the bed, moving close to the wall to free up space, then pats it. Remy hesitates, lies down. The sisters smoke quietly.

After a while, Belen chuckles. 'We'll burn the house down, together.'

'You've come down for good, Áte.' It's a wish more than a statement.

Belen takes a drag on her stick. 'Don't know. I'm down for some secret "peace talk". Again. The government said the same right after People Power.'

'You know, Áte, we took to the streets too, my classmates and I — in that bloodless revolution —'

'Don't kid yourself. No revolution is bloodless, there's always sacrifice.'

'February 1986 … we were all happy, hopeful, we ousted the dictator — I thought you'd come home …'

'*All* happy? You're still as *burgis* and clueless as ever. More so because you left. Get some perspective, Remy! That People Power was *only* a Manila event. Then what happened next? After all that peace talk shit of the government, in '87 they declared Total War against us, against the people in the countryside.'

'I was so scared, Áte …'

It's 1996 now and fear still hangs around.

'Scared for you, for grandmother.'

'I made sure she was safe.'

'Even from up there?'

'I have my own people.'

'And me — did you think of me?'

'You were fine.'

'In a house of men.'

'Father loved you.'

'So long as I did his bidding.' Remy gives up on her cigarette. 'You said you'd come back for me.'

'That was a long time ago.'

'You could have kept your promise. For once.'

'No one should promise anything in a war.'

'At least you came, now.'

Through a friend of their grandmother, Remy tracked her sister down in the hills. She arranged this meeting, she begged for it.

'You see, I can keep a promise.'

They go quiet. They have talked enough to the ceiling. They're afraid to catch each other's eye.

'Are you safe, Áte?'

'Ah, always scaredy cat.'

Hushed voices outside — Belen sits up, tensed, then relaxes. However much the voices whisper, some words are still audible. 'Darling' … 'Love you'… 'Want you.' Then laughter and next door being opened and shut. Soon, love cries and thudding on the wall. Belen puts her palm against it, 'Vibrating — ha-ha!' and Remy mouths, 'God they're loud.' The sisters giggle and have another beer.

'You are my best poet. You can arrange the language brilliantly,' Werner writes her in a short note that says he'd like to buy her books. 'Please send by post plus invoice.' Typewritten, formal yet friendly — like his salutation, 'My dear friend Remedios.' A week after she sends the books, the payment cheque arrives with a thank-you note. A brief praise of her poems, then: 'Fortunately, writing invoices is not a daily requirement for a poet as you have lost $10.00 in your additions. The correct cheque for $42.00 is enclosed.' She laughs. She finds his formally rendered humour endearing. A filial affection grows in her and it makes her sad. She has never felt this way about her own father, an ex-army colonel who said poetry is a waste of time. She grew up in a regimented house, no soft spaces. Her three brothers joined the army and the fourth did business at university. But her sister dropped out of law on her first year and went to the hills. Closely aligned with the local politicos, their father disowned her. Remy was tolerated because she always topped her class and, on his orders, took up law to make up for 'Belen's betrayal.' But she gave it up for a scholarship in Literature in Australia. To him, 'the girls' were a disappointment.

Werner drew these family stories from her on their occasional lunches and told her his own. His stepfather killed himself after he lost everything during *Kristallnacht* in Hamburg in '38 and his mother ended up in Dachau, or so he heard. He was living between Paris and London after he got away in '33 when the manager of the fabric store where he worked urged him to leave. He knew he was a Jew. He arranged to get grandmother out of Germany but grandfather opted to stay so there'd be somewhere to come home to for his wife and grandson. 'I'll be here, when *this* is over, I promise.' When it was over, Werner visited Kassel. No grandfather and only strangers living in the house or what was left of it. And no more garden.

'No flowers, no birds. No birds, no flowers. What war does, *verstehen Sie?*'

Ich verstehe — comprendo — je comprends — naiintindihan ko — I understand. She wants to understand it in all languages, if only she knows how.

'The air smells of blood for a long time,' Werner says and she nods even if she can never fully understand. She wasn't there.

They sip their coffees silently.

'Grandmother was shot in Riga.'

The five-word story hits her, her coffee spills.

'I arranged a passage for her out of Germany. I was going to meet her in Paris. But she took the wrong train. Maybe there was no more right train. I waited, she never came. She was deported to the Riga ghetto. She never got there. I go through this in my head, *ja*, sometimes I dream. I always smell blood in the air … *Blut und Blut.*'

'How did you —?'

'I found out from a neighbour who was with her on that death train. Eighth of December 1941. When they were driven out of their homes in Kassel.'

'Sir, that date … I think it was when Japan attacked the Philippines, right after Pearl Harbor.'

'*Ach*, the Pacific War — and your family?'

'It was a brutal Japanese occupation, grandmother said. Her mother was killed by the Japanese. Bayonet. She told that story to my sister and I when we were kids.'

'And now, your sister has gone to war.'

My whole family has gone to war. But she does not say this.

'Now, dessert. I think the apple strudel. It's good,' then he winks. 'But not as good as grandmother's.'

She laughs, awkwardly. 'You have a way of shifting gears —'

'To sweeten the air. The only way to live.'

'Thank you for being kind to me — and for bringing your whole family to my book launch last night.'

'Thank you for being kind to an old man, my best poet,' he chuckles then gets serious. 'You don't have family here. So I invite family.' Then he opens his leather satchel. 'Here, for you. A congratulations for your book.'

It's a yellow box: Nina Ricci.

'Oh, thank you, sir.'

'*L'Air du Temps* — "The Spirit of the Times" like — the mood or the trend, the zeitgeist, *ja*! Open it.'

'It's—it's the most beautiful bottle.'

'The doves of peace. Launched in 1948, after the war.'

Belen touches the intertwined doves on the perfume cap. 'These birds can't fly.'

'You're always contrary.'

'I took after father, Remy. The only thing I inherited from him, thank god.'

'You two fought all the time.'

Belen downs the last of her beer then puts her ear on the wall. 'I think "the fight" next door is over.'

'They're exhausted,' Remy whispers, stifling a giggle.

Belen makes heaving sounds.

Remy hushes her, the sisters giggle.

There's a companionable stupor in the room after all the beers in bed. Remy has returned the perfume to the side table. She wants to keep telling Werner's story. *Fragrances are the feelings of flowers …*'

'Mother had jasmine outside the bedroom window.'

Remy sits up. 'We had flowers at home?'

'Before you were born.'

Remy has only known a two-storey stone house with a paved driveway and an iron gate.

'Father destroyed it to punish mother. For being friendly with Nilo's teacher.' Nilo is their eldest brother.

'I didn't know that.'

'How could you? You were still in her tummy. Nilo told father that mother and teacher always talked when she picked him up from school. Then he told him he caught them having Coke at the canteen. I remember that day. I thought he would hit her. He didn't. He pulled out the jasmine from the ground and cut it into little bits. She loved that jasmine.'

'You hated him.'

'I don't hate, Remy. I just see things as they are. And I act. Unlike you. But you're a poet, so —' she shrugs.

Remy cradles the perfume on her palm. 'I told Werner about you.'

'Gossiped.'

'That you went to the hills to fight, for peace.'

'My romantic little sis, romanticising everything including a war.'

'Why don't you like me, Áte?'

'What kind of question is that?'

'Because I stayed in the house you hated?'

'You could have come with me to grandmother's.'

'You could have come back.'

'So father could beat me again?'

'Things got better, you know.'

'Only fourteen, and he beat me to a pulp.'

'You accused him of killing mother —'

'Living in fear all your life. It could kill you.'

'And you pulled that knife —'

'To defend myself — and he backed off.'

Remy was only seven then, but she still remembers it clearly. In the kitchen. How tiny her sister looked before their father and his raised fist, but how arresting her rage. It scared her, no, it amazed her. She was magnificent.

They've polished off the strudels now, though they're not as good as grandmother's.

Werner puts *Amazona*, the book she just launched, on the table and taps it, saying, 'I understand,' then he pauses, in two minds about what to say next. 'I think — you should make peace with your sister, *ja*?'

At each lunch, he tries to draw out her history. But all can never be fully told. There's always air between words. The air of the unsaid. The air of untold time. So she returns him to his own story, to Kassel. To the house with soft spaces, the house with a garden.

'What were the flowers in your grandmother's garden?'

His face lights up. '*Ach*, so many, *Rosen, Tulpen, Nelken, Maiglöckchen, Kornblumen*, I don't remember all. She loved sweet things. I used to send her perfumes from Paris, before the war. She liked them but we can never bottle flowers, she said.'

'We can never bottle feelings.'

'Right, *richtig*! I think — I think *Je Reviens* …'

'*Je* …?'

'The perfume she wore when she took that train.'

'How did you know, sir?'

'I was already in Australia, early 60s. Our neighbour Ruth tracked me down, all the way from America. *Ja*, eighteen-year-old Ruth, she lived across the road from us in Kassel. Survived the Riga ghetto then the concentration camp. She didn't stop until she found me, here in Sydney.' He tells the story as Ruth told him in a letter sent to thank Grandmother Edith, or at least to thank her grandson.

It's like an old film before Remy's eyes.

It's a very cold winter morning. Twelve hundred Jews are driven out of their homes. To be "evacuated", they don't know where. They register at the Town Hall with their luggage. They are examined: what gold or silver are they taking? Grandmother Edith arrives wearing a brown cashmere coat. The next day Ruth sits with her on the train. She's freezing. Grandmother hugs her into her coat. It's warm and smells nice, she's wearing perfume. *Je Reviens*, she tells her. How fitting, Ruth thinks. But where's

Grandfather Heinz? She hushes her. He's staying, he's hiding, she whispers. Is that possible? Three days they take the train. It stops in Skierotawa, a suburb of Riga. They get off. The SS order them to walk to the ghetto. The elderly and the sick stay to wait for a ride. They're driven to the woods and shot.

'*Je Reviens* — I'm coming back. She couldn't, she never did.'

It's half an hour to midnight. Remy hands *Amazona* to her sister.

Belen stares at the title, censures her with a look.

'It's for you, I wrote it for you.'

Belen keeps shaking her head at the image on the cover: against a splatter of red, the silhouette of a woman with an AK-47. 'I live it, you write it — is that it?'

'Please open it, Áte.'

'I'm now your new material, huh?' Belen slams the book on the side table, upsetting the perfume, and book and bottle drop. She's quickly on the floor, rescuing both. The bottle is broken and most of the perfume is spilled on the book, the floor. Remy is on the floor too, crying.

'Sorry, I'm clumsy, I break things.' Belen lifts the book, wiping it, unsticking the first pages from the cover. On the dedication page, she sees it —

To my magnificent sister,
always missed, always loved.

She can't look up because the words are blurring.

The room, the bed, the sisters smell of flowers. They're asleep. It's like how they used to sleep in the stone house. In one bed, little

Remy curled up to big sister Belen. Big sister was mother, when mother died of cancer, before she ran away to grandmother.

On the side table, the saved book and bottle cap. They had to throw away the perfume because of shards. Discard the air of time, lest they get hurt. But rescue the doves. A wing is chipped but the two birds are still intertwined and kissing. Peace broken off from its roost. Maybe this is how it should be: leave their attachment to the ground, to history, in order to fly. They will always roost again. The ground will always be here. But it can wait. Tomorrow, they will read the book together. They will start from the beginning —

Come Home, For Once

Still stone the house,
still paved the path,
still iron gated,
but not my heart.
So enter, sister,
without gun or armour,
still magnificent.

CANDIDO'S REVOLUTION

Dandansoy bayaan ta icao / Pauli aco sa Payao
Ugaling con icao hidlauon / Ang Payao imo lang lantauon —
Dandansoy I'm leaving you / I'm going back to Payao
If ever you yearn for me / Just look towards Payao

Visayan Folksong, Philippines

Perhaps he sees her. Or she sees him first. Among the *marool* trees in Broome, Australia. It's 1893. Almost four years later, he's executed by the Spanish in Aklan, Philippines.

So the story begins for the poet. It's 2019 and she's been searching for Candido. But she can't find any trace of "the Manilaman" who worked as an indentured pearl diver in Broome more than a hundred years ago. So under this *marool*, she speculates, she conjures, she hopes.

Perhaps this is how it begins: she sees him. He's perched on a branch looking out to Roebuck Bay. No, first she hears him, his sweetest sadness.

'Dandansoy bayaan ta icao
Pauli aco sa Payao
Ugaling con icao hidlauon
Ang Payao imo lang lantauon …'

She does not know this language. But she has known birdsong from the time she was born. So she knows sweetness. And sadness, well, she knows this too.

A rustle down there, he freezes.

From the next tree, a crow calls to pursue the halted song.

A distant dingo howls, as mournful.

Then just the thud-thud of their hearts.

Perhaps this is how Mary and Candido meet in 1893.

He peers down at her. She looks like one of the natives but not quite like those he's seen around town. She's wearing a long, white dress gathered by a broad brown belt, though he could be wrong. The late sun has touched everything with ochre. She's carrying a basket.

She stares up at him but can see mostly bare feet dangling from the branch and half a face shimmering with sweat and sun. It's late Sunday afternoon in September, very warm, and the sky's just starting to turn red like the earth.

'Hello,' she dares to speak first.

'Hello,' he repeats the greeting softly, peering down.

'What you doing up there?'

Silence. He looks worried.

She gestures for him to get down.

He descends, then bows, hand on chest. *'Dispensa, Señora —* sorry, Madam.'

She giggles, slapping the trunk with glee. No one has ever bowed to her before, least of all a man, and none has ever addressed her like this. Must be the dress. *Madam* — ha-ha! But she likes it.

He's perplexed. He was worried she was telling him off because he's trespassed on her tree or her land, but there's so much land here and so many trees and bushes growing this way and that, and hardly any fences, so how can he tell whose was whose? Unlike in the sugar plantation in Iloilo where he worked as a farmhand. Strict boundaries kept the likes of him in or out at the bidding of the *haciendero*, the Spanish landlord.

'I'm not *Madam*, I'm Mary.' She's still giggling. 'And you?' she asks, but he's still perplexed, so she taps her chest, 'Mary,' then points to him, 'You?'

'Candido.'

She appraises the flustered man. Handsome in a quiet way. He's blushing? Could just be the sun. 'Can — di — do.'

He nods without meeting her eyes.

'Can-di-do — Can-do —' she smiles. 'Can-do good song.'

Good song and smile he understands. This is the first time a local woman has spoken to him this close. He's surprised, pleased.

'Can-do good song,' she says again.

It sounds like a question, a request, and she's beaming now, so he starts to relax and dares to sing the first word, *'Dandansoy'* — but stops, then explains, 'Mother sing … home.' How to say it's a lullaby about going home? But he knows very few English words, so he turns to the ocean, hand pushing towards that distance.

She nods. She understands. *Mother. Home. Away.*

He smiles, stares at his feet again.

'You Manilaman pearl diver?' She's seen them around town during lay up, the *mankala* season when the north-west winds bring the "wet time". Manilamen they're called, pomaded and well dressed, always smoking and laughing, and most with a swagger, different from the serious Japanese and Malays. And they play good music and pray a lot but sometimes make trouble. Some drink too much and check out the ladies walking past. But this one keeps his eyes down. No swagger about him, instead a sadness that makes her sad.

He takes a while to nod. He does not like the name. He's a pearl diver, but he's not from Manila. He gets bold, points to her. 'You?'

'Noongar from Fremantle — and Perth.'

He finally looks up. 'Free-mantul,' he murmurs. His transit port before Broome. He taps his chest. 'Aklanon,' then finger towards ocean, 'Malinao.'

They meet each other's eyes. Then smile, at the same time. What pleasure in understanding. *They both come from somewhere.*

More than a century later, the poet sees them, or wishes to. Under the *marool* tree where she's now standing in Bedford Park, perhaps before this was a park. She's just walked from the Sisters of Saint John of God Heritage Centre where there's a *Relationships Exhibition* with photos and stories about Filipino-Aboriginal families and their links to the early establishment of the Catholic Church in the Kimberley.

She sits on the grass, relieves herself of the backpack and the guitar she's been carrying around. Her sister's guitar, for good luck — you'll approve, Áte Belen, won't you? There's a sudden lump in her throat, so a swig from her water bottle. Ah, so hot. Her shirt sticks to her back. She looks up at the *marool* canopy, thanks for your shade. There's a young *marool* in the Centre's garden. Someone told her its fruit is edible, often sour, so you must know how to find the sweet ones.

Perhaps Mary offers Candido a *marool*, a native blackberry. Perhaps she's been gathering berries. But in a long, white dress? Ah, it's because of the picture that she saw somewhere of a pearling master's family. Master, mistress and son, and behind them, their domestic servants: an Aboriginal man and two women. All in 'pearling whites' and all serious looking, except for the young Aboriginal woman in her long, white dress and broad belt. She wears the beginnings of a smile.

This could be Mary, Candido's Mary.

But would he speak to someone who looks like the Indigenous Atis at home, "those negritos" discriminated against in his time? Yes, because the poet's a hopeless romantic. She loves love stories. Or has grown to love them to make up for history. She picks up the guitar, strums Candido's song. 'Uhmm-mmm-mmm ...' The *Dandansoy*, a folksong from as early as the Spanish occupation of the Philippines. The 1500s to late 1800s — song that old?

'Dandansoy bayaan ta icao

Pauli aco sa Payao —'

Dandansoy I'm leaving you / I'm going back to Payao ... One of the saddest Filipino folksongs. They do like sweet sadness back home. She keeps strumming, eyes closed, she's cooling down. She imagines Áte, her sister, listening.

A plover tiptoes towards the shade, stops. It's curious, perhaps of the sound, not of this big animal making it. Then it returns to pecking away at the grass. It overturns a rotting blackberry. Underneath, a worm. Sweet.

'Don't ever speak to any of them again — if you don't want to lose your job.'

Candido is being censured by his friend, Francisco.

'I saw you — and what did she give you?'

'Fruit —'

'Utak bolinao — whitebait brain, dumbo!'

'Don't call me that — I didn't eat it.'

'You can't mix with those native women — it's the law!'

The friends just bought cigars at Tack's, their discreet excursion from the lugger temporarily moored close to Streeter's Jetty for some repair. They're not supposed to go into town until lay up when the cyclones start and diving stops, and all luggers take refuge on the bay. They know the routine, they've worked as pearl divers for more than two years. Left home to try their luck across the ocean and struck up a friendship when they met here in Broome. Maybe because they're from neighbouring islands and they understand each other's languages.

'She was nice. And she understood me.'

'*Sige*, you'll go to jail!' Francisco has always taken the lead in this friendship.

Evening's descended on the foreshore pearling camps of scattered timber shacks and tents. The mosquitos buzz in their ears. They light up and walk fast on the jetty.

'Next time, don't you run off like that, I was growing crazy looking for you!'

'*Nag*-walkabout *lang*' — just went *walkabout*. Candido likes the word. Learned it from the lugger's old hands. Like *pasyar*, he thinks. He doesn't understand that for Aboriginal culture, *walkabout* is not idle walk but cultural business. It's more than a walk too for the indentured labourer. It's defiance and survival. Back home, he'd take off from the masters' eyes to go walking in the jungle, listen to the birds and find wild fruit or meat, when there was not enough food at the sugar *hacienda*.

'Quick, before we're missed.' Francisco starts to run, and Candido follows. Their cigars wink in the dark.

'They're like us.'

'Who?'

'The natives —'

'No they're not —'

'The whites took their land too.'

Francisco takes a deep puff. The truth, like a knife in his chest. He thinks of his parents, his grandparents, his great- and great-great-grandparents who lost their land to the Spaniards to whom they've bowed their heads for more than 300 years.

She sees her, guitar slung on one shoulder, backpack on the other, and looking up in awe at the bronze statue of the female diver. Then she tiptoes to touch her but can't quite reach, so she runs a hand on the wave from where the diver rises — then makes the sign of the cross. From her car parked on the Conti foreshore across Bedford Park, the watching woman is intrigued. Now she's strumming? She rolls down her window to hear. She's singing too! The plaintive song carries up to the naked diver stretched towards the ocean and offering a pearl shell to the sky.

'That was beautiful.'

The singing halts, she turns around, an Asian. 'No, *she's* beautiful.'

'You were singing to her.'

'Can't help it.'

'I'm Leila,' the woman from the car extends her hand. She can't help it either. She has to satisfy her curiosity.

'Remedios — Remy,' the other takes the hand, smiling.

'Visiting?'

Remy nods, smile more earnest. 'You Filipina?'

Leila laughs. Ah, how many times has she been asked that question? 'No, I'm Bardi —'

'Bardi?'

'My Aboriginal language group.'

'Oh sorry, I'm not —'

'That's okay. My grandmother's Javanese-Bardi, that's probably why —' and she shrugs. 'You, Filipina?'

'Yes, from Wollongong.'

'Also from beside the ocean.'

'Like *her*.' She looks up to the female diver burnished in midday light.

'Our homage to the women in pearling,' Leila explains. 'The wives and mothers who gave up their husbands and sons, and the women divers who gave up their lives, for pearls — see, she's pregnant and gasping for air —'

'Oh?'

'Blackbirding days. Some pearling masters kidnapped Aboriginal women, made them dive naked, and they preferred them pregnant because they had greater lung capacity ... many died.'

She bows her head, touches the wave from where the body bursts forth. Then makes the sign of the cross.

'You did that a while ago ...'

'Don't know why, maybe habit ... when we go to church with statues of Jesus, or Mary, or the saints ... but now ...' she looks up.

Leila looks up too at the diver forever offering a pearl shell, then back to the Filipina who looks like she's about to cry. 'I've Filipino-Yawuru friends. Their families go back to the old pearling days, Remy — it's Remy, right?'

The poet nods. 'Yes, Leila ... thanks so much for telling me.'

'Check out the Historical Museum, short walk from here. You'll find out more.'

'I will, thanks.'

'Uhm ... what were you singing then?'

'A lovesong, a lullaby, both.'

Mary is back at her pearling master's house. Can-di-do. She smiles. Sweet voice, sweet man.

'What yuh smilin' for, why so long, yuh find *marool*?'

'Always asking, woman.' Mary rolls her eyes, shows Janey the basket.

'Why nah full?'

'Questions, questions.'

'Mistress been askin' for yuh,' Janey scolds. She's dressed like Mary, finds it too hot. Good thing, dressing up's only for when Master and Mistress have guests.

Mary and Janey were Mission girls, taken from their Aboriginal communities when they were little because they must be protected and educated in a Christian way, so they were told. Like many girls that grew up in the Missions, they were given to this white household for domestic service.

'Ladies waitin' long, so go! And get 'em tea things, careful not breakin', huh?' Janey hands a silver tray to the younger woman who rolls her eyes again. Hah, she's got airs, fixin' herself and speakin' like Mistress. Janey looks at her own white dress streaked with flour and eggs. I do most workin' here — but jus' look at her go! She frowns at the girl waltzing into the parlour where afternoon tea has been savoured with due justice. There's little left of the pound cake that Janey baked and the teacups have had more than a few refills.

'There she is!' Young Mistress Beatrice is relieved. 'We'll have to try this. My other girl said it can be really sweet,' and she beckons to the basket as her three guests, also wives of pearling masters and all in lacy pearling whites, crow over Mary's attire.

'Nice dress —'

'And leather belt.'

'With pearl shell buttons?' and she puts on spectacles to check.

The mistress smiles at the dress and belt. 'They were mine. I told you, we take care of our girls, we take care of our natives,' and she picks up a blackberry from the basket as the awed ladies wait for her to put it in her mouth.

We want to be the protagonists of the story, that's human nature, but the story is not only about us. The poet mulls over the thought that keeps extending as she imagines how Candido's (and Mary's) story unfolds. And even if it's about us, always there are others that walk in and out of it. But do we see them, do we hear them? Whose stories do we listen to, whose lives matter? Do we care to meet them at all? Áte Belen would have answered and argued. Isn't this trip about her anyway? Or *her* Candido? At the hotel, on the bed beside the guitar, the poet lays down the two songs copied in her sister's longhand, complete with guitar chords: the *Dandansoy* and the 1920s anti-American occupation poem, *Bayan Ko*, by Jose Corazon de Jesus that became a protest song since then and through the Japanese invasion in the 1940s, then the militant activism against the Marcos dictatorship during the First Quarter Storm in the 1970s, then on to the 1986 People Power that ousted him.

Last year when she went back home to visit, the guitar and the two songs were sent to her by her sister's comrade. More than two decades after — so late and so little. 'Effects of Kumander Belen': handwritten on the envelope that held only two pages. Did she sing in the hills, in between encounters with the military?

Again, the knife in her chest.

She traces her sister's hurried script, imagines her writing these down as she strummed and tried to find the right chords. Probably on that briefest moment of peace before the Total War that followed, after the dictator scuttled to the US and the new government militarised the countryside to crack down on communist insurgency. Though, for Kumander Belen, one of its top leaders, it was no insurgency. It was a twenty-year revolution against the corrupt regime. Remy has studied these two pages so many times and always she's struck by the faint scribble beside *Dandansoy*: 'Candido Iban, revolutionary.'

That's why she's here in Broome. To find him. For her.

Maybe she'll have better luck this time. But her thoughts are running elsewhere as she walks to the Historical Museum. She thinks of Leila, Mary, Janey, the pregnant diver, then of Candido and Francisco, then of her sister. Different times, different worlds. And here she is trying to make them meet. But writing is about meeting, right? Resolving at sentence level. Resolve the different sounds vying for attention in her head, resolve the differences of words. Make them meet, make friends. Make them kin. So each word's survival depends on the next one and the next. So a poem becomes a family of words. Only then when it's worth offering to the reader, another possible kin. But she's now venturing beyond the poem, trying to write this story. Candido's, or her sister's, or Mary's, or hers.

Around the bend to Robinson Street, a sprawl of deep-pink bougainvillea, then a mango tree heavy with fruit, uhmm, green mangoes, her mouth waters, and are those date palms? It's going to be another very hot day. Backpack and guitar are getting wet with sweat. She stops, kneels. Ah, how red this earth. She feels it between her thumbs. An old Aboriginal man is walking towards her, she says 'Good morning.' He looks surprised at being greeted by a stranger. He keeps walking, then calls back, '*Pindan* — red earth.' She waves, 'Thanks,' takes out her camera to document the earth. With footprints now, hers and his. And she thinks, resolving at sentence level is resolving at ground level: writing at the level of feet. Making different feet meet and walk together. Because it's the ground that knows: I exist, you exist, we exist.

It's the pearl shells that astonish her, not the pearls. Ah, that ghost of a rainbow, sudden and lustrous. She thinks of the *capiz* shell window at her grandmother's house in Vigan. Similar sheen, there and not there. Again, she bends over then steps back from the prized saltwater pearl oyster, the *Pinctada Maxima*, inside the glass display. She's trying to get back that sheen.

'Can I help you?'

'The sheen, it's playing hide and seek.'

The woman behind her laughs. 'Iridescence.'

'Yes, that's the word for it!'

'It's the light on nacre that does it. We have a book here, *Lustre*, that explains it — "iridescence" — "an event of light".'

'Sounds like a poem!' Later, she will discover the book *Iridescence: The Play of Colours*, and she'll think, yes, *play* and *poetry*, always an event.

The woman smiles. 'Indeed. I'm Anne, I work here — if you need help —'

'I'm Remy, I'm actually researching a Filipino pearl diver who worked here in the 1890s then went back home when he won a lottery with a friend, also a diver, and used their winnings to buy the printing press that facilitated the revolution against Spain, then became a revolutionary, then was executed — aw, sorry, didn't mean to rattle on.' She can't help it. Anne's generous smile, her own kind of light, invites her to tell all at once — or maybe it's "the poem".

'What a story.'

'I know.'

She doesn't find him here. Instead, she's led to other stories through Anne's help. But it's the hard-hat diving suit that blows her away: he went down the Indian Ocean in this. Ochre, huge and heavy looking, it's like a space suit and makes her imagine

64

Candido walking the depths in slo-mo, like when man walked on the moon for the first time.

Finally, lay up. He walks with the lugger crew into town. It's so humid, but thank God for this north-westerly. Candido's unsteady, head spinning and limbs aching, as if they'll snap out of their joints. The bends? He crosses himself, *Dios ko*, please make it mild. He did his last dive of the season yesterday, and he was fine, but now —

'Okay?' Arif, the Koepanger shell cleaner, puts an arm around him, and he nods, so the man keeps walking with the motley crew from more than a hundred luggers now docking on the bay: Japanese, Malays, Koepangers, Chinese, Aboriginals and Torres Strait Islanders. A younger man from home slaps him on the back as he staggers, '*Ay, burat ka na?*' — drunk so soon? The sundry of tongues weave in and out of the buzzing of the mangroves and the lapping of the water, but nothing beats the ringing in his ears. His head hurts! Above, kites are circling. Where's Francisco?

The sun is starting to set and the town's come alive. Along Dampier Creek, the foreshore camps are bustling all the way up to timber dwellings, boarding and food houses, stores, gambling and opium dens, and brothels. Time for rest and pleasure. The ocean has released the men, they're coming home. Wives and children will sleep more peacefully tonight.

In their whites, the pearling masters pack the porch of the Roebuck Bay Hotel to catch the breeze, drinks and smokes in hand. Faces are flushed and shiny, ah, bloody humidity. There's a nostalgic murmur about cool Mother England. Diving troubles, the haul of shells and pearls, and crew and lugger problems dominate the conversation in English. *No natives, no Asiatics allowed here*! Meanwhile up and down Dampier, the multicultural crew, who worked the luggers as family for months, gather with those "from home", cooling down with their own smokes and brews, and ultimately mixing, collected by the call of the playing cards and the stomach: all are raring for a feed on land. In front of a noodle house, a Chinese mother suckles her baby in a hammock as grandfather burns joss sticks to keep off the sandflies. The smell of cooking in all varieties wafts up and down the street.

Also in their spotless whites billowing in the wind, the English ladies promenade close to the jetty, their children held in check by Aboriginal nannies, but soon they break free, jumping with the other kids into the water for a quick swim before the sun fully sets. Mistress Beatrice breaks free too. She worries she can't see her husband among the men at the hotel entrance, so she leaves Mary with her purchases from Tack's, quickly hitches up her skirt and strides to the hotel as the other ladies gape. No decent white woman goes in there with the chaps! Not just because of the drinking but what with all that talk about the secret goings-on at the back, maybe trading in illegal pearls or something more.

Candido staggers into this scene, and it's Mary he sees first, like she's been waiting for him. *His other Mary.* Yesterday, he had a *kutób*, a bad hunch about the dive, but only fleeting. He prayed to *Santa Maria*, as his mother taught him when he was little and afraid. Blessed Mary in blue and white, smiling and arms open.

Mary moves to meet him, but catching up from behind him, Francisco wards her off, so she steps back, still looking at the man who sang sweetly up the tree.

The poet wants them so much to meet again. She wants her love story. She's walking towards The Roey, how the hotel is fondly called now. It was already built when Candido was here. Now, why did the two friends not leave the lugger together on that

66

humid December afternoon? Because Francisco stayed behind to argue with their pearling master for just pay. Both were paid only according to the number of shells they collected. But they were all-round labourers, working as diver, tender, sorting and cleaning shells, and even cleaning the lugger. The poet wants to insert resistance into the story: the men became revolutionaries.

The Roebuck Bay Hotel, Est. 1890 is emblazoned on the green billboard. On the porch, a huddle of men with their pints. An Asian woman comes out of the door, head bowed. A tall man follows, maybe Australian, and puts an arm around her.

'Hi — Filipina?' She should really stop asking, but she can't help it.

The woman looks up, and she regrets asking because the woman looks tearful, but she responds anyway with a nod.

'I'm Filipina too — Remy, Remedios.'

'I—I'm Nenita.' She's trying to compose herself, and the man smiles politely, 'Excuse us, we're rushing.'

She'll never know how *this* is as significant as the meetings she conjures. And it's real: inside, the couple met a Filipino-Javanese-Yawuru pearl diver, an elder, but she won't even notice him because she'll be quickly walking past the bar, thrown by the sight of a barmaid in skimpy shorts and bikini top, and a man ogling her breasts.

As she goes out the back looking for the hotel's Pearler's Restaurant, a sculpture catches her eye. It's a bas-relief tucked into a wall and looks like a wall itself. Arresting even in this dark back room. It's 99 or so bronze squares put together, each with intricately carved bodies in various poses of daily village life: men carrying buckets of water, women holding pots on their heads, and there's hunting, cooking, even dancing, though sinuously rendered, all the bodies seem to be dancing. How beautiful. Japanese? She's waylaid, she's all speculation. Was this here in the

1890s? In this room where perhaps the *karayuki-san*, the trafficked Japanese prostitutes, secretly waited for clients? Or were they in a nearby brothel? In their kimonos, they smiled at the door about to open, no, beyond it, all the way out and on to the jetty, towards the ocean. *Mother. Home. Away.* Or Candido and Francisco sat here waiting for the chiffa lottery to be drawn — but no Asiatics allowed in at that time. So perhaps it was drawn elsewhere. Perhaps Candido had dreamt the sign that made him choose the winning ticket. Perhaps his dream of a steamer going home matched the riddle of the *mundayi*, the Chinese manager of the game, on that lucky day in 1895.

'I read they won a thousand pesos, a lot of money at that time,' Remy says. She's telling stories with her hosts, Kristine and Phillip, in a restaurant in Kalibo, Aklan. She decided to visit after she received her sister's effects. The guitar and the songs broke her heart all over again, but it was her sister's tiny scribble that kept haunting her: 'Candido Iban, revolutionary'. Her hosts are helping her piece his story together. She doesn't tell them about Kumander Belen. Too hard.

'You're going back home to Australia after this trip?' Kristine asks.

'Home,' she laughs. 'Where is it anyway?'

'Where the heart is,' Phillip says.

'But where's the heart?'

Awkward silence.

'Anyway, I might visit Broome next year — it's Candido's pearl diving story there that hardly any Filipino knows.'

'Love to hear that,' Kristine says. 'Ah, our *inubarang manok* is here. Signature dish of Aklan, Remy.' She spoons a steaming serve over her rice. 'Native chicken cooked till tender in coconut milk with lemongrass and *úbad*, the bana pith.'

Phillip is wistful. 'For Candido, this would have been luxury.'

'I know. I keep thinking of what Malinao's Mayor Ariel told us earlier — that when he honoured Candido's family for their contribution to Aklan's liberation, they said that if great-great uncle had kept the winning money, the family could have gone to school, they could have been educated and saved from poverty.'

Kristine sighs. 'Family's still very poor … big sacrifice to give up that money for the revolution.'

'Not just money, but lives. Candido and Francisco gave up their lives.'

The pit in her stomach returns. After a while, 'I read two other Filipino pearl divers donated their savings to buy that printing press. Dalida and Rabaria.'

'Aklanons like Candido,' Phillip explains. 'All those men became revolutionaries, and that printing press allowed the *Katipunan* movement to publish their campaign materials which recruited for the cause.'

'From lottery to revolution.'

'Those men organised the Aklan uprising,' he continues. 'Under Francisco del Castillo, pearl diver turned General.'

'And they were martyred.'

Silence around the table. An angel is passing by.

'I'll take you to Lezo,' Kristine offers — 'Candido was jailed there with the other martyrs — but first, the landmarks close by. Where the rebels, dressed in white with bolos, marched into town led by General del Castillo. We'll follow his route to where he was shot.'

Shot. It's the word that always delivers the punch. She feels it in her stomach. Even after all these years. 'Do you — do you sing the *Dandansoy?*'

He's singing, or thinks he is singing. Candido's curled against the jail wall with his brother Benito and seventeen others. Their general is dead, and they were beaten to a pulp by the *guardia civiles* who tried for hours to get them to give up the names of their comrades. But the men kept silent. It's nearly two in the morning of March 23, 1897. They're still silent, dozing and leaning on each other, but he's singing. '*Dandansoy, bayaan ta icao* ...' He's perched on the topmost branch of a tree singing about leaving the beloved. '*Pauli aco sa Payao* ...' So he can go home. It hurts to sing, his mouth's swollen and bleeding, he can't open it. This singing, it's in his head. Then from outside, 'T'rik ... t'rik ... t'rik-tik-tik-tik.' A punctuation to his song. 'T'rik ... t'rik-tik-tik-tik — t'rik-tik-tik-tik.' Incessant. Then flapping of wings. Ah, the *tariktik*, the Visayan hornbill come to sing with him, or to take his song home. When he was growing up in Malinao, a hornbill used to feast on the *bugnay* berries close to their hut. He listens, but it's gone quiet. He doesn't hear the Mausers being stuck through the wall — then shots rend the air! Searing heat cuts through him again and again, he slumps, trying to reach for his brother who utters a cry and goes still, a sound echoed and re-echoed by the other men. Then again, that quiet.

'Can-di-do ... Can-di-do ...'

She's calling him. He tries to look up, or look down. She's asking him to come down from the tree, in her white dress. He tries to focus. But this light, in her, through her, hard to see, she shimmers many colours, there and not there ... like a pearl.

Ocean and seas away, Mary can't sleep. She keeps seeing the rainbow above the *marool* tree, so sudden it was, but maybe it was just the light earlier, when she visited that tree again as she's done so many times. There was a quick reprieve from the rain and the sun sneaked out, and there it was, like a halo, and she thought, how could she miss a man she didn't really know? But he bowed to her. He sang.

'*Convento, diin ang cura?*
Municipio, diin justicia?
Yari si Dansoy maqueja
Maqueja sa pag-higugma.'

The poet has also returned to the tree in Bedford Park and she's singing it again with her guitar: 'Parish convent, where's the priest? / City hall, where's justice? / But here is Dansoy charged / Charged with falling in love.' She's incorrigible in her conjuring. She will make them fall in love. They will resist history. This will be their revolution: witnessing each other in true light. *Iridescence.* 'The colour you see is your relationship to the structure in a certain light. It's an experience that isn't there when you're not there,' as anthropologist Peter Sutton explained.

You have to be there to know: this, the woman, the man I could love. Ah, that tenderness of the gaze. It makes loneliness bearable, and sadness sweet. It makes injustice resistible. It makes dying endurable. There it is again, the knife in her chest. *She wasn't there to know.* Not in 1996, at the morgue where she confirmed that the body found in the ditch was Kumander Belen, the revolutionary who had just come down from the hills. An assassination, the police said. Three bullets in the gut, two in the heart. After the sisters met at a Manila hotel for the last time. No one was charged.

Tenderness. Hope you had some, Áte Belen. Maybe in the hills, maybe with a comrade, maybe in a moment of peace or hurried pleasure. Or maybe in a story that I've wished for you again and again. Candido's story, yours. She strums again. She needs to get to the end of their song —

'*Ang panyo mo cag panyo co*
Dala diri cay tambijon co
Ugaling con magcasilo
Bana ta icao, asawa mo aco.'

Your handkerchief and my handkerchief
Bring them to me, as I'll tie them together
If they interweave
May you be my husband, I your wife.

It's about putting the pieces together. Or about wishing to put them back together. To wish, to conjure. Most times it's all we can do. But we work on it. Sometimes we get it almost right or even wrong, and that's scary, but we always try. We try to make meaning to make whole even a little piece of something inside.

The sun is setting and a crow makes its homing call.

On the open field, a father is playing soccer with his daughter. He kicks the ball, she kicks back. 'Got it, Dad!'

The poet keeps watching. From him, the ball soars to her who returns it, his arc and hers made whole.

MY TENDER TENDER

This is gospel.

Uncle Freddy Corpus

'I was born wrapped in a web. Old folks say you'll never die in the sea if you're born in a web. This is gospel.'

His tone is sure, his smile, disarming. Nenita's more than disarmed. She's charmed to the bones as she shakes the hand of 91-year-old Fred Corpus, one of Broome's and Darwin's last remaining hard-hat pearl divers. She and her husband Arvis are all smiles in this corner of The Roey. They're basking in Uncle Freddy, sunset-bright in his Hawaiian shirt and with a very cold beer in hand. 'Smothered in ice, the only way to drink beer.'

She laughs. 'You sound like James Bond! "Shaken, not stirred" — the only way to drink martini.'

As tickled by Uncle Freddy's wit, Arvis offers to buy him another beer.

'No, thanks,' he declines with a gracious smile. 'I like to get my own.'

She hears her father's fierce declaration of independence. She sees him in Uncle Freddy's combed back white hair, all spruced up for an outing, and in the cane slung discreetly on his arm. It clunks as he opens his wallet to show them a photo of young Freddy kitted up in heavy diving suit, without helmet yet but roped and ready on a lugger, its mast open and the ocean waiting behind him.

It all began a few minutes earlier. They were admiring the same photo, blown-up on the wall at the back of the bar. Man ready to take on the depths, waters waiting to take on the man. It will be a matter of life and death. But bursting with vitality and young life, only life, Freddy gleams under the sun. There are highlights on his brow, nose, cheeks, and on his suit and boots. As if he were polished for this adventure. The Western Australian Museum labels the photo thus: 'Aboriginal hard-hat diver Fred Corpus was considered as good as the Japanese divers.' As she stared at the handsome, young man on the wall, she couldn't help but see the young Filipinos in her first home. They made her heart go pit-a-pat when she was younger.

'That man — he's there.' A woman's voice behind them. French? They turn around. Yes, one of the barmaids, a backpacker from France, is pointing to the famous pearl diver drinking his beer. 'That's him!'

And so they're here at the bar. The manager sidles over, checks out Uncle Freddy's beer. 'That okay?' Uncle Freddy nods. 'I asked them to make sure your beer is okay and ready,' the manager says, gesturing towards the back room of the bar. Of course, smothered in ice.

Uncle Freddy rests his beer and opens his wallet to show them the same photo on the wall. A mini version, contained like an identity card. But Fred Corpus' history cannot be contained. It has crossed oceans and continents. He tells her that his grandfather Severo Corpus was a Filipino pearl diver from Manila who came to

Broome in the late 1880s and married local Yawuru woman Maria Emma Ngobing. Grandfather Severo was among the so-named "Manilamen", the early Filipino migrant workers who tried their diving luck far away from home.

She's delighted by the connection. They introduce themselves and she tells him she's originally from the Philippines, then asks, 'Have you been there?'

He knows nothing of his grandfather's roots or home, so no, he's never visited. 'Look at *Forty Fathoms Deep*. The story of my grandfather is there, blackbirds days time.' Blackbirding of Aboriginal pearl divers was slavery in the 1800s.

She's all ears, tropics-sweaty and leaning against the bar sans drink because they've had one with lunch and were about to leave. But not now. They're entranced by story after story that takes her home. On the wall behind Uncle Freddy, a poster on the wall says, 'Sunday Family Funday' in bright red and blue, and where she's leaning, the wood is cool to the touch.

'My father was also a pearl diver, Achil Bin Salleh, a Javanese, and my Yawuru mother is Esther Corpus, they couldn't marry because of the law then.' Later, she'll learn about this law, the outlawing of their cross-racial marriage. 'I married Nancy Koolinda. Koolinda is the name of a boat, she was born in a boat. This is gospel.' His voice is conspiratorial, his gesture, certain. There's a flash of his gold and diamond ring, and a tug in her heart. He's like her storytelling father conspiring with his listener and he never ever forgot to slip on his gold ring, a gift from a brother-in-law, before he went for an outing.

'Look at this,' Uncle Freddy invites them to look closer. With one thumb, he covers the photo at the waist, and with the other, covers the knees, thus framing a section of his diving suit. 'See: it's a face.' Yes, she sees it! A face with a broad brow, its shadowed eyes looking downwards, and there's the nose too.

'I think it's the devil,' and he laughs. 'But the priest in Darwin said, "It's your guardian angel".' He adds that at the feet of his diver father's photo, there's also a face. 'This is gospel.'

It's a declaration of certainty. Believe me, I'm telling you the truth. And she readily believes because his storytelling is so familiar. It takes her back to her first home, not so much to her Catholic upbringing in the Philippines but to its indigenous beliefs before Catholic Spain arrived with the cross and the sword. Uncle Freddy takes her back to the other world and the uncanny, like strange faces appearing in photos. And guarding us, keeping us safe.

'How did you feel on your very first dive?' she asks.

'I was excited, I enjoyed it.'

'It was a matter of life and death …'

'Yes, but I had a very good tender, Ali Laka, 40 or 45 years old. He was very careful, he looked after me.'

Tender Ali Laka keeping Freddy Corpus safe.

She read before that the 'at-tender' of a pearl diver is the one who manages the lifeline rope tied around his waist and the pump and hose from where he breathes precious air while diving into the deep. But the line goes deeper for her: it's the tenderness of an elder safeguarding the life of a boy. She can't tell Uncle Freddy this. He might find it too soft a thought about a dangerous feat of hardy men. But the thought is insistent, followed by a little niggle: for suspicious bigots these days, names like Ali Laka or Achil Bin Salleh may inspire fear, even hate. Hey, you look, sound and dress different, maybe you're Muslim, maybe you're dangerous.

Whatever happened to *tender Ali*? Like a rope, the phrase tugs at her heart and she's quickly connected to Ali's lifeline. No, it's not just her. We all must be connected, duly life-linked. It's the rope to trust: tenderness to make us kinder, kindness to keep us safe.

Not quite gospel, more like a bid for trust. And young Freddy had plenty of it in his diving days.

The bar lights beam down on him like a benediction.

'Knowing I'd never die at sea, I undid the lifeline tied around me and gave three tugs on the rope. It means an emergency. So Ali pulled me up in a hurry — and I wasn't there!' But clever Freddy rode up to the surface on the air hose between his legs. 'When I got up, Ali said, "Don't ever do that again." This is gospel.'

When you're born in the web, you'll never die at sea.

How to trust that web into which all of us are born, or are continuously woven into throughout our lives? Filipino with Australian, and Yawuru with Javanese with Japanese with French, and many more lives interwoven, sometimes by blood or by water, or sometimes by simply meeting and telling stories like this moment.

Once she facilitated a storytelling project between Aboriginal elders and Filipina migrants in Sydney. The women were complete strangers and understandably wary of each other. For three days, around the dining table they told stories about family. So much remembering. An Aboriginal elder and a Filipina discovered that they both have loved ones who got into drugs at a very young age. One died of an overdose, the other self-harmed throughout his life. She heard murmurs in a corner: how much they loved and lost, and continue to love. Then a hush, then softly, 'We're the same.' Later, an Aboriginal elder recounted the wailing of women and dogs when the children were taken from their mothers in her community. A Filipina followed with the story about how she was taken twice to 'a safe house that wasn't safe' and tortured during Marcos' time. Another hush around the table. The stories were sinking into their skin, threading them together. Then the Filipina opened her palm beside the Aboriginal elder's and said, surprised, 'Look, we're the same colour!' Everyone looked to see what she meant: that whatever is the colour of our skin, our palm is always lighter, same as everyone else. Then she took the elder's hand. By instinct, everyone did the same with the next person. Who knows how it started, but soon they were singing *Amazing Grace*. Some were crying. All of them woven into a web, duly life-linked.

They're in Uncle Freddy's web now. Linked by chance at The Roey, entrusted with his life stories. And what a very lucky life.

'Not just luck,' her husband notes. 'That was hard, dangerous work.'

'I ducked bullets during the war,' Uncle Freddy continues. When Japanese fighter planes attacked Broome, thirteen-year-old Freddy hid in the mangroves.

The mangroves of Roebuck Bay? Earlier they visited this sprawl of green on earth so red, then further up, the aqua ocean glinting all the way to the horizon and a sky so blue. It made her think of infinity. Suddenly an interjection on the thought: birdsong! And something brown, or was it grey, darted past. A few more notes, they held their breaths, then it was gone. 'Like the *mayas*, the sparrows in my mother's garden,' she whispered to her husband. No, it was probably a dusky gerygone, a mangrove bird. After a while, two bigger birds circled above. Lower and lower, and they got bigger and bigger. What grace and span of wing, what mesmeric power. Kites hunting, she found out later from Tim, a Bardi guest at their hotel. 'Take care of your pets, or else,' he warned.

'I dodged sharks,' Uncle Freddy tells them, 'and got the bends three or four times, but I recovered. That was before I learned staging.'

Mangroves to ocean, sky to water. They've to be quick on their toes as he takes them from place to place, and she's a bit lost now.

'The bends, decompression illness that that could kill. So you've got to do staging as you go up,' he explains. 'To dive twenty fathoms, you have to do six stages, half hour at sixty feet, then double to one hour, you double as you go up, I learned from a Yankee book on staging, the Japanese divers just did one stage so many of them died, you can see in the cemetery, I taught a full-blood Australian how to dive … he died at Bard Creek.'

She nods, trying to rise to the surface too, pulled up from her "technical lost-ness" in the art of diving. But story by story, trust by trust, Uncle Freddy guides her through his stages of remembering. She basks in his animation: He is my tender. His voice is my rope, steady, always with a gospel-ring. I hold on to it and marvel at the ease with which he offers me, a stranger, so many lives in one breath.

Later, when they visit the Broome cemetery, they'll see them together: different names, different lives sleeping on the same bed of red earth.

'Thank you for your stories,' she says, and her husband echoes her thanks. 'You're very generous with them,' she adds, and he smiles and tells more: in 1943 he salvaged a Dutch plane wreck. 'I saved a white man, this is gospel,' he goes on. The news said two pearl divers saved him, one of them was Freddy. But these Aboriginal divers were not named. Then onto another adventure: 'I shot a croc, largest in Northern Territory, 6.2 metres, this is gospel … the news said, "shot by a poacher".' And yet another: in 1952 Freddy and another Aboriginal diver Eddie Roe, both 25 years old, broke the record for the most haul of pearl shells. All of four tonnes 400-weight in three and a half days, which is less than a neap tide. 'This is gospel too.'

He tells story after story with a bid for trust. *This is gospel.* Perhaps to counter the listener's possible disbelief and thus the teller's invisibility? Believe us, hear us, see us: we're here, we have always been here on our land and water, and not just as stories of dispossession and loss — we are those too, but we are more.

She shifts against the cool wood of the bar, keenly aware that she came much later than all these lives he's telling them. She's not from Broome, not from Australia. She needs to listen, to learn. In that storytelling project that she facilitated, one Aboriginal elder told her rather sternly before the session began, 'First, you have to listen to our stories.' Then she took the Filipina group through a map of their land.

'I was diving in Broome, in Darwin,' Uncle Freddy explains. 'I live there now.' Over in Darwin, he was able to negotiate good pay for pearl diving.

She thinks of the self-assured Australian larrikin but he's a cut above this type. He's not just smarts and cheer. He's warmth, dignity and pride. He's lived his stories of survival, of success, long before she came.

As she listens, she hears another storytelling voice: the Aboriginal writer Bruce Pascoe and his book *Dark Emu* that argues against 'the hunter-gatherer label for pre-colonial Aboriginal Australians' — 'If we look at the evidence presented to us by the explorers and explain to our children that Aboriginal people *did* build houses, *did* build dams, *did* sow, irrigate and till the land, *did* alter the course of rivers, *did* sew their clothes, and *did* construct a system of pan-continental government that generated peace and prosperity, then it is likely we will admire and love our land all the more.'

It's Pascoe's proposition offered with generosity: *If you and your children look* (and hear and see us), then we can love our shared land together. This moves her, as much as Uncle Freddy moves her now. She thinks of the kindness of the storyteller and the listener, the kindness of the mouth and the ear. One gifts a story, the other gifts back a trusting ear. Only then can story grow. And prosper. The trusting ear is fertile. In it, the story tendrils sprout, spread and tickle the mouth to speak it again to another trusting ear, and perhaps another. We speak, we see, we believe. Together.

Before Uncle Freddy now, she's a child again listening, believing. He takes another swig of his beer smothered in ice, and she sees her storytelling father taking a swig, with great pleasure. Both love their beer.

'So how long did you dive for?' her husband asks.

'I started in 1947 and finished in 1961.'

They hear more stories. He has sixteen children and many grandchildren, he takes care of himself, cooks his own food, does his own laundry. She guesses he's on his own now, as independent as ever. Yes, he likes to buy his own beer.

'You're very lucky,' she says, 'surviving all those dangers.'

He says they should come tomorrow and he'll bring his records.

She gets more forward, playful. 'You look very young at 91. So, uhm, do you have a girlfriend?' Ah, she should have bitten her tongue. She's sounding like a *pakialamerang Pilipina*: a nosey Filipina. She's worried she's gone too far.

Eyes twinkling, he whispers, 'Yes, she's from Nigeria, she's 40.'

Her husband laughs. 'A very lucky man indeed.'

'Come tomorrow, I'll bring her picture.'

As promised, they're back at The Roey. Uncle Freddy is surrounded by friends and admiring fans. She's a new fan. She and her husband keep their distance, they don't wish to intrude. The Roey is noisy and crowding up. It's the opening of the Shinju Matsuri, the Festival of the Pearl, and Mr Fred Corpus is its longstanding patron. Yearly he's come to the Festival since he left Broome for Darwin, and, each time, every day he's at The Roey sitting at the same spot. Uncle Freddy's corner: the right side of the long bar, where the light is warm and the wood cool and polished by countless bodies that have leant on it for years.

He sees them and makes a move to rise from his stool. He leans against his cane, unsteady at first, and again she sees her father. 'Go and help him, please,' she asks her husband. He does and from where she sits close to the pool table, she sees him offer to help with the satchel he's carrying and his beer. No, not the beer, just the satchel. She smiles. He's protective of his drink. Like her father.

They walk slowly towards her, and there's a lump in her throat. Uncle Freddy is wearing a silky, pale green polo shirt, like what her father used to wear on special occasions. He's looking even more dapper today.

He sits down and takes out various memorabilia from the satchel. He opens one: it's a copy of the marriage certificate of his Filipino grandfather Severo Corpus Felipe and Yawuru grandmother Maria Emma Ngobing. She's speechless, honoured to be shared this document, and, more so, touched by this gesture affirming their Philippine connection. Severo and Emma were married by the Spanish priest Father Nicholas Emo who, she later learned, facilitated the validation of the outlawed relationships between Manilamen and local Aboriginal women from late 1800 to 1900. When cross-racial love was criminalised.

They take time to look closely at history.

Then he shows them photos of his family: first, Grandfather Severo and Grandmother Emma against a fence and trees, most likely the backyard of their home. Then, almost sepia now, one of himself with his mother Esther, brothers Henry and Richard, and sister Elsie. Then, the older Elsie and her husband with Freddy. Then, two pictures of his girlfriend Maureen. And from a newspaper clipping, one of his whole clan: sixteen children with all the grandchildren. He lays them before her with affection, with pride.

'May I get you another beer, sir?' her husband asks.

This time, Uncle Freddy nods. They've been introduced to family.

'I need a beer too, please,' she says. It's getting busier in The Roey, and warmer. She should feel at home, this is the tropics. She clips up her hair. Her collar is sticky with sweat, so is her brow. But Uncle Freddy stays cool and fresh in his shiny pale green. He tells them about his first dive, how his diver father was with him and didn't want him to go down. The elder safeguarding the boy. He pulls out more history from his satchel. There's *The Canberra Times* from 1952: 'Two Aboriginal half-castes have exploded the myth about the superiority of Japanese pearl divers and earned themselves £250 in a week doing it.' It's about how they broke the record of pearl shells haul, but 'some months ago, a suggestion was made the Japanese divers should be employed in the Australian pearling industry because Malays and Australian half-castes were not as good.'

Then, a photocopied picture of young Freddy with another Aboriginal diver, both chests bare and burnished under the sun, with the label: 'Two fine specimens of mixed blood divers ...' Smiling, Uncle Freddy points to the label, repeats it: 'Two fine specimens.' There's pride in his voice, perhaps a touch of vanity, and she remembers her father looking at his young pictures with her and her siblings, and beaming as they said, '*Guwapong-guwapo* — very handsome!'

She smiles with Uncle Freddy, and her father. But there's a niggling discomfort. "Half-castes", "mixed blood". Racial tags of that time. And "fine specimens", its colonial evocation. But who is she to judge his pleasure over this description? He knows where he stands and she's here to listen. As she looks at the photo, she wants to say to him, '*Guwapong-guwapo*,' as they said to their father.

They return to the very first photo where all this storytelling began: young Freddy in diving suit on the lugger. 'Open to page 51,' he says, he knows exactly where he is, as they look for him in *Lustre*, a book she brought with her. Then more news clippings and Broome brochures with the same shot: he's everywhere.

'You're the poster boy of Australian pearl diving!' she exclaims.

He shrugs, smiles. Beside his iconic photo, he lays down a new one: another young man kitted out for the dive. Same lugger, same ocean, same light.

'My friend, Simeon Bin Said. He took this photo of me, and I took this photo of him that day,' he explains.

But it's only Uncle Freddy now. Fred Corpus. A living history. At 91.

They're about to leave. They take the final swig of their beers.

'My father,' she starts, then clears her throat. 'He died last year. At 91.'

Silence. What to say next.

'Thank you for all your stories, Mr Freddy.'

'Yes, thank you,' her husband adds.

Uncle Freddy nods at her with a smile.

Now, how to say this next —

You gifted me my father's life. You made him come alive. You remind me of my father. You remind me that my father is guarding me, keeping me safe.

But she does not say it.

'Is it okay to have a photo with you, sir?'

He nods, he's used to this.

'Please take our photo.' She hands her husband her iPad and crosses over to Uncle Freddy's side. 'Wait, I'll undo my clip.' She shakes her hair loose. 'There, that's better.'

He smiles again, knowingly.

Yes, I'm vain too, Uncle Freddy.

She wants to put her arm around him, but all she can manage is a palm against the arm of his green shirt. It's an awkward pose. She hopes he doesn't mind.

The photo is taken and they say their goodbyes.

They walk him back to his corner at the bar where he's encircled by friends and fans. They keep walking, and an earlier thought follows her to the door: Uncle Freddy is my tender. *My tender tender.*

As they walk out of The Roey, her eyes get blurry. Must be the blinding tropic sun and this heat that feels like home.

MY FATHER'S AUSTRALIA

Makapangalag-kalag man lamang ako sa Australia —
If only I could roam my eyes around Australia.

Papa

The suit is a perfect fit. Dark blue, elegant, but unassuming like my father. All say he looks good in it. I bought it years ago from David Jones when he was set to visit Australia with my mother, and I bought her a blouse. Chiffon in butterscotch yellow, it made me think of sweet things like that summer morning.

'Smart,' he said, smoothing the lapel with some hesitance.

First time I'd seen father in a suit, and what an apparition. In the mirror, his tailored self seemed to glow beside mother's butterscotch, and outside the window, her white cattleya nodded in approbation. Late summer in Legazpi and all was well in this city at the foot of the volcano where her orchids came from.

'Now, who do you think looks older — me or the neighbour across the road?'

I laughed. 'Of course, Papa, you look much younger.'

'But,' he whispered, 'I'm two years older than him.'

Father's vanity was a joke, only for family consumption. He knew it made us laugh. 'But look at your mother, always young, always beautiful,' he said, sitting beside me, watching the one and only queen of the house take on the mirror.

'What kind of yellow is this?'

'Butterscotch, Mama, like butterscotch candy.'

'Doesn't make me look too pale?'

'Suits you perfectly,' we assured her.

She tugged at the sleeves, patted a button, straightened the collar, and shrugged so the soft fabric settled just right around her shoulders. 'What do you think?' Then she turned around for our thorough inspection.

Father and I winked at each other.

'I know, I'm vain,' she snapped.

Sweet it may be, but butterscotch has a hint of salt. Scrapes the roof of the mouth.

Another wink from him, and again she caught it. Nothing escapes her, like today.

'*Hilinga*, Nin̄i — look, daughter — the suit is almost black in this light.'

Today is more than twenty years later. It's January and humid despite the monsoon rain. Constant, as if it won't allow the ground to dry ever again. The wetness grips us all, but my mother's eyes are dry.

'That tie — your brother Roberto bought it —'

'Where's he?'

'Picking up the priest — that tie —'

'And where's Nestor?'

'He'll be here tonight —'

'Isn't he supposed to be here *now*?'

'There you go again criticising your youngest brother,' she scolds.

He does not want to be here, *with us* — but I bite my tongue.

'That tie goes well with the suit, don't you think?'

Engage "that tie", not the broken ties.

'That tie's the right shade for the suit. Smart.'

She'd rather resurrect "father's vanity", his word. *Smart.*

'So should I wear a tie too? Is this the right-smart way to enter Australia? And should I wear a suit on the plane like I'm going to a wedding?'

I remember his protestations as he shrugged off the suit and mother scolded, 'Don't crumple it.'

I always bought my parents beautiful clothes as *pasalubongs*, homecoming gifts from Australia. I shopped at big sales when designer clothes were marked down to half price. Maybe I'm the vain one, for my parents. For my father who once trudged up and down the rice-paddies with a carabao, child and beast tilling the land. For my mother who grew up caring for seven siblings from dawn to dusk each day until he married her at nineteen, the most beautiful girl in his neighbouring village. Yes, I'm vain for my parents. That's why I bought the suit and the blouse for the Australian expedition. I wanted them to look their best at the gate. I did not want the immigration official to think they came to migrate, claiming family reunion, or that my parents were poor. Look, they can afford to be tourists. Look, they're smart.

'So how is life in Australia?'

Mother's youngest sister, *Tiya* Vee, has taken me aside after also remarking how well father looks in the suit. We sit down. We say the chair is hard for our older bottoms. No, we just sat down too quickly lest our knees give way.

The screen door bangs. It's mother's friend saying, 'Actually he looks good,' in hushed tones, and *Tiya* Vee and I smile and say, 'Ah, it's the suit.'

'I don't think I'll wear it to Australia.' Again with hesitance, he ran a hand over the fine wool that summer morning years ago. 'Too smart. My hand will just get caught in it.' Rough as rough, he always said. '*Sampulong guramoy na pantrabaho* — ten fingers for work, not suits.'

'But Papa, they're the best ten fingers.'

'Uhmm ...' He stared at his unsteady hands.

Father's hands shook. '*Pasmádo,*' he said. Because he'd eaten way past mealtime all the time. Because he was always working. Manual labour and my father: twins since he was born. After farm work as a child in the village, he studied Electricals at trade school then worked in a mine, then after a brief stint teaching Electricals also at trade school, he began repairing refrigerators and air-conditioners that became the bread and butter of his eventual family. Us: four children and my mother all sent to university through the labour of his *sampulong guramoy*, his ten fingers.

The handsomeness of labour, my father's vanity: ten fingers that educated wife and children towards white-collar jobs and built a house with our mother. 'Even if I only went to trade school.' This was his favourite story, hard-earned success, which he always punctured with self-deprecation. 'But compared to all of you, I'm dumb really, I can't even speak right English — so will Australia let me in?'

Father's first job interview was with an Australian at one of the gold mines in the region. Twenty years old, fresh from trade school, holding forth the very first CV that he'd written, 'paper shaking like there's an earthquake,' to this big, English-speaking man. So obvious was the tremor of nerves, that the Australian boss said, 'I'm not going to eat you!' We always had a laugh over this story. See, Papa, we've had our Australian connection since years and years ago. He let you in, you worked in that mine. But that was *our* region's gold mine. We let the Australian in.

The screen door opens and shuts again with a bang, I see my mother flinch, and another *Tiyo* takes the last space on the sofa. Full house now all the way to the dining table where coffee cups and beer bottles are clinking. It's 5 p.m. and it's a downpour, and those who've just arrived are wiping themselves dry. There's a worried drone about this much water, what with the volcano erupting. We're used to living under the shadow of an active volcano, to torrential rains, even typhoons, but we've grown to fear the mix of water and volcanic lahar. In 2006 the rains of a super typhoon pushed down the stacked-up lahar from a previous eruption and mudflow took nearly two thousand lives, some never found again.

Worry moves around the room. The smell of wet earth rises with our breaths.

'But remember, *nabubuhay kita sa tagilid na dagâ* — we live on tilted earth.'

Someone had to remind us of this local saying. We live on uncertain, unsteady earth, but one thing is certain: the people are steady, stoic, or are expected to be. As was my father. Even if his hands shook.

The screen door bangs yet again and I hear the same noises about how well he looks, really. It's the neighbour across the road, the one who looks even much older than father now. Mother welcomes him and takes his umbrella outside, opens it on the porch, making sure the screen door does not slam. 'So no one trips on the wet,' she smiles brightly at the new arrival.

A few years ago, the banging door became a big quarrel between my parents. It was not just the noise. It signalled that father was sneaking out again, and so emphatically. Bang! Then through the iron gate. Bang! With his cane and cap, off for a *pasyar*, a promenade, at any time of the day. 'What if you fall, what if you get hit by a car, what if you lose your way!' mother scolded. Father had been falling and forgetting. Parkinson's and the beginnings of dementia, and everything went unsteady, uncertain. 'But I want out, *mangalag-kalag man lamang*— at least roam my eyes around the outside world!' he protested. Sometimes mother locked the gate.

'So when do we leave?' He was keen to discuss the trip that summer morning. 'To Oz — is that how to say it? To Oz, to Oz,' he practised and liked its feel in his mouth.

It was getting hotter, oppressively so. Suit and blouse were taken off after she aired her doubts. 'I'm never good at travelling, and how can I leave my garden, my orchids? They need daily care.'

But father was wishful. '*Gusto kong mangalag-kalag sa Australia*, Nini — I want to roam my eyes around Australia, daughter.'

Mangalag-kalag. His favourite word that English cannot approximate. English can only evoke our Bikol language.

Mangalag-kalag: to roam the eyes around a world further than our own. Even if roaming makes us unsteady, uncertain. But words are never steady or certain. Their other meanings sneak up on us.

Mangalag: "to go soul-ing" or "to go ghosting". *Kalag*: soul or ghost.

See, words are their own roaming ghosts. They enter locked gates, doors, even go through walls to surprise us. Like today, as I stare at my suited father in the immaculately white box.

Outside the rain is pouring non-stop now and *Tiya* Vee chuckles as she joins me before my father under the glass. 'Your Papa — he told me once, "Hoy Vee, when it rains, we shouldn't look up."' Giggling, she points to her nose, then to my father's. '*Dakula kaya*

92

ang lohô — because the holes are big — so we shouldn't look up, or else we'll drown.'

Yes, he makes us laugh.

My sister Lydia has just joined us and she's quickly in on the joke.

'But look,' I say. 'His nose is taller, as if with a high bridge now,' then add, 'Maybe when I'm laid out, my nose will get taller too.'

Lydia giggles. 'So there's still hope for you.'

'For me too, me too!' *Tiya* Vee pipes in.

In a country once colonised by tall-nosed patriarchs — the Spanish and the Americans — there's a colonial self-consciousness, often in banter, about noses. Mine is *pangô*, like my father's and my auntie's: bridgeless, flat. Unlike my sister's that is as patrician as our mother's from her Spanish-Chinese heritage.

Our giggling turns to laughter that brings tears. The worry drone around the room stops. There are disapproving stares. So we stop too, swallow our macabre humour before the coffin. We wipe our eyes dry.

'He's handsome in that suit,' Lydia whispers.

'He's always handsome,' I more than concur.

My sister and I share *Tiya* Vee's box of tissues. She pinches her nose and mine to coax a bridge to grow. 'But let's make it taller before we die.'

We laugh and more tissues get soiled. We cannot lock the door to the wet outside.

Whenever mother locked the gate so father could not *mangalag-kalag*, they fought. I heard about it on my phone calls from Canberra. Sometimes he cried, saying he might as well 'go home' to his village rather than be locked up like this. Much later, he could no longer tell his story, he found it hard to find and put words together. As if they were locked up too. Nor could he could put my words together. We'd struggle through simple conversation. Words were unable to roam from Australia to the Philippines and back. So he'd say, '*Dae ko na nasasabutan*, Ninì — I can no longer understand, daughter,' and he'd hand the phone to my mother.

'So tell me — will they understand my English in Australia?' I remember how he asked all those years ago, addressing the blue suit, voice melancholy. Then, 'Sshhh ...' he turned away from the suit to the window. 'Listen ... they're back.'

'Who, Papa?'

'The *kiyaw*,' he whispered. 'They're visiting me.'

I followed his pointing hand and heard them: 'Ki-kiyaw, ki-kiyaw.' Birds singing on the neighbour's golden shower tree across the path from our gate.

'*Mag-agom na oryol*,' my mother whispered — the husband-and-wife orioles. 'They visit and sing for your Papa when he sits on the porch. Sometimes they visit our back garden — ay, Ninì, *magayonon* — so beautiful. So yellow!'

A yellow brighter than mother's butterscotch.

The song went on intermittently for a few seconds, then silence.

'*Ay, nagpaaram na* — they've said goodbye,' my father sighed and returned to the blue suit at the door. 'Uhmm ... *talagang magayon* — really beautiful. Smart. Okay, I'll wear it to Australia — but, Ninì, will they understand my English there?'

Well, you made friends with the *kiyaw*, so surely ... I felt an argument brewing inside me, about language, comprehension, connection, but he was waiting for quick assurance. 'Papa, your English is fine.'

And it was. Once when my husband Arvis visited, in his finest shirt he confided to his "Ozzie guest": 'I practised my English, so we can have a conversation.' I nearly clapped my hands. Such ease in putting together a wish to be hospitable to 'your kind Australian man who makes you happy.' Because years before, he must have heard unhappiness on the phone, smelled it like when there's a dead rat in the house but you can't quite tell where it is. Each time he asked 'Where is *he*?' about my first husband, I could only respond: 'Travelling, busy, gone to the shops,' or some-such noise. When I came home and broke the news about the divorce, my mother, grandmother and aunties were quick to recover. But *Tiya Vee* whispered, 'Look, your Papa keeps wiping his face with his towel.' Our family does not do public sorrow well. So we lock out the wet. We keep steady. We survive on tilted earth.

What I remember of the wet. Copious tears at seventeen when I caught my childhood boyfriend holding hands with the prettiest Spanish *mestiza* at school. And they just kept holding hands after that without him telling me we were over. I came home to my mother all distressed, but she scolded: 'Stop crying, you're not on stage!' I stopped, I locked *it* out. But father smelled it. Each dinnertime, he knocked on our bedroom door and called me down to eat. He'd never done that before.

I'm remembering too much on this fifth day of my father's wake when the monsoon is conspiring with the volcanic lahar and we can all get swept away by the mudflow. We cannot hang on to the whiteness of a coffin. Mud is black and layered, and it runs to many places and becomes many places. *Nangangalag-kalag man ang memorya* — memory also goes roaming. And let's hope it roams with clearer eyes that can see through the murk — that it runs with its root word: *kalag*, soul. That it roams with soul and sees soul. Let's hope we remember the kindness and that we remember kindly. My father was trying to appease unhappiness and perhaps my mother did not know how to handle her eldest child's broken heart.

No one is ever smart enough.

His doubts grew as that summer morning progressed to noon. 'I'm not really sure about Australia.' Then, addressing the suit again: 'You're too smart for me.'

'But you are smart, Papa. We wouldn't have finished university without your smarts!'

He smiled. Stared at his hands. Indeed *sampulong guramoy*. Ten (smart) fingers.

But the time came when he could hardly connect the wires of an air-conditioner. Then he could no longer hold his spoon without spilling his rice. And he began forgetting, mixing up his stories, my brothers' names. But one's smarts may be recovered according to an Australian TV documentary. The brain can regrow what it lost with age or injury. If we stimulate it, if we return it to better times. So on one of my homecomings, I returned my father to his own home in the village, to old family ties. On Manila paper spread out on the dining table, we drew maps.

'So, Papa, here's the path to your family's old house where you took us berry-picking as kids.'

'Yes, *tungaw-tungaw* and *kurumbot* berries, how sweet.' Eyes alight, he followed the path that I drew.

Father roaming happy times. How sweet.

'That's the old house — and that's the road to the church where we got married.' Mother took father's hand, leading a finger along the path of my pen. His hand shook but his assent was certain. 'Yes, you were very beautiful in your wedding dress.'

Two years later, all shaking stopped. His fingers were unmoving, swollen, jaundiced. Still and speechless. Tube into his penis, into his nose to his stomach, into his throat to his lungs at the hospital's ICU. First, mother went in. She came out with cheeks more hollow, shoulders more sharp. Then we asked the nurse if all of us four children could go in as a group. We couldn't say because he's never seen us together for the last eight years. Broken ties and all that. So we went in, came out. For a while, as still and speechless. We could not find or put words together.

That we could be smart enough in grief, or that we could outsmart it. That's our vanity. So we hovered at the ICU door after our mother went back inside.

'Do you think he recognised us?' I tried to keep my voice from shaking.

It took sometime for someone to respond.

'He was always asking to see all of us. Together.'

It was my sister whispering before she finally led us to the waiting area. We were each playing the scene in our heads: at the ICU bed, all introducing ourselves to our father. 'Papa, this is Nenita — Nini, eldest daughter.' 'Roberto here, Papa.' 'Lydia, Papa.' 'It's Nestor, the youngest.' We had to keep ourselves tightly together at the foot of his bed, because he could not move his head. His eyes could not go roaming.

Mangalag-kalag. To roam the eyes, with soul. In a blue suit. In Australia. He broached it whenever I came home. 'I wish to visit you in your new home,' he'd say. 'But I'm not a good traveller,' mother would counter his proposition. So he gave up. But the wish hovered. 'When do we go?'

Strange that on this last day of the wake, I want to sit my mother down and talk and talk. About the suit or father's lockdowns, about the phone calls from Australia, about the heartbreak at seventeen, about broken ties, maybe about repair — but will she roam with me? Will she see what I see when each of us has a different map of family history?

I was home in Canberra when father was rushed to hospital for the last time. On the phone, mother and I were meticulous about what and how things should proceed — if *this* gets bad. It was past midnight and the hush made our voices sound louder. We discussed the right clothes. The blue suit for Australia came up. I said, sure, but was not really sure about anything except gripping the phone. After we put it down, I remembered why, really, I bought the suit more than twenty years ago.

I was at Charles de Gaulle airport, before French Immigration. A young Filipina was ahead of me in the queue. Very nervous, clutching a worn duffel bag. She leant towards me, confiding that it's her first time to travel abroad. 'Áte — Sister,' she said, '*Sana okay 'to* — I hope this is okay.' I assured her it is, it will be. It was my first time in France and I can't speak French, so was not confident at all. She said she was here to work as a nanny. Then it was her turn. The Immigration official began asking questions. She couldn't hear, perhaps couldn't understand the English with a French accent. She stammered, her hands shook. The official opened her bag, turned it inside out, spilling a bundle of old clothes, toothbrush, knickers. She tried to scoop them up from the eyes of the growing onlookers. 'Áte — Sister,' she called out to me, near tears. I was before another official by then, explaining I was there for an arts festival. I could not look at this sister panicking. The gate had opened for me so I just kept walking. I could not bear to look back.

She had a Philippine passport and I still had one at that time, and we had travelled to the same place. But with different maps. And the gatekeepers had their definitive one. So our eyes could not go roaming beyond who and where we were at that moment. But how far can the eyes roam at the gate? I think of the kindness of sight. Perhaps it's a kind of x-ray vision that sees through a passport, a shaking hand, through skin and an old duffel bag even after its insides are revealed. It sees soul. But sadly, in the tight, frantic space of a gate, we are all shortsighted. We see only our own maps held closely to our faces.

When I returned to Australia, I bought the blue suit and the butterscotch blouse. My parents had begun planning to visit me by then. I shopped with care, wishing for them to look their best when they land in Oz. I knew: there is not much distance to roam between vanity and dignity.

'*Makapangalag-kalag man lamang ako sa* Australia' — If only I could roam my eyes around Australia.

But he never did. My parents' expedition was shelved. Too hard. Then we all just forgot about it, but not my father. He invoked his wish whenever he opened the closet. The blue suit hung there unused for more than twenty years, until it was resurrected on that late phone call with my mother. So I quickly booked the soonest flight. In the dawn hush of my Canberra study, I imagined the blue suit that will never go roaming, that will never be able to visit me. As I clicked the pay button, I remembered his story about visitations, invoking *nagtawó*, our local belief. '*Ay*, Nini, the dying can visit anywhere to appear to the beloved.' And the beloved who sees the apparition may avert death if she cloaks "the ghost" in this moment of emergency.

The printer released my ticket. I thought, what if I'm too late? Go ghosting, Papa. Visit me.

I was too late.

The screen door bangs again. Roberto rushes in with the priest. Both are wet from the monsoon onslaught despite their umbrellas now dripping on the floor.

The way my brother shakes off the wet sends my heart off-kilter. I think of a dog who's been left too long in the rain. This brother who rushed our father to the hospital each time, who held him as he struggled when tubes were inserted, who talked to doctor after doctor, ran errands, organised nurses and carers, queued for medicines late at night, who vowed to fight *this* with our father. How grey he's grown.

Lydia offers him and the priest a towel each to dry up, and mother thanks Father Ruiz for coming. *Tiya* Vee lays a hand on her back. It straightens up quickly, like how it did for eight years of caring for her husband. I follow her cue. My heart restores itself on its perch. We steady ourselves on tilted earth.

We can't hear much of the Mass because of the rain but Father Ruiz perseveres. He sprinkles holy water on the coffin. The glass gets wet, wetter with all our unwept weep. In his blue suit father swims in our eyes, and mother breathes out.

The screen door does not bang. The iron gate does not bang. He is passing, he will roam.

Australian Immigration, Sydney. I've just landed back, I'm in the queue. Behind me, an all-Aussie voice says, 'Passing through, please.' It's a Qantas steward pushing a wheelchair with an old man in a suit. I step aside. 'Thank you,' he smiles then whispers something to the steward. In Filipino. Both laugh and keep moving through the crowd, to the gate.

NAMING THE FLOWERS

Amidst the milling crowd he stands
Eyes looking, searching for a view
A sudden flash a _____ _____
Made all the focus true.

Mama?

It's mother-daughter time unlike any other. Mother's eyes follow daughter wherever she goes, whatever she does in this bedroom with only one bed now, pushed to the wall and stacked with clothes, linen and stuff. It's the peak of summer but mother remains cool, unperturbed in floral silk jacket, champagne pearls, and her trademark self-possessed smile. A woman who knows she is beautiful.

Daughter Nenita is sweaty and voiceless.

The closet is almost empty and the stacks of clothes and linen are growing. Nenita's folding them in neat piles: mother's, father's, stepping out clothes here, house clothes there, linen on one side, towels on the other, and don't forget to sort the curtains according to the room where they belong. Then do the drawers next. But first, the important papers on the side table. She can hear the instructions in her eyes.

Nenita remembers this bed at the centre of the room, the closet shut, everything neatly put away, and the morning sun streaming through the curtains.

'I'm cold,' her mother says.

'Let's get you into these trackies, Mama — plus another layer over that sweater, maybe this hoodie.'

'Trackies, hoodie?'

'"Trackies" are these track pants and "hoodie" is this top with a hood to keep your head warm.' She helps her into the gear she brought from Australia.

'*Gari lulû*' — like a nickname, she says, face crumpling in pain.

'Yes, Australians have a way of calling stuff by their nicknames. Like "brekkie" for breakfast, "cossie" for swimming costume.'

'Ahh,' her mother smiles through the pain. 'I like the play with words.' She loves words and flowers because both are growing things. But flowers first, then words. She's an avid gardener and reader, though these passions are impossible now. 'How's my garden — have you looked?'

'Your flowers are blooming.'

'I've abandoned them.'

'But they won't abandon you. They'll keep blooming.'

'No, my orchids will die,' she whispers from inside the hood.

She tucks her under two blankets. 'Feel better?'

'My feet are cold.'

'Another layer of socks then,' which she quickly organises.

'Orchids need extra care.'

As you do, she wants to say.

'Wonder what your Papa would say.'

'Keep warm, that's what he'd say.' She tucks in her feet under the blankets. 'Okay now?'

'Thank you, Ninì,' then shuts her eyes.

Ninì, the affectionate nickname for the eldest, so they're okay.

'*Haaaaaay* …' *Hagayhay*, that long sigh of pain.

'Can I do anything else for you?'

'I'm glad you're here … and that now we know.'

They just came from her oncologist who said, 'Possibly six months.' She refused any further treatment. 'I'll just wait. I hope it's quick, but that's up to God.'

It was quick: three months.

Now she's organising her parents' effects in the bedroom rearranged time and again to meet their care needs before they died, one after another, after so much suffering that defied painkillers. Tough. She glances back at her mother's framed and blown-up photo that sat beside her coffin at the chapel. What cool beauty, what elegance. Silk through and through. She's racked with tears and coughing. Probably a virus she caught on the plane. At the funeral yesterday, she had to flash a written note, 'Sorry, no voice', to each commiserating guest who wanted to speak to her about her mother. She kept away from the teary hugs. Don't want you to catch it.

On the side table, she finds one of the many "rearrangements" of the bedroom: a floor plan in her mother's drawing and beautifully precise longhand, the envy of the whole family, on yellow pad paper for then househelp-and-caregiver Ning to follow right after father was buried. All the furnishings are duly labelled in their new posts, and at the centre, the single bed with 'my bed', 'headboard at window' and 'foot' written in red pen. So Ning gets it right. Mother's obsession for order, Nenita grew up with it. Fix this, clean that, sweep there, and the inspection after: running a hand on the jalousies that Nenita just wiped, then, 'Repeat!' if not clean by her standards. So eldest daughter must wipe all over again.

She looks around the bedroom that she's turned inside out. Closet, cabinet and drawers open, an assortment of bags strewn around, and boxes for things to give away and those to store. Sorry, Mama, won't be able to finish all before I fly back.

Then she finds the flowers.

'*Magayonon* — so beautiful,' she remembers her mother saying, pleasure rising above the pain. She sits between the linen and mother's stepping out clothes and bag that she has yet to open. Sitting on this bed at whatever time feels like only one time: always in present tense, that time with her flowers.

Before she flew back to the Philippines, for god knows how many times of to-ing and fro-ing, in Canberra she had the photos of the flowers printed and organised in this purple folder. A gift for her mother: *pang-aling*, a "feel-better" thing after her surgery that they thought would fix her up. But she got worse, so Nenita came home to take her through further medical tests, which confirmed it was cancer that had metastasised, and on the day she landed in Canberra for a break, she passed away. She had to quickly fly back for the family's fourth funeral: her father last year, Lydia's husband and an aunt's last March, and now on "the merry month of May", her mother.

Too many white flowers in less than two years. But these flowers are different. These are from her garden, photos that Nenita took after father's funeral and brought back to Canberra, plus something more. She opens the folder.

First page: *gumamela*, the hibiscus sentinel. A close-up of a newly opened bloom wet with morning rain just outside the green iron gate. Her mother's garden starts here with *gumamelas* and *sampaguitas*, a native jasmine, lining the cement fence from the outside.

'*Ang pusò garo* jewel!' she enthuses. Indeed, heart like a jewel: five stigmas like a cluster of topazes set against the gold anthers at the tip of the red pistil. From this heart glistening with raindrops, mother traces the five petals unfurling into fuchsia and turning a lighter pink, then surprisingly into peach at the edges.

How pale her hand and how blue the veins, like bruises.

'Then we enter the gate, Mama,' and she turns to the next page: the white bougainvillea draped over the gate from the inside.

Mother forces herself to sit up, propped up by pillows. '*Marambongon* — so lush! To think that was just a tiny cutting from my friend Mary.'

Bougainvillea's followed by the flowering hedge lining the fence that extends from the gate. This chronology of flowers is deliberate. In Canberra, Nenita organised the photos like a story from outside to inside.

'Look, Mama, it's the magic hedge, the star of your garden — beats your orchids, right?'

Mother makes noises of dissent. She's an orchid tragic. For years she collected different varieties: a rare *waling-waling*, a white and a purple cattleya, a peach and a white *vanda*, a white and a purple dendrobium, a white butterfly orchid, and the spotted yellow spider orchid. Cool beauties grown on the slopes of Mayon volcano, they rarely flower here and took years to flower after she bought them. Seasoned withholders, Nenita thinks, withholding their grace from ordinary mortals, like her mother who believes it's only God and her youngest son who deserve devotion. Her three older children, self-sufficient as they are, need discipline, so don't spare the rod. And it's their obligation as elders to be as devoted to their youngest brother: to care for him and excuse him from any responsibility, even if he's snubbed them for years. Care should only be one way and no need to acknowledge it in return, and if it's thrown back at you, tough shit, it's your problem.

'It is your duty to care,' her mother used to say. 'After all, you're successful so you have the capacity.'

So does the heart withhold because it's incapacitated?

Nenita holds these thoughts back as they admire the photo of the hedge, then dares to say, 'Mama, this is a lesson in amplitude,' knowing her mother loves moral lessons. 'This hedge flowers throughout the year with little care from you, and have you ever seen anything bloom in different colours all at once?' She points to the small, five-petal yellow flowers and the equally small red ones beside them, some closed like holly berries, some open with green seeds inside and others with black ones. 'Magical!'

'Uhmm, yes,' she nods.

'What's it called?'

'I don't know.'

Ah, the things we can't name.

She closes the folder abruptly now, toppling her mother's bag. Get over it, Nenita! She picks up the designer leather, a birthday gift from Lydia, as was the floral silk jacket on the photo. Both of them love shopping for their mother. Always a pleasure to buy beautiful things for a beautiful mother. Aw, stop crying! She opens the bag. Inside, an embroidered Spanish fan and a brown leather wallet, another gift from Lydia. She flips it open and finds her parents smiling at her. Better days: father's arm affectionately and proudly draped around mother's shoulder and she's leaning slightly towards him, smile generous and one gold earring winking. It's the mini version of the enlarged and framed photo that sat on her coffin during the wake, a required addition to her solo in floral silk. The happy couple, in casual blue-greys and whites, used to be the central fixture of this room, set on the drawers beside the bed. Mother kept pointing to it on her final month when she could barely speak, mumbling, 'Picture ... picture,' then, 'No make-up.'

Nenita understood: her mother was instructing her on how she should be "arranged".

She finds two other photos in the wallet: Nenita and Lydia, all smiles with their dog, and the other with parents formally seated and four siblings standing behind. Early 90s just before she left for Australia. She holds back a sob and smiles at family when they were still solidly bonded. This was mother's wish, like hers, throughout the years that she carried them around in her wallet.

And what's this? Tucked behind the photos, a folded receipt so faded, it's unreadable. But behind it, the familiar longhand in red pen:

> *Amidst the milling crowd*
> > *he stands*
> *Eyes looking, searching*
> > *for a view*
> *A sudden flash a* _____
>
> _____
>
> *Made all the focus*
> > *true.*

A poem? The thud-thud grows loud in her chest, there's a bird wanting out.

She stares at the unfolded piece: it's the size of her palm. These two blanks … was she trying to recall a poem? Or is this *hers*?

She presses it against her chest. The wings flap.

Sorting's stalled. Her mother's left a secret gift and she must unlock it. Using the unfinished verse, she's been searching for "the poet" on her iPad, but nothing. So mother was a closet poet? The writing looks hurried but clear and the red so red — so recently written? Who is the *he* standing *amidst the milling crowd*? Father? He loved roaming his eyes around the outside world. And what's the *sudden flash*? Sounds like an epiphany, because *it made all the focus true*.

After an hour of trying to figure it out, she gives up and returns to the flowers, trying to re-focus on that companionable moment of viewing them together.

'*Ano kayang ngaran?*' Mother's muffled wondering about the name of the hedge sounds other-wordly inside the hood.

'Don't worry, Mama, I'll search on the web. It's really a magic hedge, much better than your row of *adelfas* before.'

'Ah, they were pink and red.'

Mother's oleanders. She got rid of them when her friend said that if you grow *adelfa* in your garden, your daughters would end up as spinsters. It made her laugh, which offended her mother, so she made peace by sharing a fact. 'Oleanders are poisonous, Mama, so you were wise to get rid of them.'

The fourth page now: the *santan* lining the footpath towards the front porch.

'Your great-grandmother had plenty of those in our old yard in the village. *Mas mapulahon pa*' — much redder than these. 'Must have been the soil.'

What kind of soil inspires flowers to thrive? Not the question that Nenita asks as they admire the clusters of tiny red blooms close to the ground. She opts for history. 'What was great-grandmother like?'

'*Maboot na maisogon, minsan.*' A kind one who was very cruel, sometimes.

'Like your mother, Mama,' though she was tender with Nenita, her first grandchild. 'Didn't grandmother beat my *Tiyos* and *Tiyas* when they were kids?'

'Because they misbehaved, they needed discipline!'

'I remember … just before she died, grandmother told me she was sorry she was cruel.' Nenita had to say it. She wants her mother to say *it* too, but the room has grown quiet. Mother hides inside her hood.

'Almost forgot — I've something special to show you. The last page, look!'

Mother surfaces and looks at the final photo.

'Flowers from my friends in Australia.'

'And why is your father's photo —?'

'I placed it beside the flowers. Fitting, isn't it?'

She looks and looks.

Bliss mornings. How the four friends call their precious catch-ups. Aboriginal artist Jenni, Lizz from Ireland, Kate who lived for years in Papua New Guinea, and Nenita from the Philippines: all Australian poets. When it's possible, they meet at the Belconnen Arts Centre to talk poetry, art, politics, and life over tea and coffee, then lunch in a noodle house nearby. Bliss when needed, like today. Nenita has just returned from burying her father and her friends organised this bliss morning with plenty of hugs and flowers. 'From all of us,' Lizz offers the exquisite arrangement.

'We've been thinking of you over there,' Jenni says.

'Our heart is with you,' Kate whispers, hand on chest.

'Oh, thank you —' Nenita gets teary — 'it's like — don't know how to say this — our practice is we offer flowers for the dead ... at the wake ... so it's like you were there with me.'

'They're for you, with all our love,' Lizz says.

'I know, but it feels like you've given my father flowers. So, a very big thank you. This gives me so much comfort — and I'm sure he's thanking you too.' She shows them the small card with her father's photo and the prayer she composed to commemorate the 40th day of his passing, the final celebration that will conclude the mourning ritual. She can't be there for it, she had to fly back.

'What a happy smile,' Lizz says.

'A kind face,' Kate adds.

'A kind man,' Nenita nods.

'What's the prayer?' Jenni asks.

'It's in Bikol, my first language.' She reads it to them then translates:

> 'Dios ko, maogmang mamasyar
> sa dalan nin liwanag
> kung saen namumurak
> ang tunay na pagpadabà.
> My God, it's happy to promenade
> in the path of light
> where there blooms
> true love.'

Then she tucks the card into the middle of the flowers. 'Your flowers and the prayer, they go together.'

Her friends nod. They sip their tea and coffee, and name the flowers.

'Purple iris, and this, baby's breath —'

'And that's a tulip, a magenta tulip.'

'This one's red carnation —'

Voices weave into each other and words grow with the flowers. Bliss.

'And daisies — that's a white daisy and the tiny lilac ones, they're asters —'

'What about this? Looks like an orchid.'

'Yes, a pink dendrobium —'

'And this peach bud?'

'African trumpet lily — gorgeous when fully open —'

'Lasts for days — but this pink with brown flecks, I don't think I know —'

'Uhmm … maybe Peruvian lily.'

'Ah, you know your flowers. But what about these purple clusters dotted with tiny white flowers, like two flowers in one. I've seen them around a lot … you know what they're called?'

No one knows, so quickly Jenni's on her smart phone with immediate success. '*Limonium sinuatum*. Or maybe Perezii Blue.'

'Love the second name, so evocative,' Kate says.

'Stunning colour, look.' Jenni shows them photos on the web. 'Originally from the Canary Islands.'

'All these flowers are probably from somewhere else, like some of us.'

'And they've all gone somewhere else. Like all of us.'

'Bliss coming and going.'

'The amplitude of flowers.'

'Blooming their best wherever they are.'

'The amplitude of the land.'

'This land has its own flowers. They've been blooming here long before these came — lest we forget.'

Again, four voices weaving as Jenni stares at her phone. 'Latest news,' and she shows it to them. 'The PM rejected the Uluru Statement From the Heart.'

Around the flowers, a collective sigh.

'The flowers and your Papa's picture, *bagay* — good match,' her mother says, as she marvels at all ten flowers that Nenita labelled with their names. 'You have kind friends in Australia.'

She nods. 'Kindness when you're most vulnerable, Mama, a great comfort … when I was flying here for Papa's funeral, the Qantas flight attendant gave up her lunch for me, because I couldn't eat what was on the menu, bad tummy. Annie Rawson, her name — I won't forget it.'

111

'I'm glad Australians are kind to my daughter,' then she pauses, thoughtful. 'What's the Uluru Statement From the Heart?'

'Ah yes — it's the call by Australia's Indigenous People, Aboriginal and Torres Strait Islanders, to be recognised in the Constitution — the former Prime Minister rejected it.'

'What — they're not recognised?'

'No, it's a continuous struggle for them.'

'Thank God, our IPs here are recognised.' In 1997 the state recognition and protection of the rights of 14 to 17 million Indigenous Peoples from 110 ethno-linguistic groups were mandated in the Philippine Constitution.

'But they're still marginalised, Mama, even if some have a voice now in how they run their affairs — y'see, the Uluru Statement From the Heart is the First Nations People's call to have a voice to Parliament, and for self-determination and truth-telling —'

'Truth-telling?'

'Telling the truth about the injustices done to them, the violence, the dispossession not just of land, culture, language, but also of lives and dignity. It's still happening now, like with our own Indigenous Peoples here.'

'Haaaaaay ... herak man' — pity them.

'Not pity, but justice, Mama. And kindness.'

'You're right, Nini.'

'And the state must also recognise the years of injustice and unkindness.'

'Pirmi na — always! Recognise and be sorry for all the evil that it has inflicted on its people!' Her mother has sat up straighter, hood shrugged off. She seems to have been suddenly restored. This is another one of her passions: politics. She used to keep track of the local politicos' shenanigans with meticulous attention to detail.

'You know, Mama, in 2008 the Australian Prime Minister at that time made a public apology to the nation's First Peoples.

A long time coming. We were in tears watching him give the sorry speech in the Parliament.'

'You live in a good country,' her mother presses her hand. 'I'm glad.'

She presses back. 'But there's still a lot to be done, a lot of unfinished business — and here too. This is still my country too. My first home.'

'I know.' Her mother lies down, closes her eyes.

'You want to rest — shall I leave you now?'

But her mother does not let go of her hand.

'I'm writing about kindness, Mama,' she whispers. 'I'm paying homage to it.'

No answer, she's fallen asleep. Strange. Have they held hands before? Maybe when she was little. *Ay*, this bird in her chest. Unsure if it could fly out.

Be kind, Nenita, be kind. There's kindness in forgiveness even when it's not asked, and even more when it's not asked. But how can one forgive if the wrong is not named? She's still sitting on this bed and inside her, the bird is still uncertain. So are the tears. So she shuts the folder of flowers and returns to sorting stuff. *Stuff*: those bits and pieces that gnaw inside. At the bottom corner of the closet, she finds a ball of tightly knotted fabric. She struggles to open it, hears a little cry, hers, as she lays them out. A mother's stuff: the baby blanket of her youngest son Nestor that she embroidered with roses, her older son Roberto's *Wizard of Oz* costume when he was eleven, her younger daughter Lydia's green and white dress when she played Helen Keller at seven years old, and the kindergarten tie of Nenita, her firstborn. A mother's delights in a ball of fabric.

She fondles her white school tie with St. Raphael Academy printed in dark-blue. Nenita is little Ninì again, and Mama is proudly arranging the tie on her first day of school, then she pats her chest — 'there, you're ready.'

Be still, bird, be still.

Bloody tears! She gets up, opens the window. There's a little breeze, thank God, and the scent of mother's jasmine. She thinks of the unfinished poem, those two blanks. Maybe mother didn't know what to say or how to say whatever it was that needed saying. Oh, our sad, sad helplessness. 'Perhaps everything terrible is in its deepest being something helpless that wants help from us.' Rilke wrote that. He found the words, perhaps to still the bird in his chest, or to make it soar. So she returns to her mother's bed, picks up a pen and the yellow pad paper on which she rearranged this room. She copies her poem, but its lines rearranged. Flowers and words, both grow. Even from a tiny cutting. Or a cut. So she tries. She tries grafting new words to heal it.

> *Amidst the milling crowd he stands*
> *Eyes looking, searching for a view*
> *A sudden flash a   will   to understand*
> *Made all the focus true.*

How to understand the whys and wherefores. But is it comprehension that she needs? She remembers yesterday's funeral Mass, when all had to hold hands for a prayer. She did so with Nestor because he was in the closest pew. His family cared for their mother during her final months, but it was the older Roberto who facilitated their parents' care since day one. 'Nestor and I, we understand each other,' mother told her once. What about the understanding and care from your other children through the years? Beside her, just-widowed Lydia, as always stoic and brave, gripped her other hand, whispering, 'Breathe, Nini, breathe.' Maybe because her lungs seemed to have lost their capacity to find air as she sobbed. Not for her mother, but because despite the hurts, her youngest brother held her hand.

> A sudden flash an   _offered_   _hand_
> Made all the focus true.

C'mon, Nenita, re-focus, look elsewhere, and look with equanimity if not clarity. In your mother's garden, in Australia, and everywhere in the planet, *they simply bloom*. So keep this simple too. Return it to her.

> Amidst the milling crowd she stands
> Eyes looking, searching for a view
> A sudden flash, a kinder hand
> Made all the focus true.

A kinder hand, Mama. Five fingers, five petals: the magic hedge of amplitude.

THE SLEEP OF APPLES

Quiero dormir el sueño de las manzanas —
I want to sleep the sleep of apples.

Federico Garcia Lorca

I warned you,' she said, quickly swerving the Audi. 'There'll be a lot of roadkill.'

Behind them, brown fur and red.

'What was it, Ella?'

'I didn't look, I'm driving.'

That's my problem, Nenita thinks to herself. I'm looking back too much. She tries to make out the receding stain, the third as they drive out of Hobart.

'Tasmania is the roadkill capital of the world,' Ella says. 'About 300,000 animals a year, I read somewhere.'

'And carcasses everywhere on Kangaroo Island as we speak. When these bushfires are over, there'll be about a billion native animals lost, they say.'

'Whose deaths matter?' Ella murmurs.

'Whose lives matter?'

'Ask the Parliament.'

Nenita sighs. 'It's apocalyptic, with fears of extinction —'

'Stop. I'm driving, I've to be clear-eyed.'

'Sorry, Ella.'

'Don't be,' then an intake of breath as she swerves again. 'Fuck!'

This time, Nenita does not look back. They both have to be clear-eyed.

Yesterday, while harvesting dinner from her garden, Ella told her how she's been crying since these bushfires began. 'We had terrible fires here too, last year. Until now some areas haven't regrown …' She reached for the plums near the fence. 'Here, try this.'

'Uhmm … sweet and tarty, and warm.'

'I know,' she said, biting into one. 'Never really understood what golden delicious meant until I ate one still warm from the tree over there.'

'Oh, you have apples.'

'Three kinds.' She points them out, their fruit still small and green.

'She'll be apples, Ella … they'll regrow.'

'She'll be apples, that's a cliché.'

'Apples were a luxury when I was growing up in the Philippines. We don't grow apples there, they're imported. My parents could afford only two, only at Christmas.'

'Sorry about your parents' passing.'

'Thanks,' she sighs, 'but she'll be apples, right? Outdated, but I love the line. Makes me see that russet glow instantly — did Robert like apples?'

'Yes, the golden delicious ones.'

'That's the yellow-green kind. Of course not all are red — I've never really seen an apple tree in full red, ripe fruit.'

'Kidding?'

'Drew it a lot as a kid. "A" is for apple. Used up my red crayon.'

'Okay, tomorrow we'll drive to the country so you see some orchards — Tasmania is The Apple Isle.'

'Really?'

'Look.'

'What?'

'Wattlebird on the golden delicious.'

'Where?' She followed Ella's finger but caught only the slight trembling of the leaves. 'Missed it.'

'Come closer.' Ella led her to the tree. 'It's actually two apple types in one tree — one grafted onto the other.' She shows her the "two sides", both with a few unripe fruit. 'This one's the golden delicious, and this, the democrat.'

'Not republicans?' Nenita laughed.

'Cheeky,' Ella chuckled. 'Now come over here.' She moved towards a bushy shrub and cut a stalk from it.

'Looks like an overgrown dill.'

'No, asparagus,' she said, handing her the stalk. 'Taste it.'

'Crunchy, nutty, sweet.'

'Now that's how asparagus should taste.'

'It's like jade.' Nenita admired the green length, a different shade from those at the supermarket, tapering into a closed bud of multiple petals. 'Sculptural.'

'Yeah, beautiful. You should see this bush when the red berries come out.'

'Asparagus with red berries?'

'Beautiful but poisonous.'

'The sting in the tail, huh?'

'In all tails — now let's get these silverbeets.'

As they harvested the red-veined greens, Nenita tried again. 'Robert gave me a jade bracelet once.'

'Did he?'

It was awkward talking about Robert to his ex-wife after more than a decade of not seeing her. Why now? Because of the passing of her parents. Because of Krishna. Because of the jade bracelet and everything else around these mementos. Maybe because of the bushfires.

Ella sucks in her breath as she navigates a bend. 'I think that was a wallaby.'

It's a blue-sky day, what Nenita has been missing since the fires began. Where she lives in Canberra has been smoky since Christmas. It's a relief to see the horizon again and the eucalypts without the ghostly haze.

'That's Mt Kunanyi and over there, Sleeping Beauty — some say that mountain's the shape of a woman lying on her side — see her?'

'Uhmm … that's the hair, head, body, then legs …' green and lush, with a wisp of cloud over her shoulders. 'Back home, we also have a mountain shaped like a sleeping woman. Mount Makiling named after Maria Makiling, the *diwata*, a nymph, caretaker of the mountain. She blesses it with abundant fruit and animals for the hunters. She appears after a storm to heal the mountain, so it can regrow.'

'We need a *diwata* after these fires.'

'I think *diwatas* are around us, Ella, the firefighters and community volunteers, the neighbours who come to each other's rescue and support, the hand that holds the next person's through fires or storms or volcanic eruptions —'

'Oh yes, there's that volcano erupting in the Philippines right now, and you get storms all the time, don't you?'

'Yes, Taal volcano, and yes, sometimes twenty storms or typhoons a year. The science says there could be more and more intense too with global warming, so super typhoons like Haiyan —'

'I saw that in the news, terrible.'

'Six to seven thousand dead plus missing.'

Morning light ripples over the roadside gums, makes Sleeping Beauty shimmer. The cloud has lifted from her shoulder. Sweet sleep, beautiful one.

'To think we can lose all these, just like that.'

'And do we ever get them back?'

'I think we should all be *diwatas* of the planet.'

'Tell that to the climate change deniers in the Parliament.'

'Maria Makiling stopped blessing the mountain because the townsfolk abused it and because her lover, a hunter, betrayed her.'

'Parable of our times.'

'People betray people. But what hurts most is when we're betrayed by those who vowed to care … double whammy, roadkill of the first order.'

'You're being dramatic.'

'I know.'

'So, what's the story with the jade bracelet?'

Penang, 1997. They're hot and curried-out after the best Indian lunch. So into the Hong Kong Bar, an institution in Georgetown, Robert suggests. He's warmly greeted by the owner Jenny, then plenty of catch-up chatter.

'My friends, Frank and Nenita. Tiger for them, please Jenny, and I'll have a Coke.' It's Robert's dry month and he's happy. His friends have decided to get back together and he's treating them to this trip to celebrate.

'Isn't she a beauty?' he spreads his arms over the small and rather dark bar decked in servicemen's memorabilia. 'Plenty of history, plenty of character.' His gesture is generous, his smile lights up the place.

'Built in the 1920s, favourite watering hole of the RAAF,' Frank adds and to wondering Nenita explains, 'the Royal Australian Air Force.'

'Uhmm … survived a war,' Nenita says, examining the various military souvenirs, commemorative shields and photos, the Chinese lanterns and knick-knacks, all with the patina of age. 'It's like walking into a Graham Greene novel.'

'*The Quiet American*,' Robert says.

'Wrong country,' Frank counters. 'That was Vietnam.'

'That slowly heartbreaking world-weariness … Fowler could easily be sitting here at the bar,' Nenita picks up on the reference. All three of them had read the novel and discussed it once.

'So, do you feminists feel any sympathy for men like Fowler?' Frank asks. He's resurrecting an old argument.

'And do you feel any sympathy for the likes of his lover, Phuong, waiting and waiting for him to make up his mind about her fate?'

Frank shakes his head. 'You have to read it again, Nenita. She wasn't waiting. She left the Brit for the American.'

'She left because waiting was exhausting. Exhaustion is worse than world-weariness.'

'We all get exhausted, don't we, Jenny?' Robert is trying to diffuse the little tension building up. He leafs through a photo album that Jenny placed on the bar. 'That's me,' he says, pointing to young Robert — wide grin under ash-blonde curls, with the proverbial Tiger beer raised in a toast.

All look and approve, and Jenny teases 'Mr Handsome.'

'And that's me and Ella at this very same spot.'

'So young and happy.' Nenita hasn't met Ella yet, but she's heard a lot about her from Robert and Frank.

'Youth and happiness, a good pair,' Frank mumbles, then a swig.

'Now to you both,' Robert raises his Coke to his friends. 'Stay married.'

Jenny looks from one to the other. 'Just married?'

'Well …' Frank shrugs and Nenita shifts on her seat.

'Sort of.' Robert realises he's overstepped the mark with his enthusiasm, and returns to the photos.

'Jade,' Jenny whispers to Nenita. 'For luck, love and harmony.'

So they get talking about the *feng shui* of jade supposedly 'auspicious for newlyweds' and neither Frank nor Nenita correct Jenny. Too hard.

A figure appears at the door and all look, saved from pursuing the story. Hard to make out the silhouette framed by the light streaming through. It's a man in grey shirt and shorts and very worn shoes. He sits at the bar, looking weary but serene. Tom. A quiet American. He's been walking around the world since 1992.

'Everything about him was grey, Robert kept saying after we left the bar. He reckoned the man was walking something out of his system.'

'And the jade?'

'Well, after we got back to Sydney from Penang, Robert sent me a jade bracelet through Frank. No note, just the bracelet.' Luck, love and harmony for newlyweds.

'Very nice of him.'

'Robert was kind to me, Ella.'

'Kind … uhmm … you didn't see him drunk, did you?'

'Never.'

'Then you didn't fully see the man.'

'I think — I think he wanted us so much to stay married.'

123

'Of course, he and Frank, best friends,' she shrugs.

'Robert was the only friend invited to the wedding. He was the best man.'

'Yes, I heard about that.'

'When the marriage ended the first time, we returned Krishna to him —'

'Krishna?'

'His wedding present. The child Krishna lying on a fig leaf, a wooden antique, small, fits in the palm — and when we got back together, he gave it back to us saying, "Now stay married, you two".'

'Just like Robert.'

'I think it was more than that. I think … it was about his own wish to have stayed married. With you.'

'Don't!' she brakes to a quick stop. 'He left me.'

'And I left Frank, for the second time.'

'What's it with departures?'

The query takes the back seat, neither wants to respond.

Ella gets out of the car. 'There, your "she'll be apples".'

Nenita follows. Along the road, apple tree after apple tree with fruit just beginning to turn pink and Sleeping Beauty at peace in the horizon. '"*Quiero dormir el sueño de las manzanas*" … I want to sleep the sleep of apples.'

'That's lovely.'

'From Lorca's *Gacela of the Dark Death* … I wish them the sleep of apples, Ella … my parents. Not a good death.'

'I need a drink.' Ella returns to the car. 'You might as well have your fill of apples, with a kick.'

But it's only eleven, Nenita nearly says. Oh well, *La hora del Vermut*, as her Spanish friend Lola would say when they had a drink too early.

'We'll go to Willie Smith's Apple Shed. They brew the best organic cider from locally grown apples,' Ella says as they turn around the Huon highway. 'By the way, I'm starting Spanish classes next week.'

'Wonderful. You'll love the language. !*Que hermosa!*'

'Indeed how beautiful. I'm planning to travel around Spain next year. Sorry again about your parents. One never really gets over the loss of a dad or a mum.'

'More so if one has issues with mum.'

Ella sighs as she parks at The Apple Shed, an apple museum-café-bar built in 1942 that used to be a shed for packing apples. 'I was mean to my mum.'

'Or it could be that mum was mean to daughter,' Nenita mumbles as she follows Ella in. 'But when mum goes, we wish we could sweep that mean ghost away … do a spring clean of the heart.'

Ella gives her a knowing look. 'So, what do you think?'

It's like a large barn with an expansive timber ceiling, high and with the sun streaming through a row of skylights. She imagines the nave of a church, but the feel is rustic and homey, with the smell of apples.

'I mean, look over there, Nenita.'

At the far end, a wall of apples! Big and small, red, yellow and green apples, each displayed like an art piece on a grey rack with names that could be characters from a fairytale or a cloak-and-dagger novel: Beauty of Stoke, Opalescent, Merton Worcester, Lady Sudley, Jolly Beggar, Fleiner du Roi, Improved Foxhelp, Closette, Esopus Spitzenburg, French Crab, Gravenstein Early, Grand Duke Constantine, Gross Doux, Early Joe, Laxton Superb, Atalanta … She walks around them, utters each name, feeling the crunch and ooze in her mouth of the sweet and the sour, the sharp and the delicate, even the bitter and strange, and always the undeniable scent.

'You can't hide it, Ella.'

'What?'

'The scent of apple.'

As they wait for their ciders, she tells Ella about apple moments back home. A friend of her father arrives with a brown paper bag, but father isn't home so the visitor waits and waits, and falls asleep waiting. Her five-year-old sister Lydia smells apples. She gets bold, peeks inside the bag, apples indeed, red delicious, and the visitor wakes and ends up giving up one to the hovering little girl from the bag intended for his own kids. And another moment: she and her two siblings buy their baby brother Nestor a *singkamas*, a white turnip, what they can afford, saying it's an apple so he'll stop crying, and he does so all's well again with his world, their world. He's their darling.

'Our own "she'll be apples", Ella. It's the apples here,' she points to her head, then her heart, 'and here.'

'Let's drink to that.'

The Willie Smith's organic cider is ambrosial sweet, but the memories have soured. 'I think Nestor's disowned us … family politics. I try and try to win him back, I took care of him as a baby, I'm the eldest, I loved him, still do despite his repeated snubs, his judgment, the bitter silence. My mother believed her three older children deserved the treatment and that her beloved youngest could do no wrong. He and my mother looked down on us from a very high moral ground. Called us bad siblings, because whatever we gave to her beloved was never enough by their measure. She ordered us to keep giving until it hurt, even if whatever was given was barely acknowledged.' She sighs. 'All that love thrown back at our faces.'

'What's it with love?'

126

'What's it with departures?'

They finish their ciders, silently.

'Were you there when your parents passed?'

'No.'

'Were they alone?'

'No.'

'Robert went alone. I wasn't there. No one was there.'

Ella insists on paying and Nenita waits, stares at the wall of apples.

'So don't tell me she'll be apples!' Ella says through gritted teeth and walks out.

What's it with an awkward friendship moment?

'Thanks for taking me around, Ella ... and thanks for — for the last time we saw each other. You came to the hospital to wish me luck as I was wheeled into surgery. I remember Frank and I had just ended the second time. But I wasn't alone. That was the kindest thing. You came. Even when you were sick and — still grieving.'

Ella slaps the wheel. 'Fuck — more than a decade later and still grieving!'

They pass by another apple orchard.

What to say, how to get out of *this*? Both are at a loss. As they pass by another apple orchard, it dawns on Nenita that grief is familiar foreign territory. It's your house but you can't find the door. Finally she asks, 'Would you rather we don't talk about Robert?'

'I don't know yet.'

Nenita bites her tongue, Ella shuts her ears. Low clouds over the orchard now.

'I'm sorry, Ella.'

'For what?'

'For talking. For coming.'

'Oh no, don't mind me, it's just that —' Ella pulls over, looks out of the window. 'They'll get a good crop.'

She looks out too. It's now overcast. She's searching for the right words, it takes a while. 'Yes, they're good apples.'

Ella laughs. 'So you know apples, do you?'

'I know, it's so lame.'

Ella starts the car. 'Okay, love, Ranelagh next stop and we'll get you some of the best pies this side of the world. And talk away — hey, Robert,' and she looks up to the grey sky, 'we're gossiping about you, mate!'

Nenita breathes out, then, 'Actually, I came because — because I dreamt of Krishna after my mother died. Robert's Krishna. I was returning it to her.'

Ella shrugs, sighs. 'Did she also say, "Stay married"?'

Nenita falls silent.

'Sorry.'

It's starting to feel stuffy in the car.

'Really sorry, do go on.'

So she breathes out and continues. 'I was returning Krishna to my mother … in a box, but I didn't know it was Krishna, I didn't know what was in the box, you know how dreams are. She was at the other end of this long corridor, maybe it was at the hospital, it was so bright, the walls so white, I was blinded as I walked to her, I couldn't see her face but I knew it was her and I handed her the box but it disappeared, and when she opened her hand, it — he — was there, the child Krishna lying on a fig leaf and I was worried because it wasn't Jesus and my mother was a staunch Catholic so I ran back to the other end of the corridor, but when I looked back, it wasn't my mother anymore, I think it was a man … perhaps it was my father, but he was much younger, and the little Krishna got bigger and bigger, bigger than the man.'

'Whew! Heavy.'

'I remembered everything when I woke up, and I thought — maybe that man was Robert. I was returning Krishna to Robert, again.'

It's starting to rain. They listen to the drops conversing on the windshield.

She almost does not hear her whisper.

'I want to dream of Robert again.'

She reaches out —

'Don't!' Ella's shoulders hunch over the wheel as she turns on the wiper.

They listen.

Rain then gone, rain then gone with the left-right, left-right squeak on wet glass. Like how we navigate history: words then silence, words then silence.

When they reach the Summer Kitchen Bakery, it's almost blue skies again. Ella says it's best to just get some pies and keep driving so Nenita sees more of the country, then a picnic lunch by the river, if she likes.

'That dream was a sign, back home we believe in signs. So I came. You believe in signs, Ella?'

The question is left hanging in the air as they choose lunch inside the packed café and bakery. Pies sold out, so rolls: mushroom and quinoa, and spinach and feta. Plus a tart crowned with blueberries, strawberries and cherries.

'All locally grown produce,' Ella finally breaks the silence as they walk back to the car. 'We should get you some black cherries to try, the best in Australia.'

The wind has picked up, quite cool for summer but a relief after the high 30s to 40s in Canberra.

Ella looks up. 'We need more rain, more rain.'

There's a flutter among the yellow flowers of the hedge beside where they parked, then something darts up the adjacent cherry tree, sprinkling bits of rain from the leaves to their heads. Ella quietly signals for her to look up.

It blends with the leaves, but the yellow head with a bright red brow and blue cheek can't hide among the green.

Rosella, Ella mouths silently.

She's perplexed. Aren't rosellas crimson and blue?

'Haven't you heard of green rosellas?' Ella later asks in the car.

'Just like us,' she murmurs.

'What was that?'

'Nothing.'

Just like us. Rosellas, same kind but different colours. But still very much the same. Cut me and I'll bleed. Same colour.

It's a comfort, the bag of rolls warm on her lap.

'So what happened?' Ella asks as they drive off. 'I mean, after the dream.'

'I dug up Krishna from storage. Kept it hidden for years, y'know, memories.'

'Of Frank?'

She nods.

'Happy with your new man?'

'Very — the kindest man, my husband of fifteen years now.'

'Lucky.'

'What's it with luck, Ella?'

'Indeed.'

'I took out the jade bracelet too, wore it again after more than a decade.'

'History and stuff.'

'Strangely, I remembered Tom, the American we met at the Hong Kong Bar … Robert kept saying how grey he looked and how maybe he was walking off something from his soul. I wonder now if — if it was just Robert seeing his own world-weariness.'

'Exhaustion. Robert was exhausted.'

The declaration fills the car. They open the windows for air. It's gusty, something in the back seat flies about, but they don't mind. They breathe.

'Why build a nest beside a road?' Ella is furious as she swerves away from a plover and its nest. Roadkill. 'They build nests on football fields, they should be hiding their young, keeping them safe.'

'Maybe they want to be in the open, visible, with others.'

'Where's the sense of self-preservation?'

A black bird flies past. 'Crow,' Nenita says, 'off to scavenge back there,' but Ella corrects her. 'No, raven.'

Quoth the Raven 'Nevermore' — Poe's lament sneaks in and hovers around Nenita's brain as they drive uphill, past another pasture in Glen Huon.

No, there's always something more. So perhaps there's no such thing as extinction. Because we remember.

'Tom sent me a postcard when he was walking the Nullarbor. He wrote that the stars there are so large and low, you could almost pluck them from the sky.'

'Never been to that part of Oz.'

'Only a chance meeting, but Robert kept talking about him. He reckoned the man was walking around the world because he was searching for his brother.'

'What?'

'He told us his brother was a journalist. Captured by communist guerrillas in Cambodia and never heard of again.'

'Oh these men and their heartaches.'

The words sit heavy in her chest, or maybe the way Ella said it.

'Tom was an army medic. Found that out on the web only last month. He was killed in Afghanistan seven years after we met him.'

Ella sucks in her breath.

They drive quietly for another kilometre.

'Why are you telling me all this?'

'Because.'

'Because what?'

'Because we are always with others, Ella. Even when we're alone.'

Again, silence.

'So what was this Tom like?'

'Quietly smiling at that bar.'

'And Robert and Frank doing the talking, of course.'

'Hard to gauge a quiet man. But it seems — it's almost as if I got to know him because of his partner Rose. I read the transcript of her interview after he died, on the web. She said for the first time in his life, he was ready to settle down. So all that walking done … She said that just before he died, he bought a young apple tree and planted it behind their house.'

Ella chuckles, but her voice is unsteady. 'Your apple thing again.'

'She said this was his way of saying, this is my home. She said the tree doesn't even bear fruit for eight years. Broke my heart when I read it.'

'Oh you have a way of—of —' she knocks at her chest.

'I wish them the sleep of apples, Ella … Robert, Tom, my parents, that wallaby and plover on the road … may their sleep be sweet.'

Sleeping Beauty will always be awake like those rolling hills across the Huon River. Awake with vegetation and wildlife, Nenita reckons. They've reached Franklin, a bit recovered, and she's convinced Tassie is bird heaven. Throughout the drive, there were birds, some she'd never seen before and Ella named them. Rare diamond birds that flew so close to the windshield. A juvenile stump robin perched on a fence post, watching as Ella took a photo of the shaggy haired highland cattle grazing on a paddock. A wattlebird feeding on banksia. Then two rare wedgies, wedge-tailed eagles circling overhead just as they turned off towards Franklin.

They're now sitting at the end of the boardwalk of the Wooden Boat Centre, eating their rolls and looking out to the river.

'See those islands across? The Egg Islands Reserve where the bittern lives.'

'Bittern?'

'A large, streaked brown bird, always pointing its bill to the sky —'

'Telling us, look up, you lot. See that blue. Good for you.'

'Makes a terrifying cry at night.'

Terror then hope.

It's getting more windy, their roll crusts are flying about.

'So did you all enjoy Penang?'

'Robert made sure we did.'

Ella smiles. 'Of course.'

'He showed us around *his* Georgetown, we ate *roti canai* for breakfast at one of the stalls, with hot curry sauce for dipping and fried egg on the side.'

'Good memory.'

'I remember food well, and I'll remember this — so good.'

'Robert loved his food. And he could cook.'

Gust after gust from across the river, and Nenita shivers. 'Remember the sudden wind as I was going up the stairs to his flat and my skirt went whoosh to my face?'

'Yeah, that was naughty Robert.'

They finish their rolls and look out to the water.

'I remembered Penang so clearly after I dug up Krishna — and that day.'

'Can't forget that day.'

That day when Ella, Frank and Nenita went to Robert's flat to clean up after.

'The police just left the rope there after they cut him down, and the gloves that they used, thrown on the floor. Remember? I'm still so angry about that.'

Nenita lays a hand on Ella's back and this time, she does not protest.

'A man hangs himself and they leave souvenirs for the family to find?'

A large wooden boat appears from around smaller ones moored nearby.

'The Yukon, beautiful boat. You should try their river cruise sometime,' and Ella gets up. 'Come, you're getting cold.'

Silently they walk back to the car.

'Where are you going?'

'I need to get my backpack from the boot, please.'

Ella waits. The Yukon is now approaching the dock where they sat.

Back in the car now, Nenita nervously opens her backpack. 'Ella, I came ...'

Ella stares, bemused.

'I came because I want to give him back to you.'

The child Krishna lying on a fig leaf: a small dark-wood sculpture set on a cream canvas framed by lighter wood.

Ella keeps staring, tears welling up.

'I read somewhere … the god of Pralaya that brings the end of the world has no power over Krishna. The oceans rise, drowning all, the mountains, forests, continents, everything. No one survives. But baby Krishna sails on, on a fig leaf amidst the chaos, alive, unafraid, happily sucking his toe.'

Ella runs a finger around the edge of the leaf.

'This is why I came.'

Then, finger on the tiny hand grasping the toes close to the mouth.

Behind them, the Yukon has docked.

'I think little Krishna will like your apples.'

MY LOVE, MY *NERŪSĒ*

Vecā mīlestība nerūsē — Old love does not rust.

Latvian proverb

Fork, spoon, knife — no, a whole set of cutlery and plates. She's putting together "an eating kit" for each of them. '"Be prepared" should be our motto now, no, everyone's motto,' she says and he concurs to keep the peace.

'I was also a Scout, briefly in my youth, but not this OC.'

'Hah! You're just as obsessive compulsive,' she snaps.

'Not as bad as you, *mīļotā*,' he chuckles. 'Look at all these!' He means her neatly labelled packs, two of each, lined up on the lounge: medical kit, cleaning kit, loo kit, information kit, even a "happy kit" with a book, nuts, biscuits, and a chocolate bar, plus the eating kit that she's organising. Six kits for each of the two rooms, which she cleaned with militant fervour, where each of them could self-isolate in case.

'You've really gone over the top!' he laughs.

'And you'll thank me for it, if one of us gets sick — specially you!'

Nenita and Arvis are having their usual back-and-forth that has been growing a tad snappish. She's 60, he's late 70s, and she's afraid.

'What about a cuddles kit?' He takes her in his arms, 'We need more of this,' and holds her tight. He always reminds her about "tactility", as he puts it. Once, when she was too busy for days at her computer, he left a note: 'I really need some cuddles when you're able to fit these in.' He leaves her notes whenever and wherever: 'Gone shopping. xxxx.' 'Gone walking. ♥' 'Back at 6 p.m. xxxx.' Always with kisses or a heart. He's OC in affection. A sweetie, *nilalanggam*, as they'd say in the Philippines — so sweet he's "crawling with ants". He's always been that way since they met fifteen years ago when, the day after a blind date of two divorcees arranged by a common friend, he professed his commitment: 'I want to make it a mission in my life to contribute to your happiness.' She was floored. She still gets floored. He has kept true to his mission. His was a profession of constancy. But now this bloody virus is testing it, sneakily infecting his offered happiness. No, just her air. She's grown more snappish but he remains irrepressibly happy. It's heroic, she thinks, how some can shrug off the weight of darkness. But it sits on her shoulder even when she's in the light. She's having nightmares. All these deaths are doing her head in. She keeps hearing Emily Dickinson's *I felt a funeral in my brain*.

'These kits are a good idea, uhm … strategic,' he nods diplomatically then suddenly stops, squinting at the row of cedars outside their balcony. Hush, he gestures, and points to the closest tree. She hears before she sees: a three- to four-note song, clear and high and rich, with a slight slur between the final notes — or did she just imagine that? A liquid trill that multiplies like the flitting from branch to leaves to branch wet with the soft drizzle. She keeps squinting to make out the smallest of birds, olive-brown or grey with a yellow underside. A flock of them singing and feeding on what she cannot see.

Weebill, she'll learn from the web: perhaps the smallest Australian bird, about a quarter of an ounce. Like the weight of a quick kiss, yet the music goes on and on.

He smiles at her smiling at the melodic spectacle. 'You're happy again.'

Mission accomplished. Again.

The funeral in her brain has been nudged out by another line from good old Emily D: *"Hope" is the thing with feathers.* Oh the things that the reclusive poet saw and heard despite never having left her Amherst home. Seasoned in self-isolation but vision far reaching. Nenita wants to tell Arvis this, but she can't bear to hear his usual 'No metaphors for me, I live in the real world.' Her husband often lectures her on 'the economic implications of the market (and now COVID-19) on our superannuation' just as she's about to fall asleep at 1 a.m. So now she keeps the wonder to herself as the weebills make the cedar more than cedar. It's now a singing cedar. No, it's a song.

'Your birds, *mīļotā,*' he says. 'They're visiting you.' He knows her growing bird obsession of late.

Fifteen years later, her heart still soars when he calls her 'sweetheart' in Latvian. '*Mīļotā* is a song too — three notes,' she says. Like *padabà,* the endearment from her first home. Love sings in any language.

'We're lucky to be locked down here,' he says, arm sweeping the row of cedars that soften the view of the car park and street below, and the apartment buildings across. And through the spreading branches, further across they can see Mount Ainslie, echoing the lush green of the trees. *Cedrus Deodara*: evergreen conifers originally from South Asia but so at home here. Even on this bleak day, they're a treat for the eyes with these miniature minstrels just met. They're a haven for birds, mostly their neighbour magpies, currawongs, and crows calling and chattering non-stop, it's hard to sleep especially in spring when they're nesting. Then the king parrots and rosellas stop over for a feed, occasionally breaking into song after song. She hears them as professions of constancy: we're here again, as perennial as the changing of the seasons. And we'll always be here. Love sings in any language.

'Years from now when we're no longer here, *our* trees will sing too,' she says.

Our trees are two very young cedars that fill the gap in the middle of the nature strip of ten mature ones, each about twenty metres tall. "The babies" are like frail sentinels at each side of the parking ticket dispenser that's protected by two yellow-and-red iron bollards. The parking metre is protected but not the trees!

When the new apartment across was being constructed, worker vans and trucks regularly parked below, bumping against the young cedars, pushing them so far back, they looked like two children with green arms crushed and trunks about to snap. Infuriated, Arvis would write a polite note begging to 'please respect the trees' then would rush down to leave it on the windshield of the culprit car. Sometimes he'd accost the driver, again politely pleading on behalf of the trees. Nenita watched from the balcony, worried about how the encounter would pan out. Once two burly tradies got out of the car and she came down in case things got out of hand. He even spoke to the construction manager to make his case, but the trees just got hammered day in and day out. Finally he began phoning the ACT authorities and writing letters of representation on behalf of the trees. More than a year after he took the case to heart, on a sunny afternoon, he asked her to come down for a little surprise: the two cedars now had a protective iron fence around each of their trunks.

'After all that fuss, look, they're growing well now,' he says with pride.

'Not fuss, but devotion. *Our* trees, your achievement,' she says. 'They're slow growing, so we won't be here when they're grown to their full height.'

'But there'll be others who will enjoy them. They're *everyone's* trees.'

The weebills keep singing. A little reprieve from her fear.

She returns to her kits after ringing her siblings in the Philippines to check how they are. She worries a lot about them and their families and the Philippines and Australia, and the world. She's been dreaming of COVID nightly, when she can sleep.

'So how are they?' Arvis asks.

'In military lockdown. Top guy says, "Shoot them dead", those who violate it.'

He sighs. 'So different to here.'

'Of course!' she snaps. 'Those who violate the lockdown there are often the most impoverished, desperate to leave their homes to find food for their families.'

'I'm so glad we live here.' He's putting on his jacket and cap.

'Where are you going?'

'To the shops.'

'We agreed I'm doing all the shopping from now on.'

'Just check my post office box then.'

'I'll do that too — just let me finish these.'

'I need some air.'

'We'll go for a walk to the lake, together, but later.'

He's pacing to and from the door like a caged animal. 'You're being so bossy!'

'Because you're being so stubborn! We agreed you'll avoid taking risks!'

'You're not my mother!'

Heaven forbid she's sounding like her mother in those times when her father tried to sneak out for a walk when he was on "lockdown". Because she was afraid he'd fall or hurt himself. Strange, or probably not, how fear inspires our unkinder registers.

He goes out and slams the door.

Shocked, she sits down beside her kits, then thought, but he didn't take a mask!

Arvis was in ICU once. Ten days in the hospital, from Christmas Eve until after New Year. The doctors couldn't locate the site of the internal haemorrhaging. His haemoglobin kept dropping despite the continuous blood transfusions. She was terrified he'd never walk out of the hospital.

Outside the drizzle is over, the clouds have lifted, the weebills are gone, and she feels twice bereft. So unlike him to slam the door. There's a prickling behind her eyes. The afternoon sun is out and the oldest cedar is strewn with droplets of light. Tiny tears. Oh, don't be mawkish. Just keep to the task and settle that head. She checks the cutlery: one fork does not match a spoon and a knife's missing. She returns to the kitchen drawers, rummages through them.

'Which spoon, which fork?' She hears his usual question that was irritating her again last night when she asked him to set the table as she cooked.

'We've been having this conversation for more than a decade — at least pay attention and remember, please! We're eating rice, so it has to be the rice spoon that pairs with the fork of the same size. I've shown you this, time and again.'

'You're so OC! I can eat with any spoon or fork!' he barks at her.

'Forget it, I'll set the table.' Through dinner, he was contrite and so was she. He was back to his affectionate self.

'Kindness, dearest, kindness … both ways. And if we're to fight, it should at least be on something important.' Agreed — certainly not about a bloody spoon or fork!

She opens the next drawer for the right fork but discovers a different one, older, no, the oldest one. Brought by his mother when they fled Latvia at the end of World War II. The Soviets were advancing and Germany, Latvia's colonial occupier at that time, had organised a ship to evacuate the women and children out of Riga. So it was just *māte* with baby Arvis, his five-year-old brother, a few clothes, and this fork. *Tēvs*, dad, would later follow on land and meet them in a refugee camp in Germany where they spent six years before they moved to Australia as Displaced Persons. 'I played in the ruins of bombed shelters, picked up cigarette butts to sell to passing men, and my father could still go out of the camp to sing opera at the theatre, and my teacher Herr Lauterbach would give me a dinky on his bike to school, probably took pity on *der verdammte Ausländer*, "the bloody foreigner" as the older boys called me, and I learned German by osmosis.' He'd string snippets of that history for her sometimes. 'And the rare orange from the American sector — our camp was in the British one — I heard that the oranges were dumped and I imagined them bobbing in the ocean, so I wondered, uhmm … but this is not salty.' Hardly any darkness in his remembering of those years in a refugee camp. He still loves oranges.

She takes out the fork, she's forgotten this. She admired it the first time she saw it while sorting their respective cutlery when they finally moved in together. She's never seen anything quite like it before. It's fine workmanship of metal and wood: a fork with authority. The metal is slipped between two pieces of dark-wood held together by three rivets to make the handle, and below the graceful prongs, the tiny engraved ɴᴇʀᴜ̄sᴇ̄. Ah, what we take with us when we leave home, knowing we might never be able to return. 'Nerūsē, meaning does not rust,' he explained to her, and in the next breath added, 'Vecā mīlestība nerūsē — Old love does not rust. A Latvian proverb.' Perhaps for his māte, this fork was to ensure that her old love for home does not rust, constant and ever shiny in this new country. Because here, there was darkness. Arvis told her only once: how he found his brother after he took cyanide, how he died in his arms. 'The most difficult thing was going home to tell our parents.'

Old love does not rust. It cannot, must not. So the soul can sustain its sheen that reflects light. And hold fast on amplitude, that abounding capacity to shrug off darkness.

Old love does not rust. She'd like to say this now to her friends who fifteen years ago warned her against getting serious with her blind date. He's too old for you! No, he's enduring, constant in his mission to contribute to her happiness. And to be happy. This man who loves trees. A gift of a man: her love, her *nerūsē*.

She will try to match his contribution, she will try to be as enduring. They will try to be kinder as they endure this lockdown together. 'Kindness, dearest, both ways.' That was the pact they made last night after watching TV's latest coronavirus update and how the afflicted body succumbs. From what seems like an ordinary cold and cough to flu-like symptoms, then you can't breathe, you need to be intubated, put on ventilator in ICU, pumped with oxygen, then the organs start shutting down. This was how her father died a year ago, followed last year by her aunt, her sister's husband, then her mother. All their lungs gave up at the final moment. Can't breathe, can't breathe. She felt that way last night, listening to the story of dying, and suddenly all these deaths, faceless figures in an update, became her own.

How kindred we are in mortality. No, how kind we could be, when breath is still aplenty with much to share around. Because kindness cannot self-isolate, it can't be locked down for the select kin. Kindness is about making a kin, even of strangers. It moves both ways and all ways, like breath. But breath is suspect these days. She thinks of the masked faces in the streets, the fearful eyes, the urgent social distancing. The other day as she queued at Coles, the woman in front stared at her with dagger eyes, as though *this* was her fault. Because she's the only one wearing a mask, so she must be diseased? Or because she's Asian? She stepped back further and smiled to reassure her, but the dagger sharpened. Oh dear, my eyes can't smile enough.

'I don't seem to have that problem,' Arvis observed. 'They smile back at me.'

'Well, you don't walk in my skin!' This wasn't the first time that she felt uncomfortable about how she looked or about the colour of her skin. In the 90s, a parliamentarian blamed Asians for the troubles of Australia and sadly, some in the community caught the fear-and-blame virus.

The fork drops, she quickly picks it up, examines the engraving. So tiny, easy to miss, but it's a heavy fork. This weight, the substance of love that does not rust. But who do we love?

There's plenty of affection professed on TV: for the doctors, nurses, health and care workers, for the teachers, farmers, supermarket hands, and every hand that keeps daily life running. Well deserved love but often unspoken before. They're more than service providers now. They're people with families, co-survivors in this pandemic and remembered with gratitude. She too remembers the care she and Arvis received in hospitals in Wollongong, Sydney, and Canberra through the years. Ah, Rose, that young student nurse in Wollongong, her delight when she discovered that Nenita's Filipina. She had just fallen in love with a law student who promised to take her someday to his Filipino mum's hometown. Victor, she said his name was, as she helped Nenita find her next breath. She was having a panic attack before surgery and Rose breathed with her — 'breathe in, darling, one, two, three, four, then out …'

Such tender efficiency: that commitment to bring us back to our feet, or to help us depart with dignity. She remembers her parents' final days in the Philippines. Caregiver Ning taking her father for walks before he finally took to his bed, then the nurses caring beyond the call of duty. Marlon washing his hair and giving him a shave and a haircut. Alan on night shift even if his own father had just died. Thea calling her dying mother 'Mommy' as though she were her own blood. All of them kin. As kindred as the lives and livelihoods now upended in Australia by loss after loss, including the stranger under a ventilator at the other side of the globe, now made present on our screens. We hope she finds that next breath, as we do. In our bodies, we remember we're in this together, in this in-out, in-out labour of the lungs. Inside us a sadness grows, soft and strangely warm. We suddenly feel kind.

But will we be a kinder world after this? How far does a warm feeling travel?

In the streets, slums, camps and many corners of the planet are lives that were upended way before this devastation. Wash your hands when there's no water? Go on lockdown when you're already locked down? Strict social distancing when the rest of the world have long socially distanced themselves from you? Your life is as invisible as your death and dying. No place in the queue, not even a figure in an update.

And here she is worrying about forks and spoons. How middle-class, how first world we are now, Arvis. She's ashamed, ashamed of her tears. But then, old loves and histories do not rust. She stares at the fork that was saved from a war long ago.

146

She hears the door. He's back.

'Oh, my dearest, what's wrong?' He quickly puts down his backpack and hugs her. 'I'm sorry, I didn't mean to walk off like that.'

'No, I'm sorry, for being so ill-tempered —'

'Kindness, *mīḷotā*, both ways —'

'All ways.' She can't stop the tears.

'What's wrong — ?'

'Just my head,' she raps it with a knuckle. 'I'm just — I'm just so sad, so afraid for the world, and yet — and yet, so grateful for — for —' She's sobbing in privileged safety and she knows this too well.

'Why don't you sit down and relax, those kits can wait. I'll make us a cup of tea and we can have this almond slice that I got you.'

This sweetness. *Nilalanggam.* Crawling with ants.

Early evening now and it's raining. Again, a soft drizzle. Nenita has been playing her ukelele, Arvis' "get-better gift" after she returned from burying her mother last year. It felt like her eyes wouldn't ever dry up. But at least she said goodbye, she buried her. Unlike now when families weep apart or weep alone, or weep under the close watch of a gun. To grieve together and safely: sometimes, it's all that matters.

Arvis asked what she'd enjoy as a hobby, something different, something to make her happy again. She remembered how she loved playing the ukelele as a child, so he got her one. A baritone uke that sounds like a Spanish guitar, and quickly she played an old song: 'Today while the blossoms still cling to the vine ...' Learned from her high school music teacher. She's singing it now, with the soft patter of rain.

In his study, he's playing bridge on his computer. Outside the wet car park glows under the street lamp and the apartments across are turning on their lights. The cedars are mere silhouettes, "the babies" safe under their wing. She rests her uke to have a drink. When she returns, she hears them like she's never heard them before. All the trees singing! A chorus of different birds — such amplitude, an orchestration of a multitude! It's like being in the bush. She rushes out to the balcony, but it's hard to see anything in the dark. 'Arvis, Arvis! Come quickly, they're singing back!'

If you sing in the bush, the birds sing back. Her friend Jane, a sound artist and bird enthusiast, told her that once. Later, she'll wonder if they were just mobbing a predator when they chorused together, as birds do. But what a communally tuneful casting out of danger. If only we could do the same with a virus.

'What — who's singing back?' He's beside her now, perplexed. 'Sshh … listen.'

Who is singing back? They can't see. But does it matter? To sing together is what matters. To sing different tunes, timbres, pitches, volumes, in different registers. To harmonise, or not. To sing not only with our kind. To sing even with the invisible, the unknown. But always to sing. Both ways, all ways.

Ah, the thing with feathers. It knows how, it knows.

SINGING BACK

Whatever its purpose,
duetting in birds is a marvel.

Jennifer Ackerman

When we were little, *Lola* Paela taught us the songs and calls of the birds on that mountain. We need to learn or at least try to understand their language, she said, so we can call them back if they start leaving ... so they don't disappear from the face of the earth,' Andres whispers, eyes closed as if listening to birds further away than these crows calling to each other. Or so, Sinéad thinks. It's hard to know what to say, so she keeps quiet until he finally opens his eyes.

'Amazing woman, your grandmother, and amazing mountain. I like her, I like your mountain ... and I'm so sorry.' She looks away as he wipes his eyes.

An hour ago, Andres received a text from his sister in the Philippines: Grandmother is sick, maybe COVID, and she's in a bad way.

'I warned her, them — that they should strictly follow the lockdown, or else. But they have to eat.' His eldest sister, *Manáy* Clara, has been hawking the orchids that she and *Lola* Paela grow on the slopes, when the public market closed, and grandmother did the same until she was arrested for breaking the lockdown. 'Young people, nineteen and below, and seniors 60 up are not supposed to leave the house, and she's 73! But she works all the time — she has a roadside stall, cooks afternoon snacks, *sinapot*, fried bananas. The whole family warned her about going out, but so stubborn, she kept sneaking out! So now …' his voice breaks.

'Here, your sandwich,' Sinéad offers but he shakes his head.

'I'm not hungry.'

Last lunch break together at Haig Park. It's been over a month of lockdown in Canberra, and both were just told by hotel management that they'll start letting go of staff tomorrow. Receptionist Sinéad might be able to stay on Jobkeeper but cleaner Andres will have to go. He just started part time and he's not Australian.

'I can go now,' he says, 'I finished my shift —'

'Oh no, let's walk a bit, you like it over there.' Over there is the other side of the park across McCaughey Street. 'C'mon, a brisk walk will do you good.'

The crows have left. Currawongs now with their rich repertoire, including the two-note call that Andres copied perfectly the first time he heard it: first note stretched and descending onto the second. 'Like "see-you — see-you — see-you", but so plaintive as if they'll never really see you again.' But he's not listening now. He gets up from the grass. 'I've to send money to my sister for grandmother's care … and for … if she gets worse …' He looks up to the sky and she follows suit.

It's glorious autumn weather. Sky deep blue and cloudless, and the poplars are turning yellow. Yellow and blue so deep, but not quite primary colours. Maybe primal. Like this surging in his chest. *Gari unos kang bulkan* — like the raging mudflow of the volcano, as *Lola* Paela would say.

A week after they met in February, Andres told Sinéad he grew up on Mayon, an active volcano in the Bikol region, south of Luzon, and that he's the third of six children mostly raised by *Lola* Paela, Grandmother Rafaela, and his eldest sister Clara, because their parents were "taken" by the volcano. '*Nagtatao ang bulkan, nagbabawi ang bulkan*' — the volcano gives, the volcano takes, grandmother says each time the volcano erupts and always adds, "*Nabubuhay kita sa tagilid na dagâ*" — we live on tilted earth,' Andres explained. 'A local saying that's not just about the uncertainties of our geography, it's about resilience. We can survive anything on this uncertain earth, eruptions, earthquakes, typhoons, even poverty — we've gone through so many eruptions like many families, and we just all evacuate then return after to dig up our houses and rebuild.'

'But why live there?' she asked, perplexed.

'Because *there* is our livelihood, our farms on rich volcanic soil, *there* is our home.'

Told in earnest by this melancholic young man, the story blew Sinéad away and she took him under her wing. 'You'll be my little brother ... though we're so different.' She thought he was Aboriginal, quite cute, when she first saw him mopping the lobby, and he thought, what red hair and so many freckles. Then tu-dum-tu-dum went his chest when she smiled. He smiled back, with a sadness that tugged at her heart.

'I'm Andres, I'm doing a PhD at ANU,' he said, mopping towards the reception desk.

'Oh?' she sounded surprised.

'Yes,' he said, straightening shoulders as he gripped the mop, 'PhD in English, Creative Writing actually, and I'm Filipino.'

'Really?' She smiled again. 'My mother has a Filipina friend who lives with us, they work together at Parliament House.'

'Oh,' he's impressed.

'They're cleaners there, and I'm Sinéad.'

'Corazon will be disappointed if you don't eat her sandwich,' Sinéad says, packing his uneaten share. 'So take it home, and this extra one.'

'Please thank her again for me.' Andres takes the sandwiches, avoiding her eyes. He doesn't like it that she saw tears.

When Sinéad told Corazon about the Filipino student who just started work at the hotel, Corazon added an extra sandwich in her lunchbox, for him. 'What's he like, where's he from?' She was so excited about Sinéad's "new friend" — 'What, he's from Bikol, that's my region! So we're *kababayans*, compatriots — and I know that volcano!'

Sinéad's mum Orla was just as excited. 'Bring him over,' she said. Both wanted to check out this Andres who came all the way from a volcano in the Philippines to The Australian National University, on a PhD scholarship. 'Must be very bright — young, you say? Is he nice? But why clean if he's on scholarship?' Orla wanted to know more.

'Because he sends money home, mum. I think he's paying for his nephews' and youngest sister's studies. He taught at uni back there before coming here only early this year, but he's already done all sorts of casual jobs. I suspect he sends most of his scholarship stipend home. I really don't know how he lives on so little.'

'Because he's used to so little,' Corazon said and added another sandwich to the lunchbox. 'Tell him it's his take home after work.'

'Corazon and your mum — they're very kind to me, even if they haven't met me.' He hates it that his voice shakes.

'That's why you should come and visit.'

'Thanks, but I'll be busy looking for a new place.'

'Why?'

'My flatmates will give up the flat and go home to Wollongong — they lost their jobs, so … and everything's online study now anyway.' Andres met the Fil-Aussie siblings at uni and they invited him to share their flat for a small rent, but he'd have to sleep on a mat on the lounge floor — 'no worries,' he readily accepted, grateful for the perfect arrangement.

Sinéad's even more lost for words now. Lost job, lost home, and now grandmother. And she thought he was super lucky. She envied him. Doing a PhD at such a young age, and on a scholarship too. She had to stop uni last year because she lost two waitressing jobs and things got difficult. But she'll get back to it next semester, if indeed she's eligible for Jobkeeper and if this COVID thing permits. She's on her third year part-time in an Environmental Science course at University of Canberra. Her dream is to work at CSIRO, maybe on conservation.

'So I won't see you anymore,' he says, walking away and looking up at the poplars, so all the other tears don't spill. She's seen enough weakness.

'And why not, silly?' She catches up and playfully thumps him on the arm. Even if she really wants to take him in her arms — ah, silly girl. She's careful not to let on that she likes him. Because he said, 'Okay, you're my *Manáy*, my older sister.' She's younger than him but then, a head taller. Well, she started it, didn't she, when early on she told him, 'You'll be my little brother.' So now they're stuck in this awkward brother-sister thing.

A green and red zips past the poplars.

'Wh-what was that?'

'I think king parrot, green head and red belly, so female.'

He searches the sky, mouth and arms open, and rooted on the spot.

'A very early bird. King parrots usually come in spring.'

He follows the arc of the bird with his eyes, as if it were still there, flying. Then he turns to her, all earnest whisper. 'Like our *berdeng púnay*, the orange-breasted green pigeon back home. But fire not on the belly but the breast.'

She smiles, keeps smiling. That's why I like you. I like you a lot.

Again he traces the flight of the bird. 'I think it flew across McCaughey.'

'So let's walk across.'

'*Lola* Paela …' he murmurs to himself, but she hears.

'Maybe it's not really COVID —'

'Okay,' he breathes out, 'let's walk, Sinny,' movement slow and noiseless as he checks a poplar for any green and red.

'Good,' she says, pleased that he called her Sinny, though he doesn't like her nickname, because it's like "sinner", he said. 'Bit of fresh air, Andy.'

And he doesn't like the Anglicising of his name.

Avian-Human Kinship: From Memorialising to Conservation. This was the thesis that he proposed for a PhD: what probably got him the scholarship and won over my brain, Sinéad thought when he tried to explain his research one time. 'But it's really *Lola* Paela's thesis.' She was flummoxed. 'When we were growing up on the volcano, each time a bird flew past, *Lola* Paela would say, "That's great-grandfather, or great-aunt." And when a bird sang, she'd say, "Listen well, children, it's telling you a story." Then we'd try to learn the song, because "if we know them in our bodies, we won't forget them. We can sing them back if they start flying away.

154

So our *nunò*, our ancestor, will always be with us." I think it's her lesson in avian-human kinship and memorialising that … uhmm … can be valuable in conservation. But I'm still finding my way around this thesis.' Sinéad was in awe of this strange man who has a way of sneaking up on her brain from left field. 'So I'm writing these short stories about bird-human encounters inspired by *Lola* Paela's bird stories, and I might compare them with Aboriginal fiction that has bird stories, and — and try to make a connection between storytelling and conservation, if that makes sense. It's really about language — birdsong as story then *Lola* Paela copies birdsong to call them back, so they don't disappear — it's — it's incantation, like a magic spell, so storytelling is incantation too in a way — am I confusing you?'

'No, Andy, you're blowing my mind away.'

'Anyway, I'm still trying to figure this out, but I've a wonderful supervisor, Dr Lucy, so I'll be able *to nail it,* as you say here.'

'You really must meet Corazon, Andy. She's into birds too, crows. She thinks they have magic powers.' He looked at her then, held her eyes for ages, she felt.

'All beings have magic power, Sinéad, not in the supernatural sense. Just being is power — and being with each other is even more powerful. By each other's grace, we go. And that's magical.' He won her heart.

They've done this late lunch break walk a few times, and on a sunny day he always felt his chest would burst at the sight of sun streaming through rows of towering Monterey pines, Italian cypresses, and Himalayan cedars casting shadows on the grass. He read somewhere that this nineteen-hectare park has 2330 exotic trees. So where are the native gums? But he'd only walked the area close to busy Northbourne Avenue. As he entered the park for the first time, he noted that between the rows of trees, the path was patterned with strips of sun and shade interspersing, like a pedestrian lane of light and shadow converging to a vanishing point, that blur of log seats in the distance. Perspective perfect. Then black and white birds darted and crisscrossed and called and chattered, and all order was broken. 'The ones with white nape, they're magpies, the mostly black with white tips on their tails, currawongs — there'll be more further up.'

'So many birds in the city?'

'Yeah, bird haven here. In spring, all sorts come. Once, the powerful owl lived here for months. The park became its hunting ground, it fed on possums and cockatoos!' He shivered. She skipped ahead, 'Come,' and did a pirouette into the light with her big smile and red hair — ah, she glows! And his heart got re-ordered. No, went awry.

But now, he's not looking at her. He's squinting up at the branches of a very old cedar, hand on its corrugated trunk. *Lola* Paela said that if you put your hand on the trunk of a tree, you'll feel what's going on up there.

'So what will you do now, Andy?'

'Find her, that's what we'll do.' He's been stopping at almost every tree, touching trunk after trunk. They're at the other side of Haig Park now, and anyway, he no longer has to go back to work.

'Strange,' she says, 'that it came too early, really out of season.'

'Only bird knows its intent and its season.'

Faint rustle up there?

'You really think so differently, I'm —'

'Sshh …' It's up there!

You think so differently: what she said whenever he told her about his research and the volcano or *Lola* Paela, and she'd be 'blown away'. She does lunch breaks with him because he's quaint? She likes him because he's different? She likes him?

156

'Tell me more,' she'd egg him on.

'You really want to know?'

'Of course.'

Finally, one time he had to ask: 'Would you want to know *me* if — if I didn't tell you I'm doing a PhD?'

'What a question.'

'People don't talk to cleaners,' he murmured.

'How can you say that? My mum's a cleaner!'

'People don't talk to black cleaners … they don't even look at you. Oh yes, sometimes they talk to you, to say the toilet is not clean.'

Her irritation quickly dissipated. 'Andy, I'm talking to you, I'm looking at you now.'

His pulse quickened then. Those are green sapphires that are your eyes. Set on me. That was his chance, but he turned away. I'm just little brother that she's taken under her wing. And how can I presume that *this* is not about pity, sister bird?

You of little faith, he scolded himself. *Ay*, it must be all those knockbacks from girls back home, even when he was a kid. Because he's an Agta. 'Behave, or the Agta will get you,' Christian parents would scare their kids in the lowlands. They spoke about the Agta as if it were a supernatural being, a black ghoul. But the Agtas are *Lola* Paela's people! They're the indigenous hunter-gatherers of Mount Isarog, one of the various volcanos in the region. Home to *Lola* Paela and her son, Andres' father, before he married a Christian *mestiza* from the lowlands, his mother, then eventually settled on the slopes of Mayon.

'So you're indigenous?' Sinéad was taken aback. 'You never told me.'

I don't want you to pity me even more, I want to be your equal, but he couldn't say it.

Andres loves watching the constant affirmation of 'we are in this together' on TV, especially when a multitude of different voices sing, 'We are one but we are many.' He sings along though he sort-of edits the final line about all being Australians to 'I am, you are, we are Planetarian', so he can belong. He sang this to Mike, a Ngunnawal student he's made friends with at uni.

Mike laughed, 'Good one, mate, but that's really an Australian song.'

'I know, but I just want to feel included like the others here who come from "all the lands on earth".'

'Andres, the First Nations People are *of this land*, but we're still fighting to be included.'

'It's up there?' Sinéad whispers, scouring the cedar too. 'Can't see a thing.'

His eyes close, both hands now on the trunk. *Lola* Paela, *Lola* Paela, he intones in his head … then he hears the first note.

'*Talagang-talaga* — truly-truly — *Berdeng Púnay* flew into the house early in the morning before we even imagined Mayon would erupt that day. *Ay*, no warning at all. She kept flying around the house and scolding and scolding — "Ooo-o-o—krrr-krrr-krrr." Whenever your father or mother or me went to the door — we were going to the *latì*, the farm, y'see — she'd fly to the door and roost there, scolding, then she'd fly out the window and scold some more, and fly in again. Your *Manáy* Clara and *Manóy* Benjie, only eight and two then, thought this orange-breasted green pigeon was playing with them, but I knew deep down she was trying to tell us something. So when we heard the big explosion, I understood — "Ooo-o-o—krrripas-krrripas!" — run, run fast, that was what she was saying, on and on scolding, and driving us out of the house, orange breast getting brighter and brighter, *naglalalad-laad daog pa su lava* — more fiery than lava — so we ran down the slope with only the clothes on our backs!' Then grandmother paused dramatically, looking all in the eye. 'Listen, *Berdeng Púnay* was your great-grandmother, my mother — she saved us!'

It's one of *Lola* Paela's bird stories: about the 1993 eruption that killed 77, mostly farmers planting on the slopes.

'So we always have to listen to birds. They give us signs, and we should learn to read those signs. They can save us!'

'*Talagang-talaga?*' Little Andres asked.

'*Talagang-talaga* — truly-truly,' she nodded, then added the lesson of the story: 'That's why we learn their songs, so we're tuned in, so we can save them back when they're in danger — get me?'

'Truly-truly,' Andres understood. But he wanted to understand more. 'But how can great-grandmother be a pigeon? A pigeon *is* a pigeon!'

'*Ay*, you little doubter,' but she was pleased. He queried and argued like a grown-up. He'll go far, this smart grandson of hers, though years later when he tried to explain what he'll study in Australia just before he left, she asked, '*Anong doktoran mo, bayong* — what will you doctor, birds?' She thought about it for a day, then said, 'Ahhh, you want to continue asking why in Australia, so you can save birds.'

'Something like that, *Lola*.'

'Uhmm … education is about asking why, and that's good,' she gave him her blessing.

He will always credit her and his *Manáy* Clara for his successes. All their arduous labour to feed, clothe and send him and his younger siblings to school — 'I've been educated on the backs of two women.'

Presidente kang Nganta, the President of Why: how she'd call him. And she always had an answer to his why.

'But really, why's *berdeng púnay* my great grandma?' the boy badgered her long after that storytelling time.

'*Aysus*, Andres, just believe!' *Manáy* Clara scolded and *Manóy* Benjie joined in. 'If *Lola* says it, then it's true!'

'But a person can't be a bird!' Only much later will he understand why *Lola* Paela always used the proper noun when speaking about avian creatures.

'Listen,' she began to explain in her conspiratorial tone, 'Mother always wore this green dress to church and a very, very old *Eskapulario Sagrado de Corazon de Hesus* on her breast, tied with a red ribbon around her neck. Sooo old, so the red heart and red stitching around it were faded.'

'Ahh ...' little Andres considered the tale. '*Berdeng púnay* green with orange on breast, like — like faded red ... uhmm ...' but still he doubted the connection.

Years later, when he began researching birds for his PhD proposal, he'd discover that it's the male of the species that has an orange breast. So how come *Lola* Paela got it wrong? Or, why did she change the sex of the bird? Was it confusion or intent? Perhaps to memorialise a loved one? To redeem some agency? Why? Because great-grandmother was a single mother who ended up raising only one child, *Lola* Paela. She couldn't save her two older children from measles. To this day, Andres, the interrogating adult, is still trying to make sense of the bits and pieces of their family history, or whatever *Lola* Paela revealed through her tales. But at the time when she regaled them about "the rescuing *Berdeng Púnay*", the boy's only preoccupation was "the origin" of the orange breast.

'But, *Lola*, why did great-grandma wear a *kapularyo* that's sooo old?'

'*Eskapularyo*,' she corrected him. 'Because the Spanish priest who baptised her gave it to her mother, so it was her divine *anting-anting*, her talisman —'

'But you don't wear one, and you never ever go to church like us — why?'

She couldn't answer *this why*.

Back in their old home, in her green dress with the scapular of the Sacred Heart of Jesus on her breast, her mother would walk for nearly two hours from Mount Isarog to the church in the village. It was her *panatà*, her sacred vow after her two children died: to do that gruelling walk and never miss Sunday Mass, so the youngest would be saved. But when she got to the church, she wouldn't enter it. She'd hear Mass at the door because no one dared sit with her inside. Once, a child bawled his eyes out because of 'the scary Agta!' Later little Rafaela, who came to church with her mother when she was old enough to do the long walk, wondered why they never ever went in. When she realised why, she vowed she'd never go to church again.

'Weeet' — high-pitched whistle up the cedar. 'Ooo-o-o' — low, nasal whistle up his brain. Then 'krrr-krrr-krrr.' The calls repeat. Still eyes closed and hands on the cedar's trunk, he hears parrot and pigeon, present and past conversing. Then *sanong-sanong*, duetting. The sonic vibrations make his hands tremble.

Then flapping wings. Then silence. Then touch.

'You okay, Andy?' she asks, hand on his arm.

He opens his eyes, looks up. They're gone, she's gone.

'You were … away … for a while there.'

'It's a sign.'

'Sign?'

'The bird. I think … grandmother's gone.'

She drops her hand. She doesn't understand but she's loathe to ask, to intrude. She feels his trembling.

'I think we should walk back,' he says, releasing the tree.

'I think so too.'

'Daeng kasigurohan ang pagsalba — no surety in salvation. Sometimes you save, sometimes you can't. But you try.' *Lola* Paela's lesson after her storytelling, as they huddled together inside the Albay Central School that became an evacuation centre, their home for months along with many devastated families after super typhoon Reming in 2006. By the light of a Coleman lamp, grandmother had to improvise a story about another bird. The children of the other families listened, along with only *Manáy* Clara, *Manóy* Benjie, Andres, and baby Juanita now. But who knows, the little twins, Pedring and Ferdie, and their parents might still be found. Months later, the region will assess the extent of its loss: Reming and the storm surge and volcanic mudflow that it caused took almost 2000 lives, some never found again. And in November 2020, another super typhoon and mudflow will bury more than 300 homes, and these families will be back in evacuation centres at the time of a pandemic.

'*Iristoryahan kita* — let's do storytelling. Who knows the legend of Mayon?'

All hands up. It's local knowledge: Princess Daragang Magayon, meaning "Beautiful Maiden", from whose name the volcano's is derived. *Magayon* to Mayon.

'She's not beautiful, she's bad, she took our house!'

'She took my sister.'

'And my mother.'

The three detractors began to cry and tears multiplied among the huddled bodies. *Lola* Paela grew as unsettled as her audience. *Aysus*, where's your head, old woman? Wrong start, wrong story!

162

All these kids, her grandchildren included, just lost someone or something, or everything. Because of the volcano.

Then a small voice piped up, 'She died too.'

All turned to the girl, maybe seven, who's cradling her bandaged leg that was nearly crushed by a rock. 'The princess died too.'

'Because of bad people,' Andres, now twelve years old, raced to continue the story, sensing grandmother's disquiet and swallowing back his own tears. 'She died at her wedding with her boyfriend Ulap because bad Pagtuga came to stop the wedding because he wanted to marry her instead and he speared Ulap and the princess ran to save him but she got hit.'

'And her grave grew taller and taller and became a beautiful mountain,' the girl finished the tale. 'That was what my Mama always said.'

Lola Paela cleared her throat. 'So she didn't really die, did she? She's always with us, the mountain is always with us.'

'And we love her,' the girl whispered.

'What's your name, child?'

'Marina … my Mama died too … she tried to save me, she saved me.'

Lola Paela grew silent. After a while, she gathered the girl onto her lap then began improvising. 'Listen children, there was someone else, someone very special who came to that wedding — *ay*, who could it be?'

Bodies leant closer, sniffles halted.

'This special someone was watching all the time, did you know that? *Ay*, watching over our beautiful princess — it was Daragang Magayon's great-great-great grandmother *Púnay*!'

'Oh?' Awed chorus.

'Do you know *Púnay*?'

A few nodded. *Púnay*: dove, or pigeon.

163

'Now *Púnay* wanted to make sure Princess was safely and happily married, she heard about bad Pagtuga, y'see, but she's shy so she came disguised in the best clothes, startling white in front and *nagmamaris-maris*, shimmering blue-green-grey behind with a black train. But she kept her wings hidden. And when the spear hit Daragang Magayon on the breast —' she paused, taking in each rapt face — 'When the spear hit our beautiful princess, quickly *Púnay* opened her wings and flew to her, and held her to her heart and sang to her like she was a baby about to fall asleep. "Aa-oooot— aa-oooot—aa-oooot," she sang until the princess finally closed her eyes.'

All breaths held.

'That, children, was how *Púnay* got the red on her white breast. Like she's wounded too. So *Púnay* became very special, different from all other doves or pigeons anywhere. She became known as *Puñalada*, "she who was wounded by a dagger", and she still lives on the mountain to this day. She's still guarding her great-great-great granddaughter, keeping her safe.'

Andres' awe was so big and deep, it hurt his own breast. He'd seen the Luzon Bleeding Heart Dove only once, feasting on the fruit of *Lola* Paela's *atis* tree. A rare bird, a nearly threatened species in Mayon. But at that moment of story, Andres felt her. She had flown in at a time of so many wounds. He looked around and saw all the other kids' wonderment through their tears — *ay*, they felt the bird too! And they knew that someone they love or lost will always be keeping them safe. But Andres knew more even in his young heart then: that story is powerful. *It can keep you safe.*

'Sometimes you save, sometimes you can't. But you try.'

'What was that, Andy?'

'Nothing.' He walks ahead, fast.

How can you do anything with nothing? Sinéad doesn't like this sudden anger rising in her. Even after all their lunches and walks together, he's never really trusted her. She wants to help, to know, to understand, maybe to love — but 'nothing'.

He's walking past the poplars now. He stops, looks up.

She stops too, looks at the arched back, the head angled just so.

How yellow, how blue. But no bird, just sun. 'Warms my face, *Lola* Paela.'

She hears. It's something. She walks to him, tentatively lays a hand on his back, he doesn't flinch, then wraps her arms around his waist. 'I'm here, Andy, I'm here.'

GRANDMA OWL

Owl you need is love and kindness!

On Owl Mug. ED Ellen DeGeneres collection

Self-isolation, Day 2: The Parliament

Once upon a time, Grandma Owl lost her glasses —'
'So she cried and cried —'

'But she found them on top of her head — ha-ha!'

'And she was happy again — The End!'

Boy and grandmother laugh after their inside joke. He's not yet seven, she's 70. But she believes they're both as young and as wise as they wish to be. He agrees: 'Grandma Owl believes in good things, so no worries.'

'And you believe with Grandma, right?'

'Righto, Gran!' It's their pact of faith: that they believe together, whatever happens. And they believe in happy endings. So, all's well at Grandma's flat in Wollongong. Well, as well as could be.

Victor Jr. has lived on and off with his grandmother, Luningning, or Lou as she's called, because mum Rose is a full-time nurse. Boy and grandmother are more than best pals. Young Victor is very attached to grandmother and doesn't miss mum much, Rose thinks, and it saddens her. But it's convenient, because she works night shifts most days of the week. The other nurses at the hospital are envious. 'You're so lucky to have a Filipina mother-in-law. Filipinas are family orientated so baby-sitting's probably never been a problem since he was born.' But how's this for lucky? She took my son for an over-extended Christmas holiday in her hometown and they returned on the same plane as someone who's contracted the virus. But Rose doesn't tell anyone, worried it could compromise her job, even if she hasn't had contact with them since they flew back.

'No worries,' Lou assured her on the phone and was very efficient about her decision to self-isolate for two weeks when she learned about the new case. 'Even if we sat at the back of the plane, many seats away from that poor thing.'

Rose wondered whether it's her mother-in-law's ploy to keep her son for herself a little longer, but she shook off the thought. C'mon, Rose, you're a nurse, you should commend her for acting sensibly. Besides, she's not that kind of mother-in-law. She's been a comfort to you since *that* time. But she's in the vulnerable age, so she shouldn't be with your son. But who will take care of him?

'No worries, Rose, everything will be okay with the right discipline, care and prayers.' Lou was a science teacher in the Philippines, the strict sort, *but* she's also a devout Catholic. Rose is a little guilty about her *but* — but her mother-in-law has some strange beliefs and her Godspeak gets out of hand sometimes. Stop whingeing, Rose, she's your rock!

'What'll we do today, Grandma?'

'Homework.'

'But school's just starting —'

'And you're missing it.'

Lou and Rose had an argument about it on the phone. There was a family wedding so they postponed their return. 'And miss the first week of school?'

'Easy to catch up, Victor's a bright boy, so no worries.' But then there was a typhoon and their flight to Manila was delayed, so the return to Australia was set back for a second week. 'No worries, Rose.' And now, two more weeks of missing school because of the fourteen-day isolation. 'We'll be good, *no worries*.' Lou's favourite line. Grates on Rose. No worries? I'm the mother! You should have come home much earlier as we agreed. What if you both get sick?

'Let's go to the beach, Gran.'

'I said, fourteen days at home, Victor.'

'Why?'

'So we're okay and everyone else is okay — then we'll all be okay.'

'Why fourteen?'

'Because that's the time to make sure we don't get sick.'

'Can we go home to mum first?'

'We don't want mum to get sick.'

'I hate coronavirus.'

'"Hate" is a very bad word, Victor. It hurts your mouth if you say it.'

He opens his mouth wide at Grandma. 'My mouth's okay — see?'

Grandma steps back. 'No need to open. Grandma Owl has x-ray eyes. She can see that Owlet Boy doesn't mean to say it, so his mouth is fine.'

'Grandma Owl believes in good things, so no worries?'

'*Siyempre* — righto.'

'Righto,' he mumbles, then, 'So I can't see mum?'

'Mum's coming tomorrow.'

'Why not now?'

'Mum's working, my Owlet.'

Owlet. He likes it when she calls him that, not Victor like at school. 'Victor, don't do that, Victor, don't do this, Victor, don't go there,' teacher always said and he wanted to put his hands to his ears. 'Precocious kid, too bright for his boots sometimes,' teacher told Lou.

Once he asked, 'Why not Vic, Grandma? It's easy to say.'

'Because Victor is a good name, it's your father's name.'

Arms crossed and pout set: the boy is wearing a thundercloud.

'I phoned your new teacher, Mrs Hill, she's nice. She said you should stay home and no worries. But there's homework —'

He rolls his eyes to the ceiling.

She rolls her eyes too. 'Ah, I spy something with an "s".'

'Sss … no "s" up there, Grandma.'

'There's sky, blue sky — Grandma Owl has x-ray eyes, so she can see through the roof.' She plays little "owl games" with her grandson and sometimes they work, like now. The thundercloud has passed. 'So, homework. Mrs Hill said you could do a show-and-tell about our trip — that's fun, right?'

'Uh-huh.' Owlet Boy is still contemplating the ceiling.

'Come, say good morning to our owls — we missed them, didn't we?'

Lou collects them, big and small lined up on her sideboard: a porcelain Mama Owl with her owlet, where she hangs her rosary beads; a white ceramic barn owl from Matilda, her Chilean neighbour upstairs; a tiny jade owl; a wooden owl specs holder with 'Lucky' painted on its chest; a smiling brown owl, great find from St Vinnies; a crocheted pink owl with red sequins for eyes, which she made herself; and the latest: a seashell owl that they bought in Manila on this trip. Seven owls now, no eight, Victor thinks, Grandma included. Grandma Owl cuz she's round and cuddly with big eyes, and when she puts her glasses on her head, they stick out like owl ears. 'Not ears, my Owlet. Those ear tufts are feathers.' Both are into owls.

They examine the new acquisition. It's a white owl less than a foot high made of tiny nassa shells. 'You're sky and sea at the same time,' she whispers to it.

When grandmother's in this dreamy mood, Victor wants to be in it too. 'Like shells can fly ...' he runs his finger over the new owl.

'What do we call her?'

'Uhmm ...' He pats each one, reviewing their names: 'This is Mama Owl and Owlet Boy, Mattie Owl, Jadey Owl, Lucky Owl, Smiley Owl, Pinky Owl ...' Once he asked Grandma why they're all girls because she always says 'she'.

'But there's Owlet Boy, Victor.'

'Yes, that's me, me and mum!'

'So, what's her name?'

He examines the white snail shells. 'Uhmm ... Shelly Owl!'

'Okay, Shelly Owl,' she sets her at the centre, 'You be PM of The Parliament.'

'Par-lah-men?'

'Par-lah-ment. What you call a group of owls — and — what you call the people who make the law of Australia.'

'What's law?'

'Uhmm ... it's what you should do and not do. Parliament must think hard about it together, so you and me and all of us are okay. It's a very important job, a lot of thinking, so Parliament must be wise and kind to make sure the law is good for all. And whoever's PM must make sure this is so — for all time.'

'What's PM?'

'PM is Prime Minister, the leader, well, sort of, though ...' Ah, too hard to explain. 'PM's like Shelly Owl here.'

Victor digests the explanation as he studies the owls. 'Owl Par-lah-ment. Because they're wise like the people who make the law.'

'Clever boy.'

'But you're wiser, so you're PM Grandma Owl of the Par-lah-ment.'

She laughs. 'Now, shall we do homework?'

'Ring mum first.'

'No, wash hands first.'

Self-isolation, Day 3: Toilet paper — *¡qué loca!*

'We do our best and if it's not enough, we accept. God will provide.' Rose hopes she does not hear that same platitude. She remembers it now as she goes up to Lou's flat with what she's just shopped for them. It was only a month after the accident, how unfeeling, so she screamed at Lou going on and on about accepting her lot because God will provide, God will take care. She and three-month old Victor had been crying for hours as she tried to breastfeed him. She couldn't express milk. All of her body had dried up, except her eyes. She couldn't settle her son until Lou made him his first baby formula. 'Rest, Rose, God will take care of us and I'll take care of him, no worries.' And she's taken care of him, of them, for more than six years now.

'Hi, Rose.'

'Oh hi, Matilda.'

It's Lou's neighbour coming down the stairs. 'Scared of the virus?' she queries her mask, chuckling. 'We're healthy here.' Indeed. Seventy-six year old Matilda is enviably fit. Every day she goes for a walk on the beach then a swim at the rock pool. 'Stocking up before they come home?' she nods at her shopping.

'Actually, they're home.'

'But I haven't seen them —'

'They're — they're self-isolating —'

'What?'

'A passenger on their plane home tested positive —'

'*Dios mío*, are they okay — I'll come up with you — let me help with those —'

'I don't think so, Matilda — for your safety.'

'*¡Pobres queridos!*' she wrings her hands.

Poor dears indeed, including you, if you're not careful. 'They're okay, Matilda, they'll be fine — see you,' and she continues up the next flight of stairs.

She hears Matilda at the stairwell, quickly on the phone to her friend, her repeated '*¡pobres queridos!*' and 'how's the little one?' then, 'Just saw Rose with some shopping, hope she got toilet paper, they've disappeared, there's panic buying — *¡qué loca!*'

Yes, how crazy, she sighs, setting the bags outside her mother-in-law's door then phoning her —'shopping's outside, Lou' — and the door quickly opens and Victor bursts forth, arms open.

'Mum, mummy!'

A twinge in her breast, he missed her after all. 'Hello, sweetie,' she blows her son a kiss, as Lou quickly pulls him aside.

'We can't hug mum yet.'

'Why not?' he asks, struggling to break free. 'And why're you wearing that?'

'Because we don't want mummy to catch the virus,' Lou says.

'I've no virus!'

Under the mask, Rose puts on her most cheerful face. 'We're just making sure, sweetheart — Lou, two thermometers in there, keep track of your temperatures, no sharing — we'll be Skyping tonight, right, sweetie?'

'I can't see your face.'

'Mum has a nice book about owls for you, sweetie, in that bag.' Rose is trying to keep her voice steady. 'It's *Owly*, it's about a curious owl who asks too many questions like you. We'll read it together on Skype — we like Skyping, don't we?'

'I hate coronavirus!'

'We'll be okay, Rose, no worries,' Lou hugs the weeping boy.

'Love you, sweetheart,' Rose blows him another kiss then rushes down, nearly bumping against Matilda who's been listening the whole time in the stairwell.

'Don't worry, Rose, I'll help.'

As she drives off crying, Rose screams — 'Fuck! Why is everyone telling me not to bloody worry!'

Self-isolation, Day 6: Re-search

Only Matilda calls Lou by her real name: Luningning. Only she can pronounce it right. Only she knows what it means: shimmer. '*Brillar* — ¡*qué bonita!* — how beautiful, not like Lou — Lou what — what does that mean? I'll always call you Luningning!' They've been friends since their Australian husbands worked at BHP and they're even closer now that they're both widows. 'We're Aussie too — plus something else,' they tell anyone who asks, 'Where are you from?' And when the interrogator is persistent, feisty Matilda says, 'I'm Matilda,' and breaks into song, 'Waltzing Matilda, Waltzing Matilda!' '¡*Qué loca*, Luningning — I've lived here in Wollongong for years, and they still interrogate me, and you!'

'Because of our accent, Matilda.'

'They have an accent too!' Matilda was an accountant in Chile but was forced to migrate to Australia when Pinochet came to power. She knows about interrogations. She's on the phone now to her best friend, for the second time today.

'How's he?'

'Bored, sad, restless, grumpy — whew!'

'I'm baking an owl cake for him, but don't tell him yet.'

'Victor has *dos abuelas*,' Matilda tells him sometimes. 'Two grandmas — lucky you.' Matilda doesn't have children and, like her friend, she dotes on *mi querido niño*, my dear boy. She knows her neighbour's history. They've been neighbours since that accident a bit over six years ago when she took on the role of second *abuela*.

'*Haaaaay*, Matilda, what will I do without you?'

'You're doing very well, Luningning. I'll ring again when I leave this cake at your door. Have it for *merienda*.'

'Yes, perfect snack with coffee in your Christmas gift — thanks again, I love this mug — "Owl you need is love and kindness" — how clever!'

'*Sí, sí* — and on the other side of the mug, an owl science teacher, like you!'

'With chalk in hand and equations on the blackboard — I think one's "$E = mc^2$" — an Einstein owl — ha-ha!'

'Good to hear you laugh.'

'Oh, I can't give you your *pasalubong* yet, sorry, until we're sure it's safe.'

For Matilda's "homecoming present", Luningning bought an old rose *pinukpok* shawl. The woven abaca-plus-silk pounded to airy fineness doubles as a belated Christmas gift. She bought Rose one too, sky-blue, but it will have to wait.

'Fourteen days, it's a trial — and what if — but God will see us through.'

'*Dios cuidará* — God will take care, Luninging.'

'Yes, no worries.'

'How's Victor's homework?'

'We're starting.'

'Good. Now, let me finish his cake.'

On Luningning's dining table, paper, pencils and crayons, and two iPads: boy and grandma are exploring possibilities for homework. He's read and re-read *Owly* with mum on Skype and

175

is drawing the inquisitive owl. He's made six tally marks on top of the paper: six days now, eight to go. He wants to do owls for show-and-tell. But Grandma's trying to manoeuver him towards what Mrs Hill's assigned: something about their trip and maybe something along science, so they're researching.

'Re-searching — what's that?' He's grumpy.

'It's when you're looking for something to study.'

'Boring.' He's morose.

'It's when you're like Owly asking many questions.'

'Okay, I'm re-searching owls.'

The phone rings again. Cake baked so soon?

It's Rose. 'Is Victor okay, you okay?

'No cold, no fever, no worries.'

'I have every reason to worry, Lou — can you put him on, please?'

'It's mum.'

'Mum — mum!' and he's bounding from his seat, grabbing the phone from her. 'Mummy, I'm being good, I'm doing homework, a drawing for show-and-tell, and I so love Owly — when can we read him again?'

Luningning smiles. She's happy he's happy, but fear has been gnawing within.

'I'm like Owly who asks many questions, mum, I'm re-searching.'

Luningning knows re-searching. She asks questions even if it should be *no worries* because *In Him We Trust*. But asking is also a matter of faith or of affirming faith, isn't it? Re-search. To find if not answers to appease her mind, at least something to appease her heart. So she searches, and re-searches. In Him, in others, and with others. It's all she can do, and what she did at *that* time that ripped her heart out of her chest. And what she must do now,

176

again. She must return to her novenas. Add them to her regular rosary in the evening. After all, praying is asking.

Self-isolation, Day 7: The Story of Shimmer

She checks on her grandson. Under this light, asleep he looks like his father. She recognises the familiar features under the blonde hair. She turns off the lamp and returns to her bedroom. She's been going through her box of novenas after she prayed the rosary. She remembers her altar here, beside the bed, and how she packed it up after that big argument with Rose — no, it was an explosion.

'Don't you understand, Lou? It's so unhealthy. But of course, you won't listen to me. I'm just a daughter-in-law.'

'No, Rose, you are my daughter.'

'I loved him too, Lou, but please, please, time to put *that* away. My son's growing up and —'

'Don't you want him to know his father? It's like having his father around.'

'Can't you see, you're fucking up with my son's head!'

So Lou packed up her own son four years after his car accident. Victor's photo, the candle that she lit with little Victor Jr every night whenever he slept here and she'd tell him his father will always be his guardian angel, the vase that she filled with flowers weekly, and the novena for the dead, all hidden in the bottom drawer. But the crucifix stayed and the rosary she hung around Mama Owl and Owlet on the sideboard beside the main door. 'Weird,' Matilda said. She's Catholic too and she understood the altar, but rosary and owls, how's that? So Luningning told her the story of her birth.

They're at the North Wollongong rock pool. At Matilda's insistence, she agreed to do the morning walk and swim with her the day after she packed up the altar. Matilda did her laps as she dog-paddled along. They're now having the coffee that she brought in a thermos. She's not minding Victor this morning.

'Why can't she understand? I'm a mother, she's a mother, we're both women trying to — we should be in this together.'

'You're in this together differently. You're grieving differently.'

'But women must bond together. When I was doing practice teaching in the Philippines in the 70s, I had a friend who taught me about sisterhood.'

'Ah, women's lib time — but, Luningning, sisterhood can't be imposed, it's not easy, it doesn't come in a bottle. *Hermandad de mujeres* — like ours, it's good, but like all relationships, sisterhood is negotiated, we work on it. Remember, we didn't like each other the first time we met.'

What to say to that, so she spreads her towel and lies down. Matilda does the same. The friends take in the sun, lulled by the steady rhythm of a lone swimmer and the breaking of the waves at the end of the pool.

'Maybe father was right. I was born twinned with bad luck, with death … that's why my Victor died.'

Màtilda sits up.

Luningning tells it with eyes closed, her story weaving in and out of the water sounds. 'My mother said that at the same time I came out of her, they heard the cry of a *kwaw*, an owl, outside the window. As the *partera* cut my umbilical cord, she told my father that *kwaw* was my twin. My father believed owls bring bad luck, they're omens of death.' A glint in the corner of the closed eyes, it's not sea water.

Matilda scours her brain for the right words. 'We had a small farm in Santiago, with barn owls always flying around at night. Father liked them, a big help, he said. *Lechuzas blancas*. White barn owls like apparitions flying silently with that ever vigilant face … they ate mice that ate our wheat.'

178

'Ahh, angels … not bad luck.'

'*Sí, sí, angeles,* Luningning.' Not *brujas* or witches as some believe.

A week later, Matilda gave her the ceramic barn owl, 'a no-nonsense guard against those little mice running in your head.' She finally understood why her friend had hung her rosary around Mama Owl and Owlet close to the door, with her sisterhood of owls. To counter the bad luck, to keep death from entering the house.

As she goes through her novenas, Luningning hopes it does not enter this time. It's midnight now. She chooses a novena and lights a candle beside the crucifix. After this prayer, she'll ring her brother Manoling in the Philippines to ask how they are.

Self-isolation, Day 10: KV-20

COVID-19. The new word on TV, after *coronavirus.* New names to new normal. It's the third week of February. On the screen, the colourful ball floats around.

'Like a planet with things sticking out, like it's sick.'

She nods at her grandson. A planet with pustules. Bright boy, good eye.

'I'll draw it, Grandma.' He returns to his pencil and crayons.

She adjusts her glasses to read the latest figures at the bottom of the news: 76,000 cases around the world. Three deaths in Iran. The update pans a throng of masked faces in China.

The phone rings, it's a quick call from Rose checking on them. 'And Coles will deliver the groceries and fresh food that I ordered for you today.'

'Bless you, daughter, thank you.'

It rings again, it's Matilda. 'I left two rolls of toilet paper outside your door, in case you run out.'

'*Ay,* bless you —'

'I was so lucky to get the last pack at Coles — whew, you should have seen it, Luningning — ugly — people are so unkind — we need to fight this — this —'

'We need a fighter virus —'

'A kindness virus!'

'KV-20 — ha-ha!'

'Oh, we have to laugh —'

'Or we won't stop crying,' she whispers, checking if the boy's listening, but he's busy with Owly.

'You really okay, Luningning?'

'Yes, we take our temperature twice a day.' She goes to the bedroom, far from his earshot.

'Only four more days now — if you need anything —'

'So much dying, Matilda.'

'Mostly people like us. The update says it's us who can get very sick, but children, they'll be fine — but they can be spreaders, who knows — so you and Victor, I wonder —'

'Don't worry, he won't get sick, I won't get sick. God won't allow it, because I still have work to do, I have to take care of my family.'

'Take good care of yourself.'

'We are taking care — and I found my novena for the dead. I'm praying it every night now … for all of them.'

'There'll be more, I think.'

'And the Saint Jude and Saint Rita novenas — patron saints of lost causes.'

'We're not a lost cause.'

'It's what we do back home … when things are really bad.'

'We will fight this, and we will win!' Matilda knows really bad. She went through Pinochet's machinery before she fled Chile.

'Grandma, I have my show-and-tell now!'

'I better go, Victor's calling.'

'How's *mi querido niño*?'

'I think he's done his homework.'

'Bright boy, *besos* to him.'

'Look, Gran, I drew coronavirus.' He's waving his new opus: a red orb with a sad mouth and things sticking out from all over its face. 'And Owly's beside it — he's asking coronavirus why it makes people sick.' Inquisitive Owly has a frown line on his brow and a balloon coming out of his mouth with a big 'W-H-Y?' in it.

'That's very good, Victor.'

'Mummy'll like it.' They're Skyping later.

'Uhmm … Mrs Hill said show-and-tell should be about our trip — so something about the Philippines maybe?'

'Isn't coronavirus in the Philippines too?'

'Yes.'

'And owls?'

'Of course.'

'So Owly flies to the Philippines to ask coronavirus, together with all the Philippine Owlies — I can draw them too!'

She smiles. He'll make a good lawyer yet, like his father. 'I think, first you should learn how we say owl in my language.'

'In Philippine?'

'No, in Bikol, the language of my village, where we visited —'

'Where Ron-Ron and Denah live?'

'Yes, *Lolo* Manoling's grandkids — you played with them, remember? We'll ring them and they can tell you all about Philippine owlies.'

'Oh yes, yes, Gran!'

'But first, would you like to learn how they say owl?'

'Uh-hum.'

'*Kwaw.*'

'Wow — ? Owl-Wow?' He laughs. 'Owl-Wow, Owl-Wow!'

On TV an ongoing update on COVID-19 from the Victorian Premier. She hushes Victor and turns on the volume. There's another case in Victoria. Behind him and the state's chief medical officer are trees. A park most likely. As he stresses the need for social distancing, a blur darts from the leaves. And interjects.

Victor runs to the television, follows the blur with a finger. 'A bird, there's a bird there, Grandma!'

Throughout the update, it does not stop interjecting in song, and boy and Grandma cannot stop smiling.

Self-isolation, Day 13: She glows!

'The beautiful gleam appeared to come from the breast and undersides of the wings and body.' Matilda highlighted the line in the article hypothesising about the luminescence of barn owls in England and Australia. She printed it and left it at their door. She's been researching owls on the web too to help with the boy's homework. It's now *their* show-and-tell: owls, and coronavirus on the side.

'I read barn owls glow in the dark,' she told him on the phone yesterday and he was beside himself with wonder. 'Ohh … like Mattie Owl.' 'Mattie?' 'Uh-hum, the white owl you gave Gran — Matilda owl, so Mattie.' She laughed. 'So I'm an owl now?' 'Yes, like Grandma Owl.'

So today, they're close to nailing it, well, almost.

'Let's review our Parliament, Victor. Which one is the barn owl?'

'Mattie Owl!' he taps the white ceramic.

'It's a white owl — like?

'Like Shelly Owl!'

'From the Philippines.'

He jumps up and down. 'Yes, Shelly Owl, Shelly Wow! I can

take her to school for show-and-tell — and Mattie Owl too and I can draw them glowing so bright so coronavirus gets zapped away — and — and —'

'First, we must research barn owls in the Philippines.'

But they can't be sure about their findings.

What to do? Victor spends the whole afternoon drawing. He's dragged his chair to the sideboard. He draws various versions of Shelly Owl (or Shelly Wow) and Mattie Owl, and the rest of the Parliament zapping coronavirus away. He's methodical. First, sketch with pencil then colour. He's doing a lot of thinking, throughout dinner and later in bed. What to show, how to tell? When Luningning finally kisses him goodnight, he's still wondering about "the right owl". Late at night, she doesn't see him peek through the door as she prays her novena beside the crucifix and the lit candle. He's seen this before, like in a dream — in the dark, she glows.

Self-isolation, Day 14: Grandma Owl Wow

On the sideboard, it's done. But he still has to colour. When he wakes up.

ANGELS

… to try and ease fears, even if it's a matter of touch …

Dr Stephen Parnis

A S … AS …' Nenita mumbles the acronym through her shaking and the pain on her breast. Left. Where the heart is.

Rustle. 'What is it, dear?'

'AS … your name …' She's waking up from anaesthetic or trying to, but her eyes won't open and she can't still the tremors.

Whisper, maybe to another nurse, 'She's confused my name.' Then back to Nenita, 'No, dear, Sumi's my name — how's the pain, from one to ten?'

Flutter. The oxygen mask is adjusted on her face as she tries to nod, to say she did hear when she told her earlier. 'AS … Angel Sumi …'

Laughter. 'Is it the drug or me … so, one to ten?'

'Ten …'

'I'm going to give you the max for pain now,' then hand squeezes hers.

185

Can't squeeze back, shaking won't stop.

'Pain?'

'Ten,' Nenita says again, but the question is for the patient to her right who mumbles, 'I'm good.'

'Any pain?'

'Not really,' the response from her left.

It's busy at the post-op recovery ward of a Canberra hospital.

Something brushes her feet, she tries to wiggle her toes but they're stuck. No, snug inside compression socks.

Hovering, then hand on her shoulder. 'Nenita …'

She recognises her surgeon's voice, ah the brilliant Dr A-J, but her lids can't lift.

'We'll talk later,' he says.

More rustle, flutter, all flurry hither and thither. Then silence. They've all flown off.

So how did it all begin?

Over breakfast, it begins. Before her first sip of coffee, a phone call from nurse Julieann at BreastScreen ACT. There's a twinge in her breast as she asks her to return tomorrow for further examination after a mammogram a few days ago. Says she could be in for the whole day. Tomorrow comes and Arvis walks her to the appointment. It's late August, blue sky sunny but still wintry cold. Wind chill factor. She pulls down the beanie over her ears, points to the green buds pushing out of the bare trees lining Moore Street. 'Spring,' she says.

A magpie swoops over their heads, he quickly pulls on his hoodie. 'Yes, maggie season.'

'Scaredy cat,' she says and squeezes his hand. 'Look, it's probably nothing.' *Nothing* is a vast space to fill in with things.

Outside the City Community Health Centre, she puts on her mask. He does too. 'You don't have to come in with me,' she tells him but he dithers at the entrance, waits for her to finish with the COVID check. She waves to him, mouths 'Go home.' He waves back, keeps waving until she disappears into the clinic.

How can one look elegant in a blue paper gown? But she does, sitting there on one of the pink chairs at reception, snazzy leather boots crossed. Probably Indian or Sri Lankan. She smiles at Nenita, but her eyes are distant. Nenita smiles back, shifts in her old trackies and runners, beanie and gloves (with a hole), which she quickly takes off and crumples. Beside the woman, a man half-sitting, half-crouched stares at his hands. Probably husband. Another twinge. She thinks of Arvis walking home in the cold.

Inside, ten women in blue paper gowns in socially distanced seating, and soon she becomes the eleventh and the only one wearing a mask. They're strangers all but now joined at the breast, and that's comforting. The elegant woman walks past and into one of the rooms, boots in easy stride. That's comforting too. But probably husband is out in the cold now. Again that twinge.

Nurse Julieann explains how the day will proceed. Intensive diagnostic mammo of her left breast followed by ultrasound, and right after, results will be discussed with her by the surgeon of the day. If okay, she can go home by midday, otherwise she'll have to stay till the afternoon for biopsy and all will be confirmed next week. Amazingly quick and efficient. Such tender efficiency, how her breast will be handled by radiographers Karina and Catherine, and another Catherine, the sonographer, and Nenita will think, perhaps tenderness is a peculiarly wondrous wiring from her breast to theirs. But for now, they're just storytelling as Julieann checks her family's health history, usual procedure, and stories are shared. How Nenita's mother died of cancer last year and her father, the year before in the Philippines, though not cancer, but her aunt, cancer too last year. How when COVID struck, her younger sister Lydia, whose husband passed on the same month as their aunt, said, 'Let's hope the family is spared, we need some rest.' *Yes, this COVID-19.* Julieann's daughter, a star basketball player, was going to apply for a sports scholarship in the US, but oh no, not this time. Small peeks into each other's lives. Precious.

Much later, more family stories with surgeon Dr Rebecca, whose five-year old daughter is tuned in to the care of the planet that's taught at school. Nenita claps her hand. Kindred soul! As the doctor confirms the tumour and that, yes, she has to stay for biopsy, climate change and politics animate the consultation room. Nenita's reminded of her GP Dr Sharmila, their snippets of family stories woven into consultations. Perhaps care is about levelling the story field. Patient is not just the supplicant at the professional's door. Both are carers, caring to affirm the other: human, with stories, a life. And both are anchored.

Outside only four women now, and she's the fifth. It's midday and Julieann goes around with a tray of sandwiches. 'The hostess with the mostest!' one of the women says.

'All nurses should be given an award,' Nenita says.

'No, a raise,' the woman says. Murmurs of assent all around. Enervated blue gowns fill the *Nothing*.

Then it's just her and Maria, and a young woman in a hijab who steps out to make a call. Maria is Italian, maybe seventies, and her legs ache all the time with arthritis. She's worried about the biopsy, she hates needles. They talk COVID. Nenita is acutely aware of the plight of Italy. Maria says she has a very nice Filipina neighbour. Nenita almost takes off her mask to smile better, but she has a weak immune system so she keeps it on. Maria tells her about her hometown in Italy.

When her biopsy turn comes, it's with nurse Penny originally from England, and two radiologists: witty Dr Jatinder and Dr

Chat from Vietnam who has two sons whom she adores. There's anaesthetic for pain and Penny's hand. 'Squeeze as tightly as you wish,' she says. Nenita gets teary, not because of the pain but because of the offer. She can't squeeze, her hand feels limp. No, it's resting, held by Penny's and throughout the painful procedure, a line plays in her head: '... to try and ease fears, even if it's a matter of touch.' What Dr Stephen Parnis said on ABC-TV's Q&A panel of health professionals working with COVID patients. Later, she'll read the transcript of his remark. 'One of the most fundamental aspects of being a health worker is to journey with the patient, to be with them, to offer that human contact, to try and ease fears, even if it's a matter of touch. These are the sorts of things that we should always, and will, give people, whether they are mildly unwell or whether they are nearing the end of their life. It's a privilege to do that.'

This is a privilege: to have my hand in yours, Penny. *To try and ease fears, even if it's a matter of touch.* After all, care is epidermal: skin on skin, we affirm our interconnected living and dying, so we fight to live. She remembers how her father would not let go of her hand that whole night when she watched over him at the hospital. She was dozing off but he was very much awake, grip strong, alive.

Afterwards in the briefing with Penny, who has three beautiful alpacas, Nenita tells her they're all angels here and how lucky she is to be in their care. She notes her arthritic hands and stops the urge to hold them, soothe them. She suggests bittermelon tea, good for arthritic pain, or better still, get the vegetable fresh from IGA and stir-fry with garlic, tomatoes and eggs. A home remedy shared as Penny comprehensively explains how things will proceed from here, then says, 'Just go with the flow. If you're anxious, need a little cry when you get home —'

'I'm actually fine, Penny, I've had plenty of training for this in my family,' she chuckles. 'My only worry is if there's pain … my mother had so much of it before — y'know.'

'Just go with the flow,' she says again, 'and remember, you're number one now.'

It's just her now, back in her daggy trackies and beanie, when Maria comes out of the biopsy room holding onto a nurse's arm. 'Did you cry?' Maria asks. She shakes her head. 'I cried. That biopsy, whew, so painful,' and she waves her goodbye.

All quiet now.

A few minutes later, Julieann comes around, lays a hand on her shoulder. 'You okay to get home?'

She nods, 'Just waiting for my husband to pick me up,' and hopes Maria gets home okay.

'Can I make you a cup of tea?' Julieann asks.

She smiles, 'No thanks.' There's a smarting behind her eyes. They're all so kind. Now she's getting lachrymose, ugh, lachry-morose. No, she's lachrymosal. That's better. Mouth opens up as you say it, unlike the closing pout of "mose" or morose. But is there such a word? Well, if not, she'll invent one. *Lachrymosal*, like the name of a flower opening, like her mother's newly bloomed hibiscus wet with morning rain. No, like the other flower. Mama's bleeding-heart vine under her bedroom window. Flower like crimson blood as if about to drop from the whitest, heart-shaped calyx. The old folks call it *lágrimas de Cristo*, tears of Christ.

All gone now, those flowers. Last month, her brother Roberto had to uproot their mother's garden because of termite infestation that spread from the now empty family house to its surrounds. Ah, devoted son who's facilitated their parents' care and funerals, and the repair of the house and the ground on which it stands. Earth commiserating with the pain indoors. Roberto had overseen an earlier termite infestation a few months after father died, when mother was supposedly recovering from renal surgery. Left kidney out because of a tumour initially misdiagnosed as "not cancer", when in fact, it was metastasising while a new lump was growing fast on the surgical scar and two others on her scalp, and pain was constant. But mother was a gritty soul, not one to complain, not one to cry. On an overseas call, though, after the pest control job, she told Nenita, 'Naghahayà, Nini, wailing. I can hear the queen termite wailing through the wall!'

Nenita is her mother's daughter. How calm she is now, as breastscreen doctor Karen and nurse Penny explain the biopsy results: it's cancer, so surgery and treatment after. She's unfazed. Out of character, considering she's always been the "family crier", mababaw ang luhà, "tears close to the surface". But not today, not even at home and through all the preps for surgery. She feels together, almost casual, no fuss, please. This just is. Not that she's playing stoic. She just knows this health odyssey of sorts will be easier than when she got sick for a year while living alone in Wollongong. Now she has Arvis who has more questions. Each time, he raises his hand to speak, like a schoolboy. My poor love, my nerūsē. Love that "does not rust". His blood pressure has been spiking since this all began and he had to up his med's dosage. Now, her question: 'When can I start cleaning after the surgery?'

The women laugh, look at him and wink. 'Two years after,' Penny says. All laugh.

'I'm OC, y'see, with my own standard of clean.' Yes, she's her mother's daughter.

The day before the surgery, she "meets" her second Karen. She and Arvis are walking in Haig Park, through yellow cape daisies and tiny weed violets starting to awaken. Spring is happening and the birds are doing their thing. Magpies, rosellas, king parrots, weebills and crows are in choral conversation among the pines when her mobile rings. It's Karen, the breast care nurse with pre-op and post-op advice. She's impressed. Care on the ball from different sources. *For her.* She's moved. The avian chorus punctuates the call and she thinks of other winged creatures. 'You're an angel, Karen, thank you so much.'

'Anytime. You can ring breast care any time after your surgery. I'll tell you more when I visit you the day after the op.' A rosella glides past, all crimson and blue delight. She can't stop smiling. 'By the way, you'll need a post-op bra, get it at Colleen's today if you can.'

Maybe angels are human birds or bird humans. Not celestial but planetary: of the earth, where we need them.

Then, another Karen who helps her fit a post-op bra. Three tender Karens all up. A few days after the surgery, more of this tenderness when she returns to buy another bra from Gillian who had a mastectomy years ago. 'You'll get better, too,' she'll say. At this boutique that specialises in lingerie for breast cancer patients, all staff have been on their own breast cancer journey. Indeed, all joined at the breast.

'*Nag-abot su guardian angel ko*' — my guardian angel has arrived, she emails Roberto and Lydia as she awaits surgery on her designated hospital bed. Last night, she dreamt of father coming home to their old neighbourhood. He's crossing the road towards the house of their childhood, young and smiling. Her siblings email back: 'Yes, Papa is your guardian angel, he'll take care of you — good luck.' Into her ear, a bedtime prayer sneaks in: Angel of God, my guardian dear … But her angels are not divine spirits, though sometimes they're uncanny arrivals like her father and the synchronous care of three Karens. Or like the white dove that will roost momentarily on the balcony rail later at home when she's recovering from surgery. But white dove in Canberra? Roosting with a common street pigeon? She'll freeze, mesmerised: dare to care for someone different. Sudden warmth will spread around her left breast, oh joy, as the grey pigeon with its iridescent green on the nape tries to nudge the white dove that turns towards her, all shining white and pink beak, and she'll think, ah, angels … like nurse Vera at her hospital bed now, getting her kitted up in gown, compression socks and see-through disposable knickers, 'racy,' they giggle together and share parents stories. Vera cancelled her visit to her parents in Portugal because of COVID, Nenita has no more parents to visit in the Philippines. Vera grasps her toes and says, 'I'll check on you before your op.'

Like doctors with MD or other letters of authority after their names, nurses should have their own. AC: *Angel of Care*.

She waits for her surgery with Billie Holiday singing *Strange Fruit*. Who knows why she stumbles upon her 1959 live rendition of this iconic song about the racist lynching of two black men in Indiana as she watches you-tubes of orioles singing on her iPad. Must be the winged link: from bird to bird, from song to song. 'For the crows to pluck' — sang with her grimace of horror and the cutting click of her 'ck', that abrupt halt! Nenita sees the lynched bodies hanging from poplars and crows closing in. After she sees orioles, strikingly yellow and black naped, that sang for her father when he was dying. From death to death? She shivers, breath held — then three crested pigeons zip outside the glass window! Resurrection? The logic of these consonances unhinges and restores her. Breath lets go.

Soon Ash, the orderly, wheels her to the operating theatre, 'where the drama happens,' she quips and he laughs. She's received by 'my sweet lady' nurse or maybe assistant anaesthetist who prepares her in the holding area — she tells her *her* name but it

193

goes poof in the air. Ugh, brain fog too early. All she remembers is her saying, 'Now my sweet lady, we'll insert your cannula,' and that she cancelled her 50th birthday trip to Niagara Falls because of COVID, then her main anaesthetist talking to her before sweet lady nurse walks her into the theatre where her surgeon and his team smile under the bright light and lay her on a narrow bed as she keeps hearing *Skyline Pigeon* and *Sweet Painted Lady*, and she thinks, wait, wrong song, and what the hell is Elton John doing here?

All quiet now. On the next bed, Lyn, who had knee surgery, is sleeping. Tomorrow Nenita will hear her extreme pain through the curtain as the physiotherapist helps her through post-op exercises — 'Okay, darling, let's try it again, you're doing fine.' 'Darling', 'My sweet lady'. Oh these tender utterances to ease pain. Maybe this is how it is: every suffering soul becomes a beloved.

Arvis was here when they wheeled Lyn in and they heard her gasp as she was moved to the bed. Arvis winced, then kissed Nenita's brow and whispered, 'You okay, mīļotā?' His Latvian "sweetheart" made her smile through the pain. Then he said he'd grown worried because early on he was told she was already in the post-op recovery ward but it took a while before she was brought here, so he'd wondered whether something went wrong, then her surgeon came to tell him all went well.

'I'm okay now,' she squeezed his hand and it crossed her mind that she's not as worried about the cancer as with the thought of leaving him — so if I focus on Arvis, I would fight and fight and live, if this gets bad. Oh, stop being a drama queen.

'Don't worry, darling, it just takes me a while to recover from anaesthesia.' Yes, always the terrible shakes as she wakes up, and was it really surgery pain or something else?

Nurse Mini comes around again to check blood pressure, oxygenation, the breast drain bag, and administer painkillers. No 'How's the pain?' Mini's quietly efficient and so strong as she grips her arm and holds her up when she goes for a pee. But earlier she heard her chatting in the corridor with nurse Jissmol, also Indian, who cared for her initially. Conversation whispered in their language, and Nenita heard intense inflections, of worry perhaps? India's now the second country with the highest COVID cases in the world, so how are their loved ones back in the first home? How's the pain? But tall and serious Mini is the image of power as she goes about the business of care. Mini, Warrior Angel of Care. *Mini, WAC.* Later she'll read that there are Hindu guardian angels called *devas*, "shining ones". They're deities who give living things, both human and non-human, spiritual energy that help them understand the universe and become one with it.

Mini's back and after the usual checks, she kits her up with nasal cannula and intermittent pneumatic compression. Nenita's worried. She's had surgeries before but she's never used these gears post-op. She thinks of her parents, same gears and oxygen tank after oxygen tank — 'Why the oxygen, Mini? Something wrong?'

'You'll get better quicker.' Then she checks the drain bag.

'Sorry, I have to pee again.'

She detaches the gears and helps her to the bathroom.

Nenita takes a while.

'Are you okay, can I come in?'

'It's okay, I'm okay.'

When they return to the bed, she wants to ask if her parents are okay back home in India and it occurs to her that she has no more parents to worry about. Sharp twinge in her breast, she sucks in.

'Pain?'

'A little.'

She gives her two tablets, gears her up and tucks her in.

'Mini ...'

She walks back. 'Yes?'

Are your parents okay in India?

Mini comes closer. 'Yes?'

'Oh, nothing.'

In the wee hours of the morning, the nth pee, so another joint trip to the bathroom. She's unsteady, a bit disoriented.

'I should go in with you.'

'I can manage.'

She hears Mini shifting outside as she does her thing and the drain bag slips so she quickly picks it up while trying to pull up knickers but bag falls again, so pick up but knickers she can't, so she sits back on the toilet to get her bearings, seeing her mother gasping in pain as she tried to pull up her knickers after an MRI, 'Don't worry, Mama, I'm dressing you up, see?' and as she knelt to help her, her eyes smarted, *ay*, proud and proper mother so tough and together, how this moment must feel, and she wanted to hug her but they don't really hug in the family, they're formal, they're awkward touchers, so she swallowed back all that's lachrymosal but she can't now, these tears and tears and tears, as she keeps muttering, 'When I'm better, Mama, when COVID's over, I'll come home and replant your garden —'

Mini rushes in, alarmed, and quickly picks up the bag that's fallen again. 'What's wrong, more pain?'

She keeps shaking her head through the sobbing, then finally, 'It's my mother ... she died of cancer last year ... and I — I can't pull up my knickers.'

Mini kneels down and for the first time, looks her fully on the face. 'There, there,' she says as she pulls up knickers then all of her from the toilet seat, all the while clutching the bag. 'There, there.'

Nenita reaches to flush but Mini leans over to get there first, still with arm around her, it's all very awkward, so Nenita grabs and steadies her waist to keep both of them from falling.

It flushes, finally.

Both straighten up, still holding onto each other like in an embrace and Nenita feels a strange quiver under her hand and arm, under Mini's uniform, like something's waking up, pushing out. Her eyes widen and widen in wonder, her skin too, pores welcoming this intimidatingly marvellous fluttering.

Oh … maybe feathers, maybe wings.

ODE TO JOY

Seid umschlungen Millionen! Diesen Kuß der ganzen Welt!
Be embrac'd, ye millions yonder! Take this kiss throughout the world!

— *An die Freude: Ode to Joy*, Friedrich Schiller
Adapted in *Symphony No. 9*, Ludwig van Beethoven

Always remember joy,' he mumbles from the bed.

Nenita's stopped at the door, reeled back to the nineties. It's now 2018, more than two decades later. So how does Arvis know? Maybe he's just pursuing their argument last night on how to look at the world. Or maybe this is how it sneaks in, this thing called joy. She returns to him, gives him a peck on the cheek. He's asleep again so she tiptoes out with beach towel rolled around *that history*: four streets back from their hotel, for a whole year in a flat that barely got the morning sun.

'This is why,' Robert said, peering through the blinds at the brick behind of the building next door. 'You're all blocked out from the world.'

'No sun, no good,' his wife Conchita nodded, setting the *sinigang*, a sour fish soup, on the bedside table. '*Mainit pa, kain na* — still hot, eat.'

She couldn't tell them she can't because black dogs are sitting on her chest. Her nightmare the night before and still here, furry tails curling and uncurling like snakes.

'Thank you, I'll eat later,' she said and burrowed under the sheets.

But her friends were not going to leave until she ate. They never left her throughout that year of the black dogs. Conchita had her own black dog before she met Robert, when she'd lock herself in the laundry to keep herself safe from her first husband. He believed he brought her over to Australia for a better life. He believed she owed him. He couldn't get it into his head that her family had a big rice farm in the Philippines, and still has. Even now, she can't bring herself to shop in Wollongong because she might bump into him.

She must ring them, tell them she's visiting after twenty years, perhaps have a meal. Where she stands on Osborne Park, the morning sun is chasing away the cold nip of spring. She looks out to the glittering water across the road, bunching up the towel, shaping and reshaping it. She must cross now, return to the water, but her feet won't take her any further —

A flurry from the Norfolk pine behind her and two white cockatoos calling. She turns back, spreads out the towel on the grass and sits down. They eyeball her with that quizzing look under their sulphur crests: what's with you?

Can't go into the water yet.

Is it the Tasman or the Pacific? Nenita and Arvis had that little argument last night. But it was something else that she was trying to name as they looked out to the water illumined by the lampposts of Wollongong Harbour. A something else that was trying to come into the light. But it's just stories.

The cockatoos scream, then a sudden splat — she scrambles up, there's poop on her arm. Just stories — hah! She wipes off "the protest poop". It's supposed to bring *suwerte* — luck. *Pag iniputan ka ki bayong* — if a bird poops on you, as they say in her first home. Or a trick to get her back to the water. Cocky things. They scream as she crosses Cliff Road towards Belmore Basin.

The first contact makes her shiver. Ugh, water's still wintry cold. It's morning ablution on a basin with boats, the breakwater and its lighthouse. She rubs off the smell of poop with the water rushing towards the black rock where she squats. It swirls around then rushes away, revealing dips, curves and filigrees, an intricate calligraphy etched by this ebb and flow. Water writing on land. The only time she took a dip here, she was stung by bluebottles. A place can sting but trust that it salves and saves after, if one wants to be saved.

Close by, a pelican skids through the water. Oh, the size of it, the span of wings and that unmistakable bill like a pink sword. The first time she saw one, she marvelled at its exquisite manoeuvre, every part collected to do only one task: to land. Unlike humans with multiple cares and distractions, *the pelican can*.

'Go, swim.'

She turns around. An old man in a rust jumper is staring at her under a grey cap.

'Go, swim,' he says again, no, orders.

'I—I can't —' she blurts out.

'Can't swim?'

Taken by surprise, she can only nod.

'Where you from?'

'Canberra.'

'No — where you from?'

She gets up, tempted to return the question — she hears an accent — but says, 'The Philippines, originally.'

'Ah, Filipina can't swim,' he frowns, white moustache twitching, then, 'should swim,' and smiles.

What to say. So she smiles back and he walks off, tapping his cane and shaking his head, 'Should swim, should swim.'

From the Philippine islands and can't swim. She understands the surprise, or was it censure? *Should swim.* Yes. But not yet. Or not ever? This towel is only for wiping the arm, for now. Over there, the breakwater lighthouse knows. But it's the bigger lighthouse up the hill that she bonded with which knew more. She used to run to it, from her very first flat in Australia, imagining she was doing a Virginia Woolf. She'd run, run uphill to that keeper of light, press its solid, white body with her palm and run back home. It was her vector in a place just met. She ran to touch it almost every day, as if the contact with the tower of light would keep her as upright and contained, head lit and light.

She remembers her awe standing beside it for the first time and slowly turning around to take in the view: the sweep of harbour, beach and North Wollongong against the bluish-green escarpment with Mount Keira and Mount Kembla, then behind her, the water all the way to the horizon dotted by ships ferrying coal. Years later, she'd learn from Wadi Wadi poet, Aunty Barbara, that Mount Keira is Grandmother Mountain and Mount Kembla, Grandfather Mountain, both looking after all who live and come to Wollongong, perhaps above all the non-swimmers. The land knows. So make peace with the land first before going into the water.

She walks back up to Cliff Road, along the Norfolk pines. On her first month in Australia, she stood here, looking out to the water, heart heavy and missing home. Close by, there was a young man doing the same. She felt kinship with his seaward longing, then began hearing Longfellow in her head — *A boy's will is the wind's will, / And the thoughts of youth are long, long thoughts* — but he started stripping then picking up this long, white thing and running towards the water. It was her first vision of surfers.

Oh, look, two large black birds on the lamppost, also looking out to sea — a bird's will is the wind's will — she leans over the iron railing to see better. One is roosting on the lamp that seems to sprout from the banksia foliage. Both birds are still, as if posed for examination. Acute beady eyes, white chin with a yellow patch and a sculpted beak with a tiny extended downturn, ah, like a comma at the end of a distinctively sharp face that makes her pause and ponder. She never saw them like this before, or maybe she never *really looked*.

'They're great cormorants — amazing, right?' It's a half-naked man dripping wet with a surfboard under his arm and sprinting to his car.

'Thank you for naming them,' she calls out then walks up the rise of Cliff Road where the old cannons are, set up in the 1800s because of Russian invasion scares after the Crimean War. She had her own scare at this very same spot. On her first month in Australia, a bearded man stalked her here. It was broad daylight but she was terrified because the road was deserted. His face was hanging out of his van window, calling, 'Get in, darling,' as he slowed down to her pace. Her first thought was, but I'm wearing pants and long sleeves! Then, what do I do? What if he drags me into that van? Should I run? What if this urges him to act? She picked up pace yet he kept following. 'If you don't get in, I'll just give you a kiss!'

On that same month, she had her first nightmare in Australia — in her whole life really, because she never had nightmares in the Philippines.

She couldn't get over her fear of Cliff Road, until one morning when an elderly couple stopped her at this very same spot. Both smiled and in unison said, 'Isn't it a beautiful day, love?' Love?

The endearment blew her away the first time she heard it also on that same month. She was taking the Dion's bus and nearly tripped as she got on. From the front seat, a woman with a cloud of white hair, gently asked, 'You right, love?' Love! She was righted at once. It was love that was not just an Australian expression, as she'd learn later on. It was love meant for her alone. A fleeting love that helped her find her feet quick-smart on this road, despite the fear planted by the man in the van.

Don't forget the little salvings and salvations, don't forget the kindness of place.

She goes around the corner and crosses to her first home in Australia, still clay-brick with white railings and windows, like how it was when she moved in more than two decades ago: an international postgraduate student on scholarship to write about a war back home. But the oleander is fuller now and the Norfolk beside it, taller. She remembers her thrill at recognising this bush in full pink bloom then like now. Ah, *adelfa*, what her mother had in her garden back home, *so this will feel like home*. She was about to pick a blossom, but from the second floor balcony, a voice called out, 'Don't!' It was a man, probably sixties, leaning over the white railing. 'Oleander is poisonous.' So, *adelfa* = oleander. Oleander = poison. Deceptive baby pink. The doubleness of flowers, the doubleness of place. The cautioning man, Tom, and his wife, Lynne, soon lent her their old fridge, her very first "furniture" and as thank-you, she cooked them *adobo*, a chicken stew from home. Her neighbours felt sorry for her: the newly arrived student had only a suitcase. But soon, she bought a coffee table, two cushions and a mattress from a second hand shop and made a home.

It was here where she had her first nightmare after the Cliff Road scare: there's a man in the lounge room, a dark cloud over his face so all she can see is from his neck down, he's about to enter her bedroom. A scream gets caught in her throat.

The nightmare kept recurring after a sticky work issue. By then, she had begun tutoring at university. Outraged by how she had marked his assignment, a student "revised" a local paper's interview of her about the thesis she was writing on the war back home and posted it around the campus. The "new" article still had her photo but the words were changed, now with race, sex and culture ridicule embedded. Someone advised that she avoid walking home at night and this scared her. A formal complaint against the student was filed and an ethics committee hearing followed. Two of her students, bless them, testified that they heard him boast about his game plan — 'she did it to my work, I'll do it to hers!' He brought his father who acted as his lawyer cross-examining this foreign tutor on how she had wrongly marked his son's assignment. The silent ethics committee listened to the aggrieved son and father who waved the marked assignment quoting the 'unfair comments' from it.

The nightmares got worse after that. She'd be screaming in the dream but only an anguished moan would come out, waking her. So she began running to the lighthouse to clear the nightmare fog the next day. She began learning how to swim at the university pool to beat the sense of drowning, on land. 'Get physical, get strong,' someone advised her. She took swimming lessons even in winter.

She found her first winter very cold — 'malipoton!' An Australian surfer, who she married a few years later, learned this exclamation in her language because it was her mantra throughout that winter. 'Breathe with me, imagine a burning hearth within you,' he'd say, holding her close. Heart as hearth, and she'd start warming up. 'Keep breathing and she'll be apples.' It became his own mantra when the chill of homesickness or anxiety and that sneaky loneliness overtook her day sometimes.

Suddenly a crow calls from up the Norfolk pine — like a baby's cry, as if it has been left in the woods like in those old stories. Each time, it's not her ear that picks up crow but her nape then her spine as it flies down, each vertebra like a piano key playing it all the way down to her coccyx. Loneliness is primeval. It calls again before flying off and the cry sits in her bone momentarily but dissipates as she walks around the front garden.

Ah, they're still here: the ash tree, the succulents, the cana lilies, orange fiery as ever, and the frangipani. She walks to the end of the empty carpark where once she tested fruit that looked familiar. The bush had red blooms and the fruit was as velvety as the leaves, with a deep-pink heart like the guavas back home. It was sweet and tasted like flowers.

It's no longer here. In its place, a concrete fence.

A Hyundai is backing to where she stands so she steps aside. The door opens and two girls, about six and eight, alight and stare at her. The older girl is carrying a bag with a beach towel sticking out, and the younger one has a blue and pink swim ring around her waist.

Nenita smiles. 'Going for a swim?'

Both nod and the older girl points to the towel over her shoulder, 'You too?' and she nods back, saying, 'Later.'

The younger girl turns the inflated ring round and round her waist. 'Do you like my donut? It's new.'

'It's not a donut, it's a lifesaver ring,' says the older one.

'Can we help you?' A young woman, maybe mum, asks as she gets off the car. Under a red hijab, her beaming face signals "friend here".

She beams back. 'I used to live here, in the nineties.'

'Oh? My father lives here.'

'It's a good place,' she says.

'It's beautiful, so close to the beach.'

'Let's go, please, please.' The girls grab mum's hand. 'We wanna swim now!'

'I've to pick up something first upstairs,' she pulls them towards the building porch, smiling at her. 'Ah, these girls, so impatient — have a nice day.'

She hears the scamper of little feet going up the second floor. Her floor, a long time ago. There were no children in the building then and the neighbours kept pretty much to themselves, except Tom and Lynne who let her use their fridge throughout the two years that she lived here. She lived in a total of nine flats in Wollongong, moving all the time, before she finally went to Canberra. And strangely birds followed her, or she followed birds. Always, there was a bird encounter, inspiring or presaging something.

She walks away from the oleander and recalls how she heard a crow at her bedroom window at midnight all those years ago. But it was only her crying.

Now she crosses Bourke to Kembla Street where the corner bungalow still stands, its white frangipanis and Australian flag rising above the high fence as they did before. A few strides away, the cream house with the April Blush camellia beginning to flower. It was one of the delights of her run: to slow down and admire this sculpted bush blushing all over. But the greater delight, awe really, was in autumn-to-winter when the flowers shed petals that formed a pink carpet around the roots. An exquisite passing that made her stop, be still. That made her want to kneel. But winters later, she saw something else: petals suiciding.

She veers towards Corrimal Street, crossing it to one of the early block of flats built in Wollongong. That was what her neighbours, Scottish May and Dutch Helga, told her. They sort-of took care of her, worried about 'this wee Filipina', including her hand-washed laundry on the balcony dripping on the cars below. Her flat was on the top floor, like theirs. Then there was the ever-smiling Estonian Rasmus who lived a floor below them. He wore a grey ponytail and had a ruddy face — 'because he drinks every afternoon after work at BHP,' Helga whispered to her at one time. 'Aye, but he was very handsome before, lass, like a Viking prince,' May joined in. 'He's very quiet,' was her response. 'Because he knows little English,' Helga explained, proud that she could speak English even when she was still in Holland. And there were two blonde and statuesque Serbians, a brother and sister that made her gawk in the lift: how beautiful! 'From *that war*,' Helga reckoned. 'Hope they're fine,' May worried, and even more so about uni student Denise from Dubbo two floors down — 'that lass is losin' weight, goin' for long walks after dinner, if she eats, *nae guid*.' And Helga rescued the key, thank God, that a Chinese student forgot, stuck on his letterbox outside the building.

This is Australia: a mix of cultures in one building where she now belonged, and May and Helga made sure of this. They were always onto her case, giving advice at every turn. *Sticky beaks*. The first time she heard the label, she imagined poor winged things with beaks getting snagged wherever they flew or roosted, on trees and flowers and wires and roofs, and their beaks got stuck together too so they couldn't eat or sing. Her mind worked that way then, when she was just getting accustomed to the strange local turns of phrase that she grew to love. Sticky beaks: a pejorative for those nosey and meddling ones. But what if there was no sticky-beaking in a neighbourhood? Then you'll have the body of a woman getting found in a flat weeks after she died alone, as the TV would report later on.

Eighty-year old May, her beloved sticky beak, took her under her wing. She found it difficult to "hear" her Scottish burr correctly or comprehend her occasional slang, but they managed to grow a friendship. May used to come around the corner from her flat to her door, hands behind her back, conspiratorially whispering, 'I got somethin' for ye, lass.' Treacle scones, freshly baked. Sometimes they'd have some for afternoon tea with her best china and stories.

'Yer a very wee lass, eat more,' she put another scone on her saucer. 'And more jam and cream — we'll have to grow ye.'

'Thanks, May, this is beautiful.'

'Scone or saucer?'

She laughed. 'Both.'

'That's Royal Doulton antique, lass, gift from my mistress in London, aye, was housekeeper there — and those wee dancers too,' she pointed to a pair of porcelain ballerinas on the wall's hanging shelf. 'And my eldest son yonder.' She sipped her tea, eyes on a black and white photo framed in silver beside the ballerinas. 'Come, say hello. Braw, my lad.' Braw indeed, handsome with smiling eyes. He's beside a spectacular succulent with two sprouts longer than the rest, trailing like green snakes to halfway down the floor.

'Is that real?'

'Course, lass. Watch chain, it's called. Wee plant when I bought it,' and whispers, '*Crassula Muscosa*,' then finished proudly, 'I know the scientific name.'

'I've never seen it this long.'

She ran a finger on one of the chains, crooning, 'Bonnie thing.'

'Like a snake.' She was directed to touch it too. 'So, so long.'

'Aye, grew it for years, lass.'

'Green thumb.'

She smiled and picked up her son's photo. 'Robert, Robbie. Very kind, my lad, ready to help. Guid man.'

'He lives in Wollongong?'

'He died. Work accident.'

'Oh, I'm so sorry, I'm, I …' she fumbled, sorrier that she thought him alive because of Mary's present tense even if he'd died over twenty years ago.

There was a reprieve from nightmares in this building. Then she married her 'surfer man', as May called him. Charming Frank who travelled the world for work and sometimes took her on his trips for holidays. They were happy times. She was not alone, she was sharing a life. He read and gave advice on her thesis, though sometimes she squirmed when he remarked, 'What kind of English is this!' Or, worse, 'Who wrote this shit?' He introduced her to Jimi Hendrix, Leonard Cohen and Wim Wenders. He made her see Australia and beyond. But his gaze was always seaward and his will, the wind's will, always going elsewhere except home. They never lived together. He bought the flat that she rented and his surfboard lived with her.

'Ye can't sleep with a surfboard, can ye, lassie?' May once asked. So she explained that her husband is "a guid man" and sometimes husband and wife just happen to love differently. But at night, she'd cry herself to sleep. When she could sleep. Loneliness does your heart in, then it does your mind in.

The water made it easier. 'Keep swimming, keep working. Work saves us from the abyss,' Frank advised on the phone when the crying overextended. She was grateful for the long phone calls and his wise insights assuring her that she'll be apples. She was teaching full-time by then, and work, more so her students, normalised life. With them, she felt together, focused. They were her children. Frank did not want children and his travels were overextending. The marriage was fraying, or she was fraying. She continued to run, running away to god-knows-where then running home to no one. On one run, she nearly tripped over a driftwood which she took home and plonked on the dining table to mull over on her regular solo meals.

'It's very —' May could not find the word to describe the sea-weathered branch that seemed to be perpetually writhing. 'Like it's sufferin',' she shook her head at her found animal. For that was how it began to look after a week of dining with it: a driftwood that wriggles and squirms of its own accord.

'It's an animal, May — look,' she tried to make it stand on one of its curves but it kept falling.

'Uhmm … Rasmus can help ye. Guid with his hands.'

Through May's intervention, Rasmus fixed the animal, upright on a piece of wood that he fashioned as a stand.

'Alive,' he whispered, tracing it with his large, callused hand from the sharpest tips of the wood, a pair of sprouting 'Horns,' and finger sliding down to a knot with a jagged piece sticking out, 'Tongue,' then down, 'Neck,' stopping on a bump there, 'Back', and skidding further down to where it bulges, 'Stomach,' gliding all the way to its twisted length glued on the stand and rising again, a writhing in mid-air finally curving down to a sharply serrated 'Tail.'

Then he smiled at her and May, ruddy face glowing.

The driftwood had become a dragon.

May was unconvinced. 'It's a snake with horns, lass, sufferin'.'

She cooked Rasmus a meal after that. She recalls how she came down to his flat with the plate and knocked for a long time, and how she could hear foreign choral singing inside. When he finally opened the door, the music burst forth.

'Here, Rasmus, it's *adobo*, a chicken stew from my first home, and rice — thank you again for — for the —' she can't say dragon, can she?

He took the plate, beckoning for her to come in.

She hesitated. His face was flushed and there were was a finished six-pack of VB on the table and another just opened.

211

The music from the cassette recorder beside it made up for his silence.

She stepped in but stayed close to the door, which he shut. Then drunk grin on his face, he pointed to the wall beside her. 'My girlfriend.'

She shouldn't have entered. Girlfriend was a large poster of a blonde, tanned and voluptuous woman in skimpy blue bikini. She stepped back, thinking the door handle is only a grab away.

Smiling, he beckoned her to the wall across.

Should she?

He smiled again, kept beckoning, and she found herself moving closer to an old, black and white photo of a snow-clad city with spires bisecting a grey sky and a bird flying overhead.

'Home. Tallin. Estonia.'

She began to relax.

'You?'

'Legazpi. Philippines.'

He beamed then began to run his finger on the skyline, following the snow-dusted roofs, the bare treetops, then up the tallest spire, as the music from beside the VBs soared and soared, until he reached the bird.

'Free.'

This time, she smiled back. 'Great music.'

'*Ode to Joy* — Beethoven.'

After that encounter, he always smiled and tipped his head at her whenever and wherever they met. A polite gesture, as if taking off a hat, or an affirmation of kinship: we both come from somewhere.

It's only now when she fully comprehends that anxious but mesmeric moment of tracing the skyline of a city. How she wishes she were more receptive to someone sharing his home, and perhaps kinder if not knowing. Rasmus from Tallin, and back at the hotel, her second husband Arvis from Riga. Cities that went through horrific years of occupation under the old USSR. Free now, indeed.

If you want to be free, if you want to be saved, just work. Or swim. Or fly.

She moved out with the dragon when her marriage finally ended and bought a cassette of Beethoven's *Symphony Number 9*. The dragon became her mascot and she played Beethoven, but only that joyful end bit and only a few times, favouring silence in her new flat three streets away.

Should she also visit *that place*? Or should she just go for that swim?

She crosses Corrimal Street, remembering the thought that kept her sane as she packed up her flat then: love is kind but the lover or the beloved can be unkind, a human flaw, and accepting this is the kindest thing that one can leave and live with. She was the one who left the marriage, because it was saner to be lonely alone.

A crow flies overhead, crossing too, but silently.

She sensed it was time to leave the first time it happened. She thought she was having a heart attack, gasping for breath and heart on a marathon after an hour of crying in the bathroom. The doctor named it: panic. It intensified in enclosed spaces. She was terrified it would happen while she was teaching. The worst episode was on a train coming home from visiting Frank in Sydney, after he suggested that she go home because he couldn't work with her around. When the train stopped at Otford station, her breathing went haywire. She debated whether she'd handle the rest of the trip or whether she'd just get off. She got off and phoned Lucy to please, please pick her up and take her home. Ah, Lucy, her Santa Lucia. That night, her American friend Lucy drove all the way from Coogee to Otford to save her. Lucy with whom she baked orange cake, 'and don't forget the almonds,' and sang along to Leonard Cohen during the happier times before they had a falling out. Lucy who would later die of a brain tumour. She knew loneliness too, and well. Indeed loneliness does your head in.

From Corrimal to Kembla now, then walking up and down Church Street — but she can't find it! But why this meticulous return? Because her father died and her mother's ill? Thus the urge to look it in the eye. Kindly, maybe.

After another slow inspection, she recognises the three-storey brick building with two workmen on the ground floor balcony.

'Excuse me,' she calls out from the street.

The young man in orange fluoro jacket turns from his box of tools.

'I used to live here — can I come in?'

'Sure.'

Yes, the flat that barely got the morning sun. She lays a hand on the door handle and remembers how it often got stuck, so she had to keep it oiled. She should have oiled herself too. Behind this door, she got stuck in an exhausting, sunless rut. It was busier at uni and she couldn't sleep most nights. But the next day and the next, work saved her, kept her on her feet. Her students energised her, gave her moments of affirmation and pleasure, they were family. On one of her tiredest mornings, with not a wink the night before, she arrived at her office surprised to find a vase of white flowers from a bush outside. The next day, flowers again, freshly picked. Who could it be? A student, a work colleague? It was the cleaner. She said it was a pity to have an empty vase sitting on her bookcase. Teresa, her Italian "flower angel".

Around that time, she started sporting a colourful bandana around her head and brow, looking like a pirate-teacher with plenty of derring-do. Because she had begun picking her face, "fixing" her acnes at 3 a.m. It was the hour when she felt most

214

wretched, staring at her alarm clock that would ring in three hours time, so best to get up and begin her facial surgery until her brow bled. The bandana hid her handiwork.

On her work desk, the dragon writhed.

'Sure yer ookay, lass?' May asked. 'Ye look very tired, but that head cover's fetching … uhmm … but ye haven't gone Muslim, have ye?'

She went for one more afternoon tea with May. Her scones were a comfort and she served two types of jam, strawberry and apricot, and they broke into song as she told stories about working in London — now that's some memory.

'O Mary, this London's a wonderful sight
Where people are digging by day and by night —'

Her soprano harmonised with her alto, Scottish burr and Filipino accent counterpointing, but the Muslim question rendered the afternoon somewhat off-key. May had confided she was surprised to see 'a covered lady' at Woolworth's last week. She'd never seen the likes of her before.

'Head and face covered … uhmm … her little lass was covered too, but not the face, thank ye, God.'

'It's their culture, May.'

'I smiled at her, lass, but she looked away, unfriendly-like.' She sipped her tea thoughtfully, then added, 'TV said there'll be more of them coming, because of that war over there … uhmm … I'm sad for them, but …' and she took another sip. 'Yer Christian, lass, aren't ye?' then offered her another scone. 'And how's yer new flat?'

The scone felt dry in her mouth, and she didn't come for the next afternoon tea, and the next. TV was full of Pauline Hanson scaring Australia, that the country would be 'swamped by Asians.' So she was anxious where this conversation with May might lead the next time, or perhaps, dear kind May had disappointed her? She wondered: is kindness "kindness" if it's selective? Who deserves it, who does not? Now as she walks past the workmen on the balcony, the wondering returns but turned on its head. Wasn't she as selective, giving up on kindness that succoured her because of a difference in worldview? Wasn't she who had unkindly judged a friend?

Be gentle, heart, as you recall.

As she steps out of the building, she sees it: bird on a wire. Magpie or currawong? Gracefully balanced like before. That was what she hoped for then. To find her feet steady on something so thin, so tenuous. Grace in balance. Something to try to learn.

'Found your old flat?' the man in fluoro jacket asks.

'Yes, thanks.' Perhaps the question should be: found your feet, found yourself?

Old flat, old story, old self. Did these really happen?

In the sunless bedroom in there, insomnia was torture but sleeping was worse. Because the nightmares came. Bizarrely, blatantly literal: three black dogs sitting on her chest. Before she even knew about "the black dog syndrome". The horror of such black weight. She couldn't breathe, she couldn't get up. But outside of the nightmare was "daymare", as she called it then. In the morning, she could not get out of bed. Hers was a tiredness so depleting. She began to miss work. It could no longer save her. She began bleeding from every hidden orifice. The obvious one was after a session of picking acnes; she stopped only when she drew blood. Then the maddeningly itchy spots all over her body like red coins with no currency except on her tormented skin. Her mother dreamt about this, she'd tell her years later. It was her own nightmare: on her daughter's face, blood-red rubies. The red spots itched at night, with no relief until the morning. They grew bigger on her scalp and arms, like red islands — dermatitis then psoriasis, the doctor named them. But the worst was the sorrow. She never thought it could be that deep, she never seemed to hit rock bottom. Never thought weeping could be unstoppably foreign. It was as if someone or something was singing in a language she could not understand. She wanted to shut its mouth, but she couldn't see it.

Maybe sorrow is a bird too, foreign, invisible.

Then she began considering ways on how to kill herself, at 3 a.m.

She crosses Church Street, takes in the light-ochre brick building for one last time. Here, she was undone. And here, she was succoured. Her friends, Robert and Conchita, used to leave a full meal at her doorstep when she wouldn't open the door. She couldn't let them in on the full story. She couldn't say she was terrified she was growing mad. But she told two friends interstate about her 3 a.m. "considerations": Jacquie and Helen who made her promise to ring should "they" come, at any time. So she'd ring Jacquie in the early hours of the morning and wake her two-month old baby. Jacquie came to Wollongong once, when she was still married and Frank was on a trip, to care for her after a surgery. She cooked her 'Mum's soup' with sweet anise and medicinal herbs. And Teresa once invited her to come to Christmas lunch. 'I'm cooking *quaglia*, quail wrapped in bacon — *delizioso!*' Strange that she remembers the comfort food so well. Like her first taste of olive bread in a Sydney restaurant where her Faculty Dean and her husband took her for a meal after a book launch. She suspected the treat was strategically organised after Sheila, her secretary, relayed an odd phone call. It was one of those non-stop weeping days when she'd go through her phone book wondering, who can she ring? She rang her Faculty.

When *it* was finally named as Chronic Fatigue Syndrome, CFS, her Dean facilitated a sick leave for a whole semester. She remembers her now, and warm olive bread dipped in olive oil with balsamic vinegar. Perhaps it was HFS, Heart Fatigue Syndrome. So: feed the stomach to feed the heart.

'We can try Prozac,' her psychologist suggested but she refused to be medicated. 'My head's already messed up, I can't mess with it any further — is there another way?'

'When your body starts getting better, your head will follow. So take care of your body, do something physical, get strong.'

She took heed of the advice and added her own: *You must want to be saved.* She forced herself to get out of bed, open the door, get out of the flat, get some sun, and walk back to the water. Slowly her dragon began to look different, no longer writhing but bristling, horns sharper, puncturing the air. Perhaps it was her mascot that conjured its reptilian cousin in her office when she finally returned to work. One late afternoon, a long, olive-browny thing zipped from the bottom of her bookcase, over Neruda's book of poems towards her desk, grazing her feet. A snake! After a while, from the opposite bookcase, it poked its head, stuck out its tongue, testing the air or probably testing the company. Is she friendly? It was a garden skink. She called it Neruda. It lived in her office for a week, perhaps a welcome for her return or an assurance that she's out of the deep now and solidly on *terra firma.*

She's back on Cliff Road. The Tasman is a sheet of silver and along the beach, the runners, amblers, baby strollers and dog walkers seem to glow. She walks down to their path. Time to return to the water.

It was the water that returned her to some equanimity during that breakdown. Now, she can name it: break-down. She steered clear of the word before. Whenever anyone spoke it, she'd hear the vicious snap at "break", then see a body hitting the ground face down. Frank named it too, called it her "nervy". The word grated on her.

Past the beach kiosk now where a young family are finishing their fish and chips. Baby toddles towards the huddle of squawking seagulls on the grass. Mother runs after baby, seagulls fly, one roosting on the head of the statue of a surf lifesaver poised to run to the water, to save. He wasn't here before. Nenita watches as mother picks up baby struggling to return to the birds. She wanted so much to have children.

It's time to return to the rock pool.

She remembers practising her strokes in that pool after a run, and she'd feel renewed. Because all runs lead back to water, she tells herself now, however far we stray from it. When we drink, wash or have a dip, we're returning to who we've always been before there was even land. We're flowing back to the amniotic. No wonder the rock pool always received her with such expectation and ease all those years ago, as if it had known her before she even knew herself. The trust of water. But she had to learn how to trust it back.

'Why are you always swimming that way?' A pool regular stopped her laps once, taking off her goggles to query her better.

'I'm not getting in your way, am I?' She always practised her free style along the edge of the pool, swimming only its width so her feet could still touch bottom.

'I mean you're not swimming across,' the woman said.

'I — I'm scared of the deep end ...'

'Come swim with me, I'm Debbie,' she said, leading her with slowed-down strokes to the other side and before the return swim saying, 'She'll be right.'

And she was. She often wondered why "she'll be apples" or "she'll be right" means "it will be all right". Maybe it's women who are often not all right, or maybe it's women who know how to make it right. She must ask Debbie whose great-great- grandmother came from England on the first fleet. But a month later, her swimming buddy had a change of heart about her rightness.

'You missed a swim yesterday.'

'I was in Sydney —'

'Visiting?'

'No, joined the Free East Timor rally —'

'What?' Debbie looked perplexed, then hurt, then angry. 'Why would you?'

'It was the anniversary of the Dili massacre —'

'Stupid girl!' And she launched into a fervid sermon about loyalty that ended with, 'My country is Australia, I want to protect our own freedom, our democracy!'

'But what does supporting East Timor's freedom got to do with hurting your democracy, Debbie?'

It was like they'd slapped each other. Debbie never spoke to her again and she stopped venturing in the deep end. Both of them made sure they always swam away from each other. Kind Debbie helping her with her strokes versus unkind Debbie excoriating her "disloyalty"? Too simple, too fixed. And what about her own outrage? Like people, kindness is more complex, watery, ever-shifting in its impurities.

Ah, seaweed! She stops walking, oh, this smell, breathes in deeply, holding it all in. She always stopped at this spot during a run, breathing it all in when the rocks below had turned green with freshly washed-away seaweed, like now. But days later, she sped past this same spot, holding her breath, because of the stench of rotting weed with huddles of seagulls feasting on maggots and flies feeding on decay. The kindness of place depends on the state of the place, or the state of one's place?

After this hillock hiding the view, the rock pool. Close. Her breathing picks up. Relax, she'll be right.

More than twenty years ago, when she came here that last time, was it to swim?

She slows down, stops.

Or was it to fulfil the 3 a.m. "consideration"?

She leans against the hillock. Breathe in, breathe out. Maybe best to turn back. After a while, she finds her feet again. There's the pool now and a red swimming cap, no, it's a hijab. It's the young mum she met earlier seated on the pool's cemented edge. Then a yellow dot zips across the water to the other end: ah, older daughter. Close to mum, the younger one cheers.

'I can do that too!'

'No, Noora, not yet.'

She hears the argument better as she takes the stairs from the path down to the beach where the pool is.

'You've got your new donut, don't you like it now?'

'But I can swim out there too, mum, I know I can.'

'When you're better at it.'

She walks over to them. 'Hi again.'

'Oh, hello,' mum smiles. 'Good to see you again.'

'I do like your donut,' she says to the girl in frilly pink bathers, and mum nods.

'See, the lady likes it — by the way, I'm Fatema,' and offers her hand.

She takes it, warm. 'And I'm Nenita.'

'Swimming?' the girl asks.

'This is my daughter Noora, and over there, Sara, my eldest,' pointing to the girl in yellow bathers leaning against the rock at the other end.

'Swimming?' Noora asks again, taking off the swim ring from around her waist and setting it on the cemented edge before paddling away.

'Uhmm … yes,' she answers. 'Maybe.'

'Come back here, Noora,' Fatema scolds, holding out the ring, 'And put this back on,' but Noora keeps paddling away.

'I'm better now, Mum, look!' and she moves further away in free style.

'Noora!' Fatema screams. Mum has now stepped into the water, frantically holding out the ring. 'Noora, come back!'

From the other side of the pool, a zipping yellow swoops up the pink frills and the two girls are beside Mum in no time, giggling.

'Don't ever do that again, Noora!'

'It's okay, Mum, she can swim,' Sara puts an arm around mum's waist, sitting her back down on the edge. Her sister is still giggling.

'These girls, these girls,' Fatema wrings her hands. She's wet from the waist down and she's not in bathers.

'Oh, look, *Jiddo*, *Jiddo*!' Noora rushes up the metal steps, Sara close behind, waving, 'Grandpa, Gramps!' They run off to meet the old man in rust jumper and grey cap, slowly descending the stairs with his cane and a picnic basket.

'It's my father — oh, these girls,' she sighs but proudly looks at them, now relieving *Jiddo*, Grandpa, of the basket.

'Ah …' Nenita smiles and sits beside her. 'I met your dad, early this morning actually, at Belmore Basin.'

'You did?'

'He scolded me. He said I should swim, sounded like an order — *should swim.*'

'That's my father.' Fatema goes quiet, then, 'My mother drowned …'

'Oh, I'm so, so sorry, I —'

'Thanks.'

A soft wind fills in the pause.

'Actually,' Nenita breathes out, 'I almost drowned. Here.'

Fatema grabs her hand.

'But a boy saved me.'

She stares at her, wide-eyed.

'Over there in the deep end. He was swimming by, so I called out, "I lost my strokes," and he just swam over, put out his hand and said, "Hold my hand and we'll swim together."'

Behind them, the girls' laughter and Grandpa's murmurs ebb and flow.

'He was probably nine … didn't get his name.'

'We —' Fatema starts, breathing hard. 'We were in a boat. From Indonesia … there were too many of us … it sank.'

A small wave breaks against the end of the pool, then another.

'I was twelve, couldn't swim.'

The girls are asking what Grandpa brought them.

'My father could only save one of us.'

'Fatema, come, I have snack.' His cane clicks behind them, closer, then stops. 'Ah, the Filipina.'

'Yes. Should swim,' Nenita laughs, discreetly wiping her tears before turning around. 'Hello, sir.'

'This is Nenita, *Baba*,' but Fatema can't turn around yet.

Fatema's *Baba*: Father. But she hears something else, something more from home: almost interrogative in tone, the final "a" sliding up, songlike, ending in a glottal stop. *Babâ*: the more affectionate truncation of *padabà*, beloved, even if love can never be truncated. Not even by the water.

'Mum, Mum, I told *Jiddo* I swam — there!'

'Gramps brought lamb *samoon*, Mum, and humus and falafel and *kleicha* and my favourite *sharbat*, ohhh, yummy!'

'We eat and if Filipina lady like, she eat with us.'

To be saved by food. It's fated. The Iraqi family left her sated. All she could say was a profuse thank you. But her gratitude felt short, not enough to share around from the Philippines to Australia Iraq Legazpi Wollongong to Osborne Cliff Road Corrimal to Dundee London Tallin Riga Serbia Holland China East Timor to Sydney

223

Canberra to flats harbour home lovers strangers friends to camellia frangipani guava to Frank Dean Sheila Teresa to Cohen Woolf Wenders Hendrix Beethoven breakwater rock pool to Fatema Sara Noora *Jiddo* to swimming boy driftwood dragon skink Neruda to Robbie May Crassula Muscosa Debbie Helga banksia lighthouse Longfellow Norfolks ash tree *padabà* to Jacquie cockatoos Helen cormorant Rasmus crow Arvis seagulls Ron Carina currawong magpie to oleander cana lilies to doctors psychologists Tom Lynne Lucy Aunty Barbara to students surfers to Mum's soup *samoon sinigang* scones *adobo* humus *quaglia* olive bread falafel *kleicha sharbat* tea to Wadi Wadi Grandmother and Grandfather Mountain to rock beach seaweed bluebottles maggots flies to land water wind sun and to all yet unseen, unnamed but rendering air alive, like her —

> '*Seid umschlungen Millionen!*
> *Diesen Kuß der ganzen Welt!*'
> 'Be embrac'd, ye millions yonder!
> Take this kiss throughout the world!'

How to feel, what to think as Beethoven plays in her head, and what to say here now in the water, and why this strangest crying that feels like home. Shhh … listen. As primeval as loneliness.

Name it.

Joy. *Freude*.

Sounds close to "Free".

It laps around her, like silk.

Now open arms, give in.

Let it lift you.

Eyes to sky.

For a start.

Float.

ACKNOWLEDGEMENTS

To artsACT for funding the research and creative development of this book and De La Salle University Manila for the visiting fellowship that furthered this development;

To Uncle Freddy Corpus, The Hon. Linda Burney, Annie Parmentier, George Roberts, Werner Rares and Stephen Rares, Lydia Nichols, Candido Iban, Nicolas and Amparo Bobis, Jennifer Ackerman (*The Bird Way*, 2020; *The Genius of Birds*, 2016); Dr Stephen Parnis (*Q & A program*, ABC TV, 6 April 2020); Peter Sutton (*Iridescence: The Play of Colours*, 2015; 'Iridescence', 1988); Bruce Pascoe (*Dark Emu*, 2014); Emily Dickinson (*Selected Poems 1830–1886*, 1959); Heinrich Heine (*Wit, Wisdom and Pathos, From the Prose of Heinrich Heine, With a Few Pieces from the "Book of Songs"*, 1888); Federico Garcia Lorca ("Gacela de la Muerte Oscura": "Gacela of the Dark Death", *Selected Poems*, trans. J.L. Gili, 1960); Ellen DeGeneres (owl mug); Friedrich Schiller and Ludwig van Beethoven (*An die Freude*, 1785: *Ode to Joy*, trans. William F. Wertz; *Symphony No. 9*, 1824), from whose insights, words, music and lives the stories grew;

To Faiqah Faizol, Aliah Husaimi, the staff and cleaners at the Australian Parliament House, Kristine Sumugat, Phillip Quimpo, Mayor Wilbert Ariel Igoy, Jeff Darvin Igoy Repedro, Dinanara Nepomuceno Molina, Mendel Jay Iscala, Angela Powell-Dep and the Broome Historical Museum, Kevin Puertollano, Ellen Puertollano, Sarah Keenan and the Sisters of Saint John of God Heritage Centre, and Andrew Wood whose indispensable assistance helped my understanding of the context of these stories;

To the knowledge bearers that enriched the writing — 'Fairy-wrens Sing Secret Passwords to Their Unborn Chicks', *BirdNote* 2013, 2018/2019 (Todd Peterson, Mary McCann); *Are you my mother?* (PD Eastman); 'Mama' (Connie Francis version); 'My Banishment to the East', Diary entries, 8 Dec 1942–26 Jan 1945 (Erika Mannheimer Oppenheimer); 'The Nineteen Martyrs of Aklan', *Ibajay Homepage*, 1997 (Plaridel E. Seneris); *Re-imagining Australia. Voices of Indigenous Australians of Filipino Descent*, 2016 (Deborah Ruiz Wall with Christine Choo); 'Emerging Consciousness: Acknowledging the Past and Embracing the Future', *KASAMA* 22.3, 2008 (Deborah Ruiz Wall and Dee Hunt); 'Heriberto Zarcal. The First Filipino-Australian', *Navigating Boundaries. The Asian Diaspora in Torres Strait*, 2004 (Reynaldo C. Ileto); *Deep Diving & Submarine Operations. A Manual for Deep Sea Divers and Compressed Air Workers*, 1951 (Robert H. Davis); 'Lustre', *Griffith Review 47*, Jan 2015 (Sarah Yu, Bart Pigram, Maya Shioji); *Lustre. Pearling in Australia*, 2018 (Eds. Tanya Edwards and Sarah Yu); *Selling Sex: A Hidden History of Prostitution*, 2007 and 'The History of Female Prostitution in Australia', 1994 (Raelene Frances); 'Kimberley Women: Their Experiences of Making a Remote Locality Home', PhD thesis, Edith Cowan University, 2004 (Elaine Rabbit); 'Crossing the Great Divide: Australia and Eastern Indonesia', *Macassan History and Heritage: Journeys, Encounters & Influences*, 2013 (Anthony Reid); *Migration Revolution: Philippine Nationhood and Class Relations in a*

Globalized Age, 2014 (Filomeno V. Aguilar Jr); *Western Australian Museum* website; 'Women Recognised for Love and Death in Broome Pearling', ABC, 29 Nov 2010 (Vanessa Mills); *Old Broome. Five Great Stories that Bring Broome's History to Life*, Documentary film, 2006 (Goolarri Media Enterprises); *Sisters, Pearls and Mission Girls*, Documentary film, 2002 (Rebel Films); on "Pearl Diver Myth", *Canberra Times*, 1952; *Forty Fathoms Deep*, 1937 (Ion Idriess); 'Giant Crocodile Captured in Australia to Stop It Going to Town', *Sydney Reuters*, 10 July 2018 (Paulina Duran); *Sharing Our Stories Around the Dining Table: Aboriginal and Filipino Women*, March 2007 (Aunty Betty Little, Aunty Ali Golding, Aunty Sylvia Scott, Aunty Joyce Ingram, Bet Dalton, Miguela de Lara, Maria Elena Ang, Deborah Wall); *Letters to a Young Poet*, 1929 (Rainer Maria Rilke); 'Army Medic's Journeys End in Afghanistan', *NPR*, 7 May 2006 (Steve Zind); Tom Stone and Rose Loving; *The Quiet American*, 1955 (Graham Greene); 'The Raven', 1845 (Edgar Allan Poe); 'Tasmanian Wildlife Carers Express Concerns Over Road Kill', *Mercury*, 26 Dec 2014 (Roger Hanson); a moment with Dolores Herrero, Oct 2009; 'Today', 1964 (Randy Spark); *Owly*, 1982 (Mike Thaler); 'A Review of Accounts of Luminosity in Barn Owls *Tyto Alba*', 2006, *The Owl Pages* (Fred Silcock); 'Strange Fruit', 1959 rendition (Billie Holiday, Songwriter: Abel Meeropol); 'Skyline Pigeon' and 'Sweet Painted Lady' (Elton John); works of Virginia Woolf, Jimi Hendrix, Leonard Cohen, Wim Wenders; *Uluru Statement From the Heart*, 2017; *The Indigenous Peoples of the Philippines*, 2007 (National Commission on Indigenous Peoples); 'Dying Traditions of the Agta in Bicol', *The Manila Times*, 31 Oct 2017 (Frank Penoñes, Jr); 'Philippines' Quarantine Restrictions Based on Age Slammed', *The Star*, 30 April 2020; '2003 Statistics on Philippine Protected Areas and Wildlife Resources' (Department of Environment and Natural Resources); 'Mayon Volcano Natural Park', 20 March 2015 (Philippines National Commission's submission to UNESCO); 'Wild Birds of Bicol'

FB Posts; '10 Most Common Urban Birds', *eBON, Official Newsletter of the Wild Bird Club of the Philippines*, 3 July 2013 (Maia Tañedo); 'Mayon Volcano and Its Frequent Eruptions' http://factsanddetails.com/southeast-asia/Philippines/sub5_6h/entry-3922.html; *Birds of the World* (The Cornell Lab of Ornithology), *Canberra Birds* (Canberra Ornithologists Group); 'Urban Bird Watchers' Guide to Hobart', *Australian Geographic*, 15 Feb 2017 (Ellen Rykers); *Birdlife Australia* website; 'Stone the Crows! Could Corvids be Australia's Smartest Export?' *The Conversation*, 27 Jan 2012 (Stephen Debus); 'Guardian Angels in Hinduism', 27 April 2019 (Whitney Hopler); 'My Lost Youth' (Henry Wadsworth Longfellow), Lizz Murphy, Kathy Kituai, Jennifer Martiniello; Aunty Barbara Nicholson; Amanda Gorely, Jennifer Byrne; *Tiya* Baby, Uncle Rey and all the kind aunties and uncles; Mama Ola, Karola, Maria and the wise elders of this world, and all those met by accident or grace that illumined story and storyteller;

To Gail Jones, Jennifer Ackerman, Lucy Neave, Alvin B. Yapan, Elizabeth Lisners, Reinis Kalnins, Anne Brewster, Lea Bobis-Torres, Rolando Bobis, Friederike Krishnabhakdi-Vasilakis, Subhash Jaireth, Faiqah Faizol, Jana Berzins, Lizz Murphy, Kathy Kituai, Jennifer Martiniello, Paz Verdades-Santos, Cecilia Quiros Cañiza, Uncle Freddy Corpus, Annie Parmentier, Linda Nichols, Stephen Parnis, Peter Sutton, Julieann Solway, Penny Vethanayagam, Karina Allwell and staff at BreastScreen ACT for reading the stories with generous insight and heart;

To May, Randy, Conchita and Robert, Sharon, Sheila, Rike, the boy who saved and swam with me, and all Wollongong friends; "Bliss Women" Lizz, Jenni and Kate; Lucy, Annie, George, John; Jacquie and Helen; Annie Rawson; Jane Ulman; Lucy Berzins; Julieann Solway, Penny Vethanayagam, Karina Allwell, Catherine Flood, Catherine Patterson, Dr Chaturica Athukorala, Dr Jatinder

Shekhawat, Dr Karen Pahlow, Dr Rebecca Read and BreastScreen ACT; breastcare nurse Karen McKinnon; Dr A-J Collins; Dr Sharmila Sambandam; nurses Sumi, Vera, Jissmol, Mini, orderly Ash and the healthcare workers at National Capital Hospital; Karen and Gillian at Colleen's — and all who restore health and hope, or ease soul and body in one's 'most quiet need'.

To Ning, Lyn, Thea, Marlon and Alan, and those who generously cared for my parents in their final days; and all health care and frontline workers around the world who comfort and sustain our living and dying with dignity;

To all who lose and grieve, and those who kindly succour them, for the tenacity, kinships, affirmations of kindness and the interweaving of lives and histories;

To my Australian publishers, Susan Hawthorne and Renate Klein, for their ongoing passion and persistence in bringing a multitude of women's voices and stories to the world; to my editors Pauline Hopkins and Susan Hawthorne for the ever-tender care for story and the word; to artist Deb Snibson for the beautiful cover and design; to Lynne Kowalik for the notation of the kindness song; Helen Christie for the splendid book design; and to the Spinifex Press family for the invaluable and unwavering commitment to women's publishing;

To Anvil Publishing (Philippine edition) and Maureen Alexandra S. Ramos Padilla for instantaneously welcoming this book, Arlyn Dimayuga for facilitating it, cover designer R. Jordan P. Santos, and all at Anvil for ensuring that my stories are heard in my first home;

To my beloved family — parents Nicolas and Amparo, and siblings Rolando, Lea and Noel who, in spirit, engendered this book — and most especially to Rolando and Lea for the clarity of vision and steadfast support;

To Reinis, my love and *nerūsē*, for the amplitude of care and joy;

229

To all who see, listen, feel, think and act with kindness across racial and cultural differences, and across human and non-human borders for believing that *we're all in this being-and-becoming together*;

To Bikol, Wadi Wadi Country and Ngunnawal Country for nurturing my living and dreaming of stories;

To Mayon Volcano, Haig Park and Lake Burley Griffin, and the mountains and waters of Wollongong for the lessons in eternal resurgence;

To trees and flowers, your restorative vibrance;

And to birds, your gifts of delight, solace, uncanny illuminations, and "trust in air" that has taught me how to breathe,

With deepest gratitude, I offer these stories to you.

Also available from Spinifex Press

Locust Girl, a Lovesong
Merlinda Bobis

Winner, Christina Stead Prize for Fiction,
NSW Premier's Literary Awards

Juan C. Laya Philippine National Book Award
for the Best Novel in English

Shortlisted, ACT Book of the Year Award

Most everything has dried up: water, the womb, even the love among lovers. Hunger is rife, except across the border. One night, a village is bombed after its men attempt to cross the border. Nine-year-old Amadea is buried underground and sleeps to survive. Ten years later, she wakes with a locust embedded in her brow.

This political fable is a girl's magical journey through the border. The border has cut the human heart. Can she repair it with the story of a small life? This is the Locust Girl's dream, her lovesong.

Don't be lulled by the lusciousness or lured by the love but make sure you are warned by the politics. Typically inscrutable, relentlessly seductive, Bobis uses a different quill ... and Australia can use the sweep of a different wing.
—Bruce Pascoe, author of *Dark Emu*

ISBN 9781742199627

If you would like to know more about
Spinifex Press, write to us for a free catalogue, visit our
website or email us for further information
on how to subscribe to our monthly newsletter.

Spinifex Press
PO Box 105
Mission Beach QLD 4852
Australia

www.spinifexpress.com.au
women@spinifexpress.com.au